HIDE ME AWAY

The Bishop Smoky Mountain Thrillers
Book 1

LAUREN STREET

STERLING & STONE

Chapter One

RILEIGH BISHOP STEPPED out of the bright sunlight into the dimly-lit interior of the Rusty Nail Tavern and was immediately as certain as sunrise on Easter Sunday morning that she was wasting her time. Smitty was tending bar, which meant the owner of the establishment, one Walter Thomas Collins, AKA Pinky, had somehow gotten wind she was coming and split out the back door as she was coming in the front.

Great.

The cash register in her head that dinged when she scored — delivered a summons or turned in a surveillance report or uploaded pictures of Mr. Can't-Keep-His-Pants-Zipped cheating on his wife with Stella the Stripper — was as silent as a tomb. She worked for "**G**atlinburg **I**nvestigations …The Good **GI**'s" and only got paid when she *completed* an assignment.

Every minute she spent trying to find some jackass like Pinky who was hiding out from a summons cost her money.

She slumped down onto a stool near the door.

"I'm looking for Pinky," she told Smitty. As if he didn't know. "Is he here?"

"Nope."

"Just between you and me, was he here say, oh, I don't know, five minutes ago?"

Smitty shrugged.

"Couldn't tell ya." He paused. "But there's a reason that bar stool you're sittin' on feels warm."

Rileigh sighed.

"Give me a Fat Tire."

As he retrieved a cold mug and began to fill it with ale, Rileigh looked down at the bar, saw the water ring that'd been made by the last mug of beer. Somebody had put a couple of drips of water inside the circle and made a smiley face out of it.

Rileigh's older sister Jillian adored smiley faces.

Jillian.

Rileigh took a sip of beer and let herself settle into the memory. Why not? It was a bright, sunshiny Monday morning and she didn't have anything better to do.

IT STINKS IN HERE. Smells like dirty socks. It's a closet full of shoes and boots— sneakers and goulashes, but it doesn't smell like shoes. It smells like dirty socks. The smell is gross.

But Rileigh stays where she is, still as a rabbit, even though the stink is upsetting her stomach. She'd covered herself with shoes and if she doesn't move, even if somebody opens the door—

The door opens and a shaft of light from outside makes Rileigh squint. She can't see who it is, but she knows. She can smell the crew cut gel on her cousin's hair even over the stinky socks.

There's a pause. She holds her breath. Then the door closes and she is left in darkness again. Rileigh's not afraid of the dark, though. She's a big girl, just turned six, had lost her two lower front teeth, and

2

big girls aren't scared of the dark. That's what Jillie told her and Jillie never lies.

The door opens again, but this time it's flung wide and she looks up, squints into the bright light ... at an angel. It is the most beautiful being Rileigh has ever seen. The bright sunlight from behind glimmers all around her, sparkles in her golden curls, shines through the bride's veil that's as delicate as a spiderweb, makes her pure white dress glow like a firefly.

The angel stands in the doorway for a moment. Then she kneels down— in a white dress and veil— in the pile of dirty, muddy shoes, and begins to pick up the ones Rileigh had piled on top of herself. One by one, she removes the shoes until Rileigh is just curled up in the corner in her pink taffeta dress, with nothing to hide her.

"You ready to come out now?" the angel asks. "We can't start without you."

Of course they can't start without Rileigh! She's the flower girl and Jillie said hers was the most important part. She's supposed to walk down the aisle in front of Jillian, tossing rose petals on the floor. She can't wave or say hi to anybody in the audience, can't even look at them. Her job is to throw the rose petals on the floor — not all in one place, but scattered, like tossing feed to the chickens in the coup in the backyard.

She's supposed to walk in front of Jillian, so of course they can't start without Rileigh— that's why she'd crawled into the closet among the dirty shoes to hide.

They can't do the wedding rehearsal without Rileigh. If she hides, they'll have to call it off — and the wedding, too!— and Jillian won't move out!

Rileigh had only figured out that part this morning, when she heard Mrs. Hicks talk about how her son David, who was the groom, had already moved his things into the new apartment where he and Jillian would live ... but Jillian hadn't even started to pack.

Jillian was going to leave. Nobody'd told Rileigh that her big sister getting married meant she would leave! That she'd move out of her bedroom down the hall from Rileigh's and go to some apartment somewhere and live with David Hicks.

Rileigh couldn't let Jillian go away! Who'd sneak into her bedroom after bedtime and hide under the sheets with her, reading her stories by the light of a flashlight? Who'd tie the ribbons in her hair? Mama's bows were clunky and ugly. Who'd be there for her to run to in the middle of the night when the Boogie Man came after her?

"Ellie Hicks told me you heard her talking about my new apartment and you got upset … do you think I would move away and never come to see you?"

Rileigh starts to cry and the angel folds her into her arms, holds her so tight the little pearl things on the front of her dress make dents in Rileigh's cheek, but she doesn't care.

"I'm sorry I made you sad. It's all wrong and I'd change it all if I could … but it's too late for that now. I have to go through with it. We all do. But I'll visit you — so often it'll feel like I'm still living here!"

Visiting wasn't the same thing as living here, but Rileigh didn't say that.

Today's wedding rehearsal was the last one, a dress rehearsal where you had to put on your outfit but you didn't have to fix your hair, and the groom had to stay away so he wouldn't see Jillian's dress until the real wedding tomorrow afternoon.

Now that they'd found Rileigh, the rehearsal would continue. And Jillian would get married tomorrow and move out. Tonight was the last night Jillian would be here where she was supposed to be. And Rileigh couldn't do anything to make it different.

"You're okay now, aren't you?" Jillie asks, letting go of the hug and holding Rileigh out in front of her. The love on her big sister's face is so bright it makes Rileigh want to start crying again. But if she does, she might never stop. All she can do is nod.

"Okay then, let's see a smiley face," Jillie coaxes.

Jillian loves smiley faces. She plasters smiley face stickers all over her textbooks and has a huge one on the wall above her bed. Will she

*put that in a box and take it to David's apartment and hang it over
her bed there?*

*Rileigh can't smile, but she does anyway — pulls up the corners
of her mouth so her face looks like it's smiling.*

"KNOCK, knock. Earth to Rileigh. Your beer is getting
hot," said Smitty, wiping the bar with his rag — a movement he performed a thousand times a day. The swipe
erased the watermark smiley face and the memory disappeared with it. "Warm beer tastes worse than yak piss."

"Drink a lot of yak piss, do you?"

"Only when I can't get warm beer."

"You know you could help me out here, you could tell
me when Pinky's around so–"

"Could, but won't. He don't want to go to court on
that DUI. I wouldn't neither if I's him."

"It's only putting off the inevitable. Sooner or–"

The door to the ladies room at the other end of the bar
banged open and the Rusty Nail's only waitress stormed
out, yelling at somebody on her cell phone.

"... you think I won't tell, don't you," Tina Montgomery said to whoever was on the other end of the line.
"Well, you've got one or two more thinks coming if you–"

"Hold it down," Smitty snapped at her, nodding with
his chin at Rileigh. "We got paying customers."

Tina glared at Rileigh as if it were somehow Rileigh's
fault that she'd gotten in trouble. Tina was one of those
"too much" girls who'd have been pretty if you scrubbed
all the makeup off her face. How'd she keep those rhinestones and false eyelashes from falling off — Super Glue?
The thought of having to remove them every night made
Rileigh cringe.

Tina looked up when the bar door opened and three

men entered. She hissed some final invective into her phone before disconnecting, hurriedly tucked her shirt, hot pink with the Rusty Nail logo on the back, into her skin-tight jeans and pasted a fake smile on her face to greet the customers.

Like the fake smile Rileigh had pasted on her face in the closet all those years ago.

She'd thought then that Jillian moving out of the house would destroy her whole world. It didn't, of course. The blood all over the sheets did *that* ... and the blood splattered on those little pearls sewn to the front of the wedding dress crumpled in a heap on the floor. And the thing. The bloody *thing* on the bed ... those images had shattered Rileigh's world into so many tiny pieces there was no way to put it back together.

No, it wasn't the images that had done it. It was that nobody'd believed her. Rileigh had tried to tell them all and they'd said she'd imagined it. *That* was what had destroyed her world.

Putting a couple of bills down on the bar, Rileigh slid off the stool and headed toward the door.

"Don't rush off," Smitty said as he scooped up the money and swiped his rag to erase the mug ring. "You going somewhere special this afternoon?"

"Nope. Just gonna hang out in Georgia."

Chapter Two

THE YARD, what there was of it, was littered with toys — plastic trucks/dinosaurs/dragons and superhero action figures. That's what they called dolls for boys, action figures. Most were missing key body parts, the trucks were in various states of disrepair. Rileigh managed not to run over any of them as she pulled her tired old Ford car into the gravel space in front of the double wide trailer house belonging to her BFF. The two of them had gone to kindergarten together at Black Bear Forge Elementary School. Gwynneth Anne McGinnis had put chewing gum in Rileigh's hair during recess the first day of school and Rileigh had punched her in the face. The teacher'd been so horrified she put them both in something like permanent time out and they became best friends as they stood with their noses in opposite corners of the supply closet.

In fourth grade geography class, Rileigh realized that Gwyneth Anne's initials, GA, were the abbreviation for Georgia. Gwyneth McGinnis was a tongue twister, so Rileigh nicknamed her Georgia. By the time they graduated from high school, only her family still called her Gwynn.

Rileigh could hear Mayella's shrieking before she got out of the car. She might have pulled back out onto the road and driven away, if she hadn't been fairly certain Georgia had seen her pull up.

Mayella was three years old and the sound she was able to produce with her little lungs was genuinely impressive. Rileigh was sure that under the right circumstances, it would shatter crystal. The child used her singular ability as a club to beat the entire family into submission.

What Mayella needed was a genuine, sincere, heartfelt butt-busting — more than one— and Rileigh would cheerfully have volunteered for the task. But Georgia doted on the little girl — finally! — after four boys. Unfortunately, discipline wasn't Georgia's strong suit with the boys, either, which meant "hanging out in Georgia" required a high tolerance for chaos.

But Georgia was a loyal friend and those had been in short supply in Rileigh's life in the past year. Nothing like having a national scandal to separate the wheat from the chaff in the friendship department.

Rileigh reached down and unhooked the holster from her belt. It was an IWB holster — sounded formidable but all it meant was that it fit inside the waist band of her jeans. The clip made it possible to put the gun and holster on her belt without having to unhook the belt.

But more important was the fact that the gun, once clipped, was firmly against the skin of her right side—not affixed to the outside of her pants. All she had to do was pull her shirt down over it to avoid a tell-tale bulge at her side.

Rileigh carried a Glock model 43X 9 mm, and had willingly turned in the .40 caliber Sig Sauer P229R DAK that was the duty weapon of the Memphis Police Department. The only people promoting that semi-automatic double action-only pistol were police administrators who knew nothing about handguns and had no faith in the training they provided their officers. Her opinion, of course ... one shared by every officer she'd ever met.

What she had always wanted, what she drooled over in gun stores, was a Springfield Armory XD .45. But that pistol had a double-stacked magazine with a really wide grip. Her hands were flat out not big enough to use the weapon effectively. And she had *tried*.

Besides, on a woman her size, a handgun that big would be just about impossible to conceal. Not that the law demanded she conceal it.

The state of Tennessee didn't require a concealed carry permit, didn't require a permit of any kind to openly carry any firearm, loaded or unloaded. The same went for carrying a weapon in her car. Rileigh kept her pistol in the console. It was closer there, easier to get to than in the glove box, and if she were in an accident where the passenger side of the vehicle was damaged, it might be impossible to open the glove box.

She slipped the weapon into the console and shut the lid. She would not carry a loaded weapon into a house with five inquisitive children. And it was, ten plus one, which meant that she'd loaded the single stack magazine and chambered the first round, then removed the magazine and replaced the round she'd chambered.

Georgia opened the front door and began talking at once.

"Come on in this house and let me get you some ice tea — Eli, stop poking your little brother, Conner, get your dinosaur collection off the chair so Rileigh can sit down — you look beat, girlfriend, like somebody just pissed in your

Cheerios–" Turning on her oldest, Georgia continued, "And don't you *even*, Liam. No, you are not allowed to say "pissed," we've talked about this so don't ask."

She spewed out the distracted greeting in one long breath as she swept a herd of plastic dinosaurs off onto the floor when Conner ignored her, and popped a chunk of banana into Mayella's mouth. That kid had taken to bananas like an addict to crack and the only sure fire way to get her to shut up was to stuff her mouth so full of them she could barely draw a breath.

"When Daddy was on the phone, he said he was pissed off–"

"I see a time-out in your future, young man, if–"

"Ding! Ding! Ding!" Rileigh cried. "I'll give a dollar to any child who draws me a picture of a ..." What? "A pink and purple cat with two heads. You have fifteen minutes starting"—she looked at her watch— "now! Go!"

Liam, Eli and Conner raced out of the room, leaving Mason, four, who pounced on the abandoned toys he never got to play with when his three older brothers were around.

Georgia stuffed another hunk of banana in Mayella's mouth as Rileigh sank into a kitchen chair. What appeared to be a gob of grape jelly was stuck on the table in front of her and she was careful not to set her arm down in it.

"You shoulda said half an hour." Georgia plopped ice into glasses and poured in amber liquid from a pitcher in the refrigerator. It was a magic pitcher, Rileigh was sure, since she'd never seen it empty. The tea had so much sugar in it you could trot a mouse across the surface.

"I plan to offer a fifty cent bonus for a matching dog picture."

Setting a glass down in front of Rileigh, Georgia observed, "You look like death on a cracker, girlfriend."

Rileigh retorted with their standard childhood come-back to insults. "You're ugly and your mama dresses you funny."

"Do you *ever* eat?" Georgia answered her own question. "I didn't think so. Well, I made your favorite — pineapple upside-down cake— cause I knew you couldn't resist a piece."

When Rileigh hesitated, Georgia said, "If you don't eat it, I will." She patted her generous backside. "The only two pairs of jeans I can still zip look like I was melted and poured in them."

Same conversation, different day.

Georgia had battled the pounds all her life. Rileigh, on the other hand, was a stick.

Well, she liked to think of herself as "thin and willowy" — rather than Mama's description of "scrawny." She once overheard her aunt tell a woman in the grocery store, "Rileigh's so skinny her striped pajamas ain't got but one stripe." Of course she'd "filled out" in high school, and "bulked up" in the military. Now though … yeah, she was a stick again.

Georgia placed a plate on top of the glob of jelly that held a piece of cake roughly the size of a catcher's mitt.

"I can't eat all *that*—"

"No sense saving any for Chigger. He went running out of here a little while ago like his pants were on fire. No telling when he'll be home. He's out … you know."

"You know" was selling drugs, of course. It wasn't something the two friends talked about. Roger Albert Stump —Chigger — had been doing something illegal, selling drugs or fencing stolen property or who knew what else ever since Georgia met him. If Rileigh had been home at the time, she'd have done everything up to and including duct taping Georgia to a chair to keep her from marrying the bum. But Rileigh had been in the army. By by the time she got home, Georgia was ready to pop out the first of their five children.

Rileigh had set aside her personal feelings about Chigger a long time ago — had to when she'd been under at least the implicit obligation to arrest him for what she knew he was doing.

But it still chapped her butt that he was even a failure at that— selling drugs. Everybody else Rileigh had ever known in that line of work made a fortune. They also got addicted themselves, died of overdoses, got killed in some kind of turf battle, or ended up locked away on a manda-tory-twenty-year minimum. But while they were still gain-fully employed in the sale of illegal substances, they'd lived like kings.

Chigger — and by extension, Georgia and the kids— lived in a rundown double wide trailer house affixed to the mountainside with a satellite dish stick-pin. It'd just been shoved into a wide spot beside the road up against a rock cliff face. No back yard for the kids to play, and a front yard so small they were always in imminent danger of getting run down in the road.

If Chigger was going to risk his life and freedom to be a drug dealer, why couldn't he at least be good at it?

"If I ask you what's wrong, will that spoil your appetite so you don't eat the cake? Because if it will, I don't want to know that bad."

"Same old same old," Rileigh said, taking a small bite of the mound of confectionary on her plate. It was good and she was suddenly ravenously hungry. When had she last eaten anything? It'd been … sometime this morning, or last night. She couldn't remember.

Speaking with her mouth full, she continued, "I've had

three assignments from the Good GI's this week. Two summonses and a stake-out."

"Stake-out where?"

"Nothing interesting." Interesting was when your hours of boredom sitting in a car watching a house where nobody was home were rewarded by the arrival of the "subjects," and shooting close-up pictures of the two star-crossed lovers in a groping embrace.

This stakeout was a landlord who wanted a call if the delinquent renters showed up to move out. During stake-outs, Rileigh occupied her time listening to audio books. But if business didn't pick up, she would soon have to settle for reading books from the half-price bookstore.

"Pinky Collins has been dodging me for almost a week and I thought I had him this afternoon, but …"

"Considered changing professions?"

"You about to tell me McDonalds is always hiring?"

"No, I was going to respectfully suggest you get an application from the Gatlinburg Police De–"

Rileigh cut her off. "I'd rather stand at a window and ask if you want fries with that order. And I'd have a better shot at landing that job."

"But you have so much experience. And it's been a long time. People have short memories. Who still remembers or cares now?"

I do. She didn't say it out loud, though. And how about the old lady who'd been screaming? They were almost five hundred miles away but the images had never stopped prowling the dark hallways of Rileigh's mind.

When Rileigh didn't respond, Georgia played her Ace.

"You're not a quitter. Jillian wouldn't want you to throw up your hands and give up."

Bam. Right in the solar plexus.

Rileigh was saved having to respond by Mayella's

shriek. She'd swallowed the last of her banana plug. Following on the heels of her banshee cry was Eli running into the room with a piece of lined notebook paper covered in some kind of Rorschach-test blob that was either a two headed cat or a cancerous kidney.

"I got it, see!" he cried.

A dollar was a small price to pay to escape the chaos that was about to explode in Georgia Stump's kitchen.

Chapter Three

RILEIGH HADN'T MEANT to take a nap when she got home from Georgia's house, but it was quiet and still, and she hadn't slept well, so she nodded off. It was late evening before her eyes popped open, instantly awake and alert, the tattered wisps of the nightmare that had catapulted her from sleep dissipating like the smoke from a dying campfire.

Surely the swing on her mother's porch was listed in some book of world records somewhere —the only authentic, half-a-century-old porch swing that was mute. Not a sound. Not a squeak. Every other such swing in Rileigh's experience — including the ones on the porches of all her friends' houses when she was growing up — squawked and squalled and emitted all manner of finger-nails-on-a-blackboard noises that were soothing in some indefinable way, a sound unique to each swing, each house, and each friend. Georgia's grandmother told her once, "a porch swing'll talk to ya, if you got ears to hear."

Rileigh was grateful for the swing's silence tonight, though, as she moved it gently back and forth through the warm summer air. She had come down the stairs from her attic bedroom quietly, reluctant to face her mother and her aunt quite yet.

Now, she sat listening to the crickets tuning up under the porch and the tree frogs harrumphing in the woods. Oh how her heart had ached for the Smoky Mountains when she was in the army, moving from one ugly military post to another. She had *lived* in the mountains as a kid, with the whole half-million-acre Great Smoky Mountains National Park within rock-throwing distance of her home in little Black Bear Forge — just "the Forge" —Tennessee.

She'd hiked the hundreds of miles of park trails — the ones for tourists— and twice as many more that only the locals knew. She could recognize all the wildflowers — mountain laurel and columbine, of course, but others you didn't see unless you went deep into the woods. Turk's cap lily, almost the same orange as flame azaleas, wild geraniums and dutchman's breeches, fire pink, crested dwarf iris, pink lady's slippers and blue phlox that was more purple than blue.

She could identify the calls of just about every one of the forty bird species in the park, too — from the raucous caw of the blue jays, the cooing of mourning doves, and the hooting of barred owls to the lonely cry of the red-tailed hawk sailing high above the trees. She'd even seen a bald eagle swoop down out of the sky and snatch up a rabbit out of a meadow. She'd played in the little creeks as a child and shot the Class III and IV rapids on the Pigeon River as a teenager. She was still in middle school the day she'd faced down a mama black bear with three cubs. Yelling swear words she'd overheard when her grandfather and his friends played poker (for surely obscenities had great power), she'd waved her arms in the air, jumped up and down and made faces. Rileigh liked to think she'd scared the bear away. It was more likely the mama bear left laughing.

Without those images to fill her mind, to warm her heart like the morning sun on a frosty windowpane, Rileigh would have died in Iraq or Afghanistan. Her soul would have withered away to nothing in the face of such unspeakable horror, and even if her body had survived, she'd have been as hollow as a rotten stump. Images of the mountains had saved her sanity in war, and when she returned a shattered veteran almost a decade ago they had renewed her.

Could they do the same thing now, heal her again? She really didn't think so, not a second time. Not after what she'd done. But she was here. She would see.

The silent swing swished back and forth. Back and forth.

The night was peaceful. Rileigh was not, of course. Her financial situation would have been dire.

The spring on the screen door squawked — it *wasn't* mute — and Rileigh's aunt, Daisy, stepped out on the porch, a woman whose mane of white hair had for twenty years remained in a permanent state of bed head. Right now, her hair was stuck to her skull, like she'd taken a shower and didn't even bother to towel it dry.

She sat down beside Rileigh on the swing, wordlessly, like she didn't see her.

"Evening, Aunt Daisy."

The old woman ignored her, placing a small black box on the swing seat beside her and staring blankly ahead into the firefly-twinkling darkness. The box looked familiar, like — why, that was Rileigh's box, the one she—

"B'lieve I'll get me some lemonade," Daisy announced.

Turning to Rileigh as if she'd just noticed her, she asked, "Want me to get you some?" Without waiting for a reply, Daisy stood and marched with purpose back into the house, allowing the screen door to bang shut behind her.

Rileigh stared at the box, then slowly reached out, picked it up, and placed it in her lap. Opening the lid, she looked down into it, studying the contents. She picked up the badge first, held it high with the porch light glinting off the surface. It was gold, of course. The patrol officer badge she'd turned in for this one had been silver. The detective badge she'd longed for was silver, too. But the badges of a sergeant, lieutenant, captain, deputy chief and chief badges were all gold.

She ran her fingers over the raised lettering. Badge number—871. "Sergeant" and "Memphis' in all caps, bracketing the insignia in the middle. It was riverboat on a square light blue background, with Memphis, Tennessee, and Shelby County on the four sides.

It felt strangely heavy. Had it felt that heavy when it'd been pinned on her chest? She didn't think it had, like maybe it had gotten heavier and heavier the longer she wore it, until in the end she flat out didn't have the strength to lift it anymore.

Putting the badge back in the box, she pulled out the name tag: R.J. Bishop. She appreciated the irony of the initials, and liked to think her older sister would have, too.

Yeah, Jillie would have smiled at the way life had come full circle since her eleventh-hour demand for a concession to Rileigh's femininity all those years ago. As the story went, Jillian had gazed in adoration down at the brand new baby sister who'd just been placed in her arms and burst into tears.

"Rileigh Joseph is a boy's name!"

Well, duh. Of course it was, and not just any boy's name, either. It was a— drum roll, please— family name. Sort of. Joseph Riley Bishop. Senior. Junior. The third. And now ... well, it appeared there wouldn't be a fourth — so her father had grasped his last-straw chance to pass on the family name in some form or another by hanging it like an albatross around the neck of his second daughter, whose traumatic birth had ensured there would be no children following her.

"No it's not." Rileigh's mother, Lily, had stepped in to keep peace. "We'll call her Rileigh Jo... and spell it Rileigh— like Vivien Leigh."

Of course, the spelling had done nothing to change the boy's name into a girl's name — and at that time in American culture such things had mattered. It had merely sentenced Rileigh to a lifetime of needless, tedious spelling and pronunciation discussions and to wasted hours trying to trick spell-check into allowing the name to pass muster the first time around.

"Rileigh Jo, you out there?" Daisy called from inside. Rileigh *Jo*. Her mother and her mother's sister, Daisy, were the only people in Rileigh's life who still sometimes used both names. "You're not hiding from me, are you child? You know I don't hold with such foolishness."

"Yes and no," Rileigh called out. "Yes, I'm out here and no, I'm not hiding from you."

Daisy reappeared behind the screen door without the lemonade, which had apparently left her memory and gone wherever forgotten things went. Stepping out onto the porch, she sat down where she'd been sitting before the forgotten lemonade. The worn wooden slats of the swing — unlike the vinyl of the bar stool at the Rusty Nail — hadn't likely retained her butt's heat from a few minutes before. Gesturing with her chin toward Rileigh's lap, she asked, "Where'd you get the box?"

Rileigh didn't answer, just batted a question back into her aunt's court.

"How'd you get it down?" Rileigh had put away every mention of her time as a police officer on the top shelf of her closet, a shelf too high for either her mother or her aunt to reach.

Daisy had managed it somehow, though. How, and why she'd gotten it down in the first place were tangled up in that jumbled space between her aunt's ears where her functioning brain was rapidly being replaced by dangling synapses that fired at random and made no connection to each other or to any other part of her mind.

Dementia. That wasn't actually a true weasel word—a word aimed at creating an impression that something specific and meaningful had been revealed … when the word actually concealed reality. Or at the very least, distorted it beyond all recognition. Dementia had, however, in its myriad shapes and forms— frontotemporal dementia, Lewy body dementia, vascular dementia — been lumped with all the other brain malfunction words like Alzheimer's to take the place of a perfectly useful broad term that didn't need so many synonyms. Crazy.

"There's rats in the storage room," Daisy said, either unwilling or unable to hook her contribution to the rest of the conversation. "I need me a rat trap." Rileigh's father had added the storage room onto the back side of the garage when he had moved his family in to stay with his mother before Rileigh was born. It was far more likely that rats had taken up residence in some other part of the house but Daisy was certain she'd heard something scratching around in the storage room.

As soon as Rileigh promised to bring home a trap, Daisy's mind flitted like a water spider to some other thought and she dropped her voice to just above a whisper.

"I seen my cat's shadow in the moonlight a little while ago." Daisy's cat had died sometime during the pandemic, and the moon had not yet risen above the peak of Pine Mountain. "Some'um real bad's 'bout to happen. I seen it in the coffee grounds when I threw them away this morning, too."

She looked around, as if she didn't want to be overheard. "Somebody's 'bout to get theirselves kilt, gonna wake up in the morning on the wrong side of dirt."

Chapter Four

"SHE SAYS IT'S REAL IMPORTANT," Deputy Mullins said from the doorway. "Says her daughter didn't come home last night."

Exactly why a teenager out playing bump and tickle with her boyfriend after curfew had risen to the level of a police matter was not readily apparent. But there was nothing for it but to talk to the woman.

"Well, go get her and bring her in so she can tell me her story," Sheriff Mitchell Webster said while shuffling the clutter of papers on his desk into a less jumbled pile.

Still trying to impress, even three months into the job. At his core, Mitch was not a people pleaser. He had become one, however, when the sheriff of Yarmouth County, Jedediah T. Mumford, (folks called him Mum) had called him into the office three weeks after he was hired and announced that he was about to become acting Sheriff indefinitely.

. . .

"IT'S EITHER you or picking among all the other four, and all of them are good men, who work hard, are good at making nice with the tourists, but when it comes to real police work, not a one of them could pour water out of a boot if the instructions was on the heel."

Mum smiles, revealing piano-key white teeth.

"The only real police officer on tap right now is you, Mitch, which means your apple just bobbed up out of the water. The docs have been saying for years that I need two new knees. Ruined them both in the army — airborne, jumping out of perfectly good airplanes. Last week, this one here," he gestures toward the lump stretching the fabric of his brown uniform pants taut, "blew up on me. And now if I don't get both of them replaced next week, they say I could mess them up so bad I'll never walk again." He rubs his jowled chin. "Hard to pass a department physical on crutches. I won't be back to full steam for six months — that's minimum. The way that one doctor looked at me, I figure he thinks it'll be closer to nine months. Maybe a year."

Mum smiles again. He smiles a lot. Fact is, Mitch can hardly remember any occasion on which he wasn't smiling. What that might or might not mean about his character was not for Mitch to say.

"And while I'm sitting on my butt getting fat on Martha's fried chicken and beer, you're going to be holding down the fort."

THE DOOR OPENED and Deputy Mullins showed Charlotte Montgomery into the room. She was a a short woman, almost as broad as she was tall, walked on a lumbering waddle.

Mitch had an aversion to classifying people as "fat," it sounded judgmental. There were lots of reasons for excess weight. Hormone problems. Heredity. Medications. A lack of self discipline was only one explanation.

But looking at Charlotte Montgomery, Mitch couldn't help the mental assessment that, in her case, the extra pounds had been produced by excessive consumption of moon pies and RC cola.

He stood and approached the woman, held out his hand.

"I'm Sheriff Mitchell Webster and I understand you are—"

"Charlotte Montgomery. Folks call me Lottie. I come to talk to you about my girl, Tina. She didn't come home last night."

Mitch returned to his chair and gestured for the woman to make herself comfortable in one of the two chairs that faced his desk.

She sat with an audible sigh.

"So tell me—"

"She never come home, that's all the story there is to tell. And she ain't one of them that stays out til all hours, drinking and carousing and the like. Tina's a good girl. Graduated from high school last year and went to work for BTB."

"BTB?"

"You know, Back to Basics, them vitamin supplements. She was a regional manager."

Translate that, she was on some middle management level of some quasi-legal pyramid scheme. He'd seen them before, where you had a party at your house and signed up everybody you knew to join you in selling some kind of widget, and the real money came from signup fees and the requirement that everybody take an auto-ship order of it every month.

"She went to Knoxville three times a week to pick up the product and to meet with her sponsors."

Sponsors — who took two cents out of every dime that passed through your hands, and through the hands of all the people on lower rungs of the ladder, the people you sponsored.

"She works hard, got herself a side job waiting tables at the Rusty Nail. She goes to church every Sunday. She ain't wild."

"When did you last see her?"

"She's getting ready to go to work and I told her to bring home some of them peanuts from work. The Rusty Nail has buckets of peanuts sitting all around for people drinking beer. Folks just throw the shells all over the floor, so Tina comes home with peanut shells in her shoes. She said they have to change the peanuts, have to throw out the ones in the buckets that didn't nobody eat and fill them up with fresh ones every day. It's a health department rule or some such."

She ran out of air at the end of the sentence and had to pause. Either she had some kind of lung condition or carrying around so much extra weight was putting stress on her heart and lungs.

"Anyway, I asked her to bring me home them leftover peanuts cause they're real good. And she said, Sure, Mama, sweet as could be. Come around the table and pecked me on the cheek. Said I love you as she was going out the door. You see. She's a good girl, and she wouldn't have stayed out late 'less something happened to her."

"What time did she normally come home?"

"This week her shift ends at noon. Last week, she worked the noon to eight shift and next week she'll work late — eight until closing. That's when you make the best tips, the late shift. Folks is good'n drunk by then and feeling no pain."

"Did she always come home as soon as she got off work?"

"Oh, no. Not when she's on first shift. She's a busy girl,

has lots to do, lots of friends. But she don't hardly ever stay out late and when she does, she calls and lets me know."

"So you know what time she gets home every night. You're still awake—?"

"No, not usually. It ain't like I wait up for her or nothing like that. But when her car pulls off the road, her headlights shine in my bedroom window and I know she's home even if I'm not up."

"So you're saying you don't know exactly what time—"

"Don't you be putting words in my mouth. She's a good girl. And even if she is a little late sometimes, she ain't never stayed out all night before."

The woman's voice was rising in both volume and pitch as she spoke, and the final words rode a sob out of her throat.

"Somethin's wrong, bad wrong, I know it. I can feel it."

"When did you notice she was missing?"

"This morning when I got up, I looked out the kitchen window and seen her car wasn't parked beside the house like usual. I thought maybe she'd got up early and went somewhere, but I checked and her bed was still made. She didn't sleep in it last night."

"And you've checked with her friends—"

"I called everywhere I could think. Hadn't none of her friends seen her. Smitty said she left work soon's her shift ended same as usual."

"So this Smitty person is the last person who saw her?"

"Far's I know. What are you going to do about it? What are you gonna do to find my Tina?"

Mitch felt uncomfortable and tried not to show it in his tone or demeanor.

"There isn't anything I can do right now, Mrs. Montgomery. By state law, a person has to be missing at least twenty-four hours before we an fill out a missing person's report–"

The woman got to her feet, moved fast for a woman her size.

"I knowed it. I never shoulda wasted my time coming here. Mum woulda done something, if he was sitting behind that desk 'stead of you."

"Please come back and fill out a report if your daughter isn't back by–"

He spoke the words to her back as she started for the door.

"Can't figure why Mum left you in charge," she fired over her shoulder without looking back. "You ain't been here long enough to know diddly squat about this county. 'Round here, we don't hold with outsiders."

"Mrs. Montgomery –"

She opened the door and marched away down the hall before he could finish the sentence.

Chapter Five

RILEIGH HEARD the doorbell ring as she sat at the kitchen table tapping a pencil unconsciously on her teeth, staring down at the pile of bills in front of her.

She'd never intended to get into such financial trouble. But then nobody ever does, do they?

The pile of bills represented what had accumulated since she'd left the only job she'd ever had that paid a reasonably decent salary. When she came home to the Forge to live with her mother, she'd had outstanding credit card bills, a car payment, and other miscellaneous other bills. It all added up. She wasn't extravagant. She certainly wasn't a clothes hound or a compulsive shopper. She lived within her means. The problem was that her means had shrunk. The bills had not. Now she was struggling to catch up.

And there was also the envelope that lay unopened. Wasn't any sense in opening it, because there was nothing she could do about the contents. It was the bill from the attorney who had represented her in her... *problems*... with the Memphis, Tennessee police department.

He had been recommended to her as the best in the business and at that time she was so frantic and desperate that's what she wanted —the best. Well, you get what you pay for. He was the best and he charged like the best, but she didn't get what she paid for, because what she paid for was to make it all go away. He couldn't do that.

But she still owed him thousands of dollars for the effort.

She could hear voices from the other room, her mother and somebody else she didn't quite recognize. The voices were coming her way and she caught the tail end of her mother telling somebody:

"…in the kitchen working on something. And you ain't interrupting her, so don't you worry yourself about that a bit."

Rileigh hadn't noticed until she came home how much of her mothers speech was consumed by a rambling babble that went from nowhere to nowhere through nowhere with no point Rileigh could discern. Oh, she wasn't crazy like Daisy. But she was getting on in years and her mind wasn't as sharp as it once was.

Her mother showed a large woman into the kitchen through the double doors in the dining room. Rileigh didn't recognize her.

"Sugar, this here is Lottie Montgomery," her mother said. "You might not remember her, but she used to work in the cafeteria at the Forge middle school when you was going there. She come 'cause she needs to talk to you."

Turning to the woman, her mother said. "You just sit yourself down right here and let me get you some coffee. Or would you rather have tea? Hot tea? Ice-tea? We got juice, orange and apple and–"

"Mama, just get us both a cup of coffee and let me find

out what it is Mrs. Montgomery wants to talk to me about," Rileigh said.

Rileigh's mother went to the cabinet to get out some coffee mugs. As she filled them from the pot she had started earlier in the day, Rileigh turned to Lottie Montgomery and smiled.

"So tell me what—"

"My Tina didn't come home last night," the woman said. "She went off to work same as every other day, but this morning I seen her car wasn't in the driveway and she didn't sleep in her bed. I'm worried to death about her. "

Tina... Tina...

Then Rileigh made the connection. "Does she work at the Rusty Nail?"

The woman nodded her head. Tina *Montgomery* was the girl she had seen yesterday when she was looking for Pinky. The one who came out of the ladies room in an argument with somebody on her cell phone.

"It was a good job and she was good at waitressing. But it was just a side job. Her real job was BTB."

"BTB's still around?"

Those pyramid marketing schemes came and went, so these vitamin supplements must have worked for somebody.

"It didn't take a whole lot of her time, just going back and forth to Knoxville three times a week. She was industrious, though, didn't just sit around on her butt, got herself a second job at the Rusty Nail."

"And she didn't come home last night?"

"I didn't know it until this morning. So she's been gone for hours."

"You sure she didn't just go off—"

"Tina was a good girl! She wasn't like them others that run around, drinking and doing drugs and such. She went to church with me every Sunday. She wouldn't of stayed out all night without telling me. She knew how I worried about her and she would've called me."

Rileigh didn't know quite what to say. She was certainly sorry that Mrs. Montgomery's daughter was missing, but she didn't have any idea what that had to do with her. Before she could ask the question, Lottie Montgomery answered it.

"I know you work for that private investigations firm in Gatlinburg. I heard of them, The Good Guys. The woman who lives down the road from me said her brother-in-law hired them to track down a fellow who owed him a whole lot of money. And they done it. Found him in three days." Lottie suddenly reached across the table and took Rileigh's hand in her chubby ones. Her palms were sweating.

"So I figured if you worked for them, you was an investigator too, right? You are aren't you, right?"

"Well, yeah…"

Lottie opened a purse about the size of a diaper bag and began to dig around in it.

"I ain't asking you to do this for nothing. I know private investigators is expensive. But I got money." She finally found what she was looking for in her purse and hauled out a wallet and opened it. Rileigh could see that it was stuffed with bills.

Rileigh's mother was busy at the other end of the kitchen, had recipe books spread out on the counter, obviously looking for one in particular.

So Lottie Montgomery leaned close to Rileigh and spoke softly. "Don't nobody in my family know it, but I hit it big. The state lottery! I liked to wet my pants when they called out that last number and I seen it was the same as the one on my ticket. Wasn't nobody home at the time. Bob had took the littles to see his sister in Tupelo for the weekend or I'd a'told everybody. By the time he, Tina and her two brothers got home, I'd done decided I wasn't gonna tell nobody. I decided I was going to save this money for something important. Maybe have a little stash so if something bad happened we'd be prepared for it."

She shoved the full wallet toward Rileigh. "Here. You take what you need to go find my Tina."

Rileigh pushed the wallet back toward Lottie Montgomery. "Now Mrs. Montgomery, I couldn't possibly—"

"Please don't tell me no. I done been to the sheriff and he told me no. Don't nobody understand that I know my Tina. She's my girl. I know she wouldn't of stayed out all night and not called me 'cause she knows how bad I worry. Something's happened to her. And I'll pay every dime I got to find her."

Tears streamed down Lottie Montgomery's cheeks and dripped off the jowls on her jaw. Rileigh felt sorry for her. But she couldn't take the woman's money to go looking for her daughter. She wouldn't know where to start. Just because she could serve a summons, and had been a patrol supervisor in Memphis, didn't mean she possessed the skill set to be a detective.

"I'm sorry, Mrs. Montgomery, but you don't understand. I'm not a detective. I just work for a private investigations company. I don't know how—"

"You know more than them others. That fella at the sheriff's department that Mum appointed to take his place while he was out getting his knees fixed. He ain't from around here. He ain't local. He don't know nothing. Ain't no way in the world he could find Tina, and he done said that he wouldn't even start trying for twenty-four hours. Twenty-four hours! I can't imagine what kind of bad things could happen to my girl in twenty-four hours." She squeezed Rileigh's hands in hers.

"Please! Please help me."

"I can't just—"

"Look here," Lottie Montgomery dug around in the wallet and pulled out three $100 bills. She laid them on the table, and then scooted them toward Rileigh.

"This here's a fee for you to start looking." Before Rileigh had a chance to protest Lottie Montgomery held up her hand. "Ain't expecting nothing. I'm just paying you $300 to try. That's all. I just want you to try. Somebody's got to try."

Three. Hundred. Dollars. As mama would say, the truth in longjohns with the butt flap down was that Rileigh was broke. She needed the money. Needed it bad. And what was the harm? The woman only wanted her to help to find her daughter. Maybe Rileigh could help.

"OK, Mrs. Montgomery, I'll tell you what. I will try to find your daughter, but I can't guarantee anything. You have to know upfront that I am not a professional investigator. You could hire somebody from the Good Guys in Gatlinburg and—"

"I don't want nobody from Gatlinburg. I want somebody from here. Somebody who knows us. Somebody who's local. Them folks from away from here, they don't know us and our ways. I'd rather have you, no matter how little you know, than some fella I never seen before."

"No guarantees, are we clear on that?" The woman nodded her head. Rileigh sat for a moment thinking.

"All right. I'll give it my best shot."

The look of joy on the woman's face about broke Rileigh's heart.

Swell. Where do you start to find a missing person? Well, Rileigh figured the best place to start was with the person herself. She needed to find out everything she could about Tina Montgomery.

And shoot, she was sure the girl would turn up just fine in a couple of days. She'd probably just gone off with her boyfriend and was embarrassed to tell her mother about it. Or she and some friends got drunk, and she was still hung over. There were plenty of reasons why an 18-year-old girl might not show up at home on time.

Rileigh was certain there was a reasonable explanation, and if it would put her mother's heart to rest to know that somebody was working hard to find her daughter, Rileigh was happy to oblige her.

She looked down at her own empty coffee mug and couldn't remember drinking any of it. Lottie Montgomery hadn't touched hers.

"Let me get another cup of coffee. Then I want to ask you some questions about Tina." When she stepped to the coffee pot, she glanced out the kitchen window where she could see Daisy, her bonnet snug on her head, tossing feed out in the chicken yard.

The chicken coop had been built by Rileigh's grandfather. The birds out there pecking at the dirt now were descendants of the ones that'd been pecking at that same piece of dirt when she was a little girl.

Then she remembered what her aunt had said last night. "Somp'um real bad's about to happen. Somebody's about to get their selves kilt. They're about to wake up in the morning on the wrong side of dirt."

The stupid premonition unaccountably raised the hairs on Rileigh's arms.

Shaking it off, Rileigh got the coffee pot and sat down at the table to talk to Lottie Montgomery about her missing daughter.

Chapter Six

AFTER LOTTIE MONTGOMERY LEFT, Rileigh showered and got dressed, trying to figure out the most reasonable steps to take to try to find somebody who was missing. She had gotten from Tina's mother the names and addresses of all of Tina's close friends.

Mrs. Montgomery said that Tina had a steady boyfriend and he didn't know where Tina was, but Rileigh wasn't buying that. The young woman who'd come bursting out of the bathroom at the Rusty Nail yesterday didn't strike her as the kind of girl to have a "steady boyfriend." In ten seconds, Rileigh had sized her up as a flirt. She was too vibrant and sexy and full of life not to play the field.

Which led to the logical question: if she wasn't telling her mother about her love life, what else was she not telling her mother about?

Rileigh tried to think back on being eighteen. But so much had happened between now and that time in her life she had trouble getting back to it. It was like crawling through the ruins of some great city: nothing but rubble and broken things for miles.

OK, that wasn't entirely accurate. It hadn't all been ruined. There'd been some good in there. And what wasn't good— the war, the battles, dead friends, mutilated children, the constant rattle of gun fire, the smell of blood and smoke — she had managed to wall off when she got back. She'd come home to Black Bear Forge and healed.

Then she'd gone to Eastern Kentucky University's renowned school of criminal justice to study law-enforcement. And she'd gotten a job in Memphis as a police officer. Those years had been good.

Well, up until the end.

At eighteen, Rileigh didn't tell her mother anything. And she would bet the rent Tina Montgomery's mother thought she knew a whole lot more about her daughter than she did. That was the way of it. Their daughters told them what they wanted to hear and it was easier and more comfortable to believe the sweet lie then to go digging around too deep in it to find the ugliness.

Rileigh was sure that Tina Montgomery had a life of her own. And it was one her mother not only didn't know about, but wouldn't have approved of if she had.

So how did that help Rileigh locate the missing Tina? She knew what her mother thought about Tina's life. She had to go find some more objective observers.

She stopped herself in mid-conjecture. She was running out in front of her own headlights. It was entirely possible that Tina Montgomery was sleeping off a drunk at some friend's house, male or female, or some other place that did not put her in as eminent danger of death and dismemberment as her mother feared. That was what Rileigh had to check first, rule that out before she moved on.

Getting into her car, she put her phone in the hands-free device on the dashboard and punched the first of the numbers that Tina's mother given her. There was no answer and Rileigh left no message.

When she got home yesterday, she'd pulled backward into the space in front of the fence where she parked — always did, just in case her mother or her aunt forgot and left their cars out front rather than pulling around the house to park out back. There was little space to turn around in front of the house, and *nobody* could back a car down that steep, bumpy driveway.

She waited until she'd maneuvered down the drive to Bent Twig Road before punching in another of the phone numbers Lottie Montgomery had given her. And so it went as she drove from her mother's house to the Forge. She only found one of Tina's friends at home, and she hadn't seen Tina in a week.

Rileigh was also reluctant to open up about why she was looking for Tina, so she didn't press. It would be easier to get the girl's friends to be open and honest about her if indeed she was missing, but she didn't want to sound the alarm too soon.

By the time Rileigh got into town, she's called all the friends that Tina's mother had provided for her and she'd come up bone dry. So she made her way to the Rusty Nail. Hey, she might get lucky and find Pinky there.

Not.

But she did find Smitty, the bartender, and when she told him that Tina didn't go home last night, he merely raised an eyebrow.

"Looks like that doesn't surprise you," Rileigh said.

"Let's just say that Tina had more going on in her life than her mother knew. "

Just as Rileigh had figured.

"Like…?"

Smitty dodged the question. "I might not be the person to ask about all of this."

"Aw come on Smitty. If you know where Tina is, or might be, spill it. Whether justifiably or not, her mother is worried about her. If you really liked Tina, you'd help me help her mother."

Smitty tossed the wet rag he used to wipe down the bar onto its shiny surface and looked at Rileigh for a long moment. "Where you need to start looking is at the sheriff's office. I don't think Tina ever got charged with anything, but I do know she was into some really bad shit." He paused. "With the kinda people you don't want to get on the wrong side of. I'm sure her mother didn't know anything about it."

The courthouse in Black Bear Forge, Tennessee, looked like small town courthouses all over the south — Tennessee, North Carolina, Kentucky. The whole town was laid out around the courthouse square, and in the center of the Square was the building itself. The original courthouse had been destroyed by a fire in the early 1900s and they kept the basic architecture of the south when they built the new one. There were big broad steps that led up to a wide porch where white columns sat on pedestals to hold up a roof over the entrance. The doors were oversized, ten or maybe twelve feet tall.

Once inside, big steps lead both up and down. The upstairs held court rooms and the county clerks office. District court was held on certain days in the smaller rooms on that floor. Circuit court was held in the big room on the top floor on the other days.

What Rileigh was looking for was in the basement. The Yarmouth County Sheriff's Department occupied the whole basement, with offices on both sides of the hallway.

In counties that contained cities big enough to have their own police departments, the sheriff's departments did what they had originally been created to do... which was to deal with crime outside the city limits, but more importantly, collect county taxes.

Black Bear Forge did not have its own police force. Crime and criminals in Yarmouth county were the responsibility of the sheriff's department and its deputies. And they could call in the Tennessee state police in a pinch.

Rileigh hadn't known Mum — Sheriff Jedidiah T. Mumford — but he was legendary. Sheriff was an elected position, and Mum had been elected to it repeatedly for something like 25 or 30 years. Rileigh had only seen Mitchell Webster, the interim sheriff, absence at a distance. He was tall, broad-shouldered and lean, and — she wasn't blind – good looking in a rugged kind of way. But she'd never spoken to him.

Pushing through the doors into the sheriff's department, she walked to the reception desk. The receptionist smiled.

"How can I help you?"

"I'm here to make a public records request," Rileigh said. The woman's welcoming smile began to drain away. " I'm interested in what you can tell me about a young woman named Tina Montgomery. Her mother – "

"—is Lottie Montgomery, right?" Came a voice from behind her.

She turned to discover that Webster was even better looking close up. "Why are you interested in Tina Montgomery?

"Because Tina's missing. Lottie said she reported it to you, and you wouldn't do anything about it."

Rileigh watched the man's face close up.

"There isn't any information we can give you about

Tina Montgomery because it's part of an ongoing investigation."

"Open investigation? Lottie Montgomery said you told her you couldn't investigate until Tina had been missing for twenty-four hours. So how could there be an investigation now?"

The big man paused, then gestured toward a door at the end of the reception counter. "Why don't we talk in my office, Miss …"

"I'm Rileigh Bishop."

"This way, Miss Bishop."

Rileigh realized he didn't know who she was. And she greeted that understanding with mixed feelings. On the one hand, it was a bit disheartening not to be recognized in your own hometown. Everybody else in the office knew who she was. And *what she'd done*. Which was the other side of the he-didn't-recognize-her coin. The acting sheriff might not have already formed an opinion of her based on what'd happened last year in Memphis.

Rileigh followed him into his office, noted that it was as bare as a monk's cell. There were no pictures on the walls, none on his desk either. In fact, there didn't appear to be anything personal at all in the whole room. Maybe this had been the previous sheriff's office, and he had moved Mum's things out but hadn't had time to move his own in yet.

But somehow she didn't think so. Though she had known him less than 90 seconds, she had felt a clear sense of "separate-ness" about him. She suspected that this man didn't put any private things out for other people to peruse because he was a private person and didn't share who he was with anybody.

She sat down in the chair facing his desk. He sat behind it.

"Why did Lottie Montgomery ask you to go looking for her daughter? Do you have—"

"She came to me because I work for the Good Guys, a private investigation firm in Gatlinburg." She hurried on, before he could ask any questions. "I'm not an investigator, but she thought I was and—" she paused, and studied him, wondering if she should be honest, tell him why Lottie had to asked her to look into the case. She went for it. "She didn't think you would do anything about her daughter's disappearance because you're one of 'them.'"

"Them?"

"If you didn't grow up in the Forge, if you can't trace your ancestors back to before Davy Crockett went off and got himself shot at the Alamo, you're not to be trusted. You came from 'away from here'."

"Is that like a place out there somewhere — Away From Here? I'll have you know I was an upstanding citizen of that fair community, played on the Away-From-Here little league team, graduated from Away-From-Here high school — didn't go out for football, though, I was a band kid — and joined the Away-From-Here Unitarian Church where I filled up those little plastic communion cups with grape juice every Sunday."

Rileigh couldn't help smiling.

The big man settled back in his chair "Well, contrary to Mrs. Montgomery's opinion, I am looking into the disappearance of her daughter, even though legally I can't classify her as a missing person for 24 hours. And I am looking into it because, also contrary to Mrs. Montgomery's opinion, I actually *do* give a shit about the people in this county."

Before Rileigh could say anything else, one of the receptionists opened the door a crack and and put her head into the room.

"Sheriff, the guy on line one says he heard you were looking for Tina Montgomery. And he knows something that might be helpful."

Sheriff Webster looked at Rileigh.

"I'm sorry, but you'll have to excuse me Miss Bishop. I have to take this call."

He was dismissing her.

Rileigh stood, reluctantly, tried not to show how irritated she was. "Well, thank you for your time."

She turned and walked out of his office. And down the hall, down the steps, out the big front doors, down those steps, and got into her car parked at the curb … where she sat until she saw the sheriff exit out one of the side doors of the building, get into his cruiser, and drive away.

Rileigh followed him.

Chapter Seven

THE SHERIFF's cruiser headed out along the winding roads in the steep mountains around the Forge. Rileigh had no trouble following him. On these roads, there was nowhere to pull off, so she figured he had probably spotted her riding his tail. If he hadn't, he wasn't much of a police officer. But then, cars always stacked up one behind the other like a freight train on mountain roads, because there was nowhere to pass. Get behind some nervous tourist who kept looking at the drop offs on every hairpin and it could take you over an hour to get to Gatlinburg.

Of course, Rileigh knew Yarmouth County like the back of her hand, and she begin to think she might know where the sheriff was headed. It wasn't like there was much out this direction from town. Just woods full of black bears. Once the woods would have been full of moonshiners. Now the abandoned stills had grown up with weeds and the lingering aroma of liquor had been enticing black bears to come sniffing around for half a century. Moonshining days were over, but if the sheriff was going where

43

she thought he was, somebody had put him on to taking a look at the grass hut.

When Rileigh pulled her car off the road onto the small piece of horizontal landscape beside it, the sheriff was standing by his cruiser's open door waiting for her.

"You're going to tell me why you followed me out here?"

Well, at least he'd noticed she was back there. That was a good sign as far as his law enforcement acumen went. She walked around the back of his cruiser and came to stand in front of him.

"You're looking for Tina Montgomery. I'm looking for Tina Montgomery. You got a tip on where she might be, and it's a free country. If I happen to want to drive out Shady Creek Road on this fine Tuesday morning, there's no law against it."

"Can you say obstruction of justice?"

"I'm not obstructing anything. You can't obstruct from behind. All I did was follow you."

Sheriff Webster looked annoyed. He knew there was nothing he could do to make her leave, might even know she understood the law as well as he did, which opened up the can of worms of her past. Maybe after she left his office this morning, he'd asked around about her. God, she hoped not.

"Why are you so interested in this case?" You could hear the frustration in his voice.

"Full disclosure – I need the money. Tina's mother offered to pay me $300 to go looking for her daughter." She held her hand up to silence him and he swallowed the protest in his throat. "I told her there were no guarantees. I made sure she understood that all I could do was some poking around, shaking a few trees and seeing what fell out. You and I both know, that the girl probably isn't missing at all. Certainly not in any legal sense. She's just off somewhere, sleeping off a drunk, or shacking up with her boyfriend, or any number of perfectly reasonable activities that an eighteen-year-old girl with big brown eyes and a nice ass might be engaged in."

Rileigh changed the subject, trying to keep him off-balance. "So who told you to come poking around at the grass hut?"

"What do you know about the grass hut?"

"A hell of a lot more than you do. And you didn't answer my question. Who told you to come poking around out here?"

The sheriff didn't bite, just pressed his lips tight together, so she asked again. "What do you know about the grass hut?"

There wasn't anything to know about the place that Rileigh didn't know. The meadows in this hanging valley in the mountains were just about the only pieces of flat ground with good sun in the whole county, which meant they were the only place you could grow weed. And it had been the location of choice for many a weed grower over the years.

She didn't know exactly who had built the hut. But somebody had, long before she was born. It was just a hut, a shack, stuck back in the bushes under the trees so you couldn't find it if you didn't know it was there. But hell, it was an open secret, even back then. Law-enforcement knew who was growing weed, where they were growing it, who they were selling it to, and what the going rate was. And they turned around, closed their eyes, and pretended they didn't see a thing. It was just weed.

The shack reminded Rileigh of those lean-to things they put up on the Appalachian Trail. Places where hikers could get out of the sun or the rain, with no amenities at all. The shack was one big room, and at one time there had been cots for the growers to sleep on. Somebody even put in counters and cabinets and a sink with a pump on it, rather than a faucet, bringing water in from the creek. No facilities, though. No outhouse. If a bear could shit in the woods, so could the humans.

Rileigh had been out here several times for various reasons, had even brought her aunt here a time or two. There was a special patch of weed here that was grown just for her.

"What I know about the grass hut is what everybody else knows about it: that it was built by weed growers, and when they didn't need it anymore, it just sat empty. Well, except for my Aunt Daisy."

"Your Aunt Daisy… What does she have to do with this with the grass hut?"

Rileigh would have to back up quite a way to tell it so it would make some sense for the sheriff. It went all the way back to her childhood, when Georgia would come over to play and they would sit on the back porch with baby dolls or Barbie dolls, pretending they weren't poor mountain kids, pretending they were somewhere exciting and exotic instead of living their lives with only a few hours of direct sunshine every day. The sun didn't come up above the top of Scarecrow Mountain until about ten o'clock in the morning, and it went down again in the west about three. Hard to get a decent suntan with only that much sunshine.

Sometimes Georgia's older brother Ian would tag along with her when she came to visit Rileigh. Daisy took a shine to that boy from the get-go. In fact, it was clear that she liked Ian a whole lot more than she liked Georgia. Daisy was downright mean to Georgia sometimes, and Rileigh never knew why that was.

But she would bake cookies for Ian, give him cold milk

and set him up at the big people table when he visited. Over the years, the two of them had developed an odd friendship. Even after he graduated from high school, sometimes Ian would drop by the house just to hang out with Rileigh's aunt.

And Lord knew Daisy didn't have many friends. Folks shied away from her after she had that mental breakdown and got sent away to the sanitarium. She never was the same afterwards, but Ian didn't seem to mind. Or maybe she'd simply never shown him anything but the sweet old lady persona she could summon whenever she needed it.

When she got breast cancer, she took chemotherapy treatments that made her hair fall out and she got as scrawny as Rileigh's mother had said Rileigh was. Ian came by the house one evening with a bag of weed. Everybody knew he was growing it out by the grass hut. He told Daisy he'd read that smoking weed, or putting it in brownies or spaghetti sauce or some other tasty dish, would help with the nausea she suffered from the cancer drugs. She was miserable from the effects of the drugs, and she would've tried anything. And wonder of wonders, it worked.

Ian kept her supplied with "special weed" as he called it, a special mellow strain he grew just for her. When the treatments ended and Daisy was declared cancer free, she depended upon Ian to supply her with weed for her own personal recreational use. Often, he took her out to the grass hut with him to help "cultivate the garden." That had continued for years. Long after Ian got out of the weed business, he still grew a special patch just for her.

Every now and then he'd come by and pick her up, take her with him to tend the patch, because there wasn't much in life that Daisy enjoyed more than gardening. To Ian's credit, even though she sank so far down into dementia she only had a few functioning synapses left, he still brought her weed and sometimes even hung around to enjoy it with her.

"I'll make you a deal. You tell me who sent you sniffing around out here and I'll tell you what my Aunt Daisy has to do with the place."

"You first."

"Seriously. You think I won't keep my end of the bargain?"

"Hedging my bets."

Rileigh gave him a withering glance and then told him the story. When she was done, she demanded payment of the debt.

"I don't know who it was who called," the sheriff said. "But I've got a pretty good idea it was that fellow who tends bar at the Rusty Nail. What's his name?"

"Smitty."

Rileigh had asked Smitty what he knew about Tina and he'd held out on her.

"He said he heard I was looking for Tina Montgomery and he'd just thought of something I might want to know, that she'd mentioned the grass hut once, hinted that she went there sometimes for 'privacy' with her boyfriend."

"Who's her boyfriend?"

"He said her boyfriend's named Aubrey Tucker, but he didn't think that's who she was talking about, said she was very secretive about it."

"And so you came out here hoping she might be here, shacked .. well, hutted up with her boyfriend."

"Longshot, sure, but it was a start."

"I could have saved you a trip if you'd told me where you were planning to go. The grass hut isn't the sort of place where you spend the night, and half the next day shacked up with your honey."

She looked around. "And there's no car."

"And no tire tracks, at least not as far as I can tell—because *you drove in right over them.*"

"On these rocks, there wouldn't be any track marks."

He said nothing.

Rileigh sighed. "Well, she's not here now, but I guess it's possible she came here yesterday. Let's see if she left anything behind."

Rileigh turned to head up into the woods, but the sheriff didn't move. When she turned around questioningly, he said.

"Remind me when it was I agreed to include you in my investigations?"

Rileigh threw up her hands in disgust.

"Look, we either go together or you leave me here and I'll follow. You pick."

He sighed. "Come on."

Chapter Eight

EVEN THOUGH THE weed growers tried to take different routes across the meadow and into the woods around the grass hut, their constant back and forth trips wore a trail anyway. The last time she'd been here, the trail had been easy to follow, meandering across the meadow, scuffed dirt, crushed grass and bent over weeds marking the winding route. This time, it was harder to find. It had probably been years since someone had been growing up here.

Rileigh had to study the ground to locate what was left of the path, careful not to deviate off of it as she lead the way out across the wildflower strewn meadow, where butterflies danced in the sunlight and bees hummed a drowsy song.

"You better be grateful I came along. Do you think you could have found this trail without me?"

"It wouldn't have been easy, but I would've found it eventually."

"So you're saying you don't need my help at all, "she said, as she found her way through the grass and up the hill side to the trees.

"You said it, I didn't."

Rileigh stop talking, concentrating on staying on the thin line of trail that lead up into the woods where the hut was located.

Of course, this hadn't been a meadow back in the day.

Once you got into the trees, it would've been difficult for anybody to find the hut if they didn't know it was there. Whoever had built it knew what he was doing in terms of camouflage, because the stand of bushes that protected it from sight looked like any other bush and brush pile.

When they crested a small knoll in the woods, Rileigh stopped and pointed down the hillside to the brush that concealed the shack, then beyond it to the secluded meadow where generations of weed growers had grown their crops.

"Just be glad I don't charge extra for the scenic tour." She gestured toward the meadow and the brush pile and asked, "you see it?"

"Sure, I do." But Rileigh could see his eyes seeking out some change of shape that would indicate something in the woods that hadn't grown here. He was bluffing. But she didn't call his hand on it. There was no sense in rubbing his nose in the fact that she knew way more about this place — and this county— than he did.

If he was as smart as she hoped he was, he would figure out quick that he needed her help. But he had to come to that conclusion on his own. So she stepped out in front of him and continued down the side of the hill where are the trail had completely vanished now.

Coming around a big oleander bush, Rileigh stopped in her tracks and gestured toward the rundown building that age had bleached gray. The wood looked soft, like the coat on a gray pony.

"Thar she blows." The two of them went together to

the hut. Rileigh reached out to open the door and he grabbed her arm. "Don't touch the knob."

"What? Do you think there might be fingerprints on it that will lead us to Tina?" She couldn't keep the derision out of her voice. He didn't rise to that bait either, though.

He just turned the knob by grasping where it fit into the door, and pushed the door inward. The place was as empty as Rileigh knew it'd be.

As soon as the sheriff got a good look at it, he wrinkled his nose and she realized that there was a distinct musty, leafy smell to the interior of the building that was unpleasant. She had never noticed that before. She was sure if they opened the door and the two windows and let a breeze flow through, it would wash away the stink.

"Why would anybody come here to rendezvous with their boyfriend?"

"Well, not to put too fine a point on it, but there is a floor here to lay on, if laying down is necessary to the activity you came here to do. But I'm sure the real draw of the place is its isolation.

"So why was she hiding?"

"I only got to talk to one of her friends, the names her mother gave to me," Rileigh said. "Her name was G.G. Masterson, and she hadn't seen Tina in a week. When I asked her if Tina had a boyfriend, she said yeah, Aubrey Tucker, the same guy Tina's mother mentioned. I heard a 'but' … in the response and pushed her, and she said she suspected Aubrey might not be the only one."

"So she's sneaking around to see this guy behind her boyfriend's back. Maybe that wasn't the only reason Tina was hiding the identity of this guy from the whole world?"

Rileigh lifted her eyebrow. "Meaning?"

"Meaning maybe he didn't want anybody to know he was seeing *her*, either."

The two of them looked around the big empty room. There was nothing to indicate anybody had been here. No trash, cigarette butts.

The sheriff ran his hand across the countertops and then lifted it and looked at his palm. "No dust."

Rileigh hadn't noticed that, but when she came to look it was true. There was no dust on the countertop, though it was thick on the windowsills.

"Looks like somebody has been here recently." He turned to Rileigh. "I need to look around outside."

"For what?"

"I'll know it when I see it."

"Like maybe Tina's secret boyfriend dropped his business card — land line, cell phone numbers and his email address —in the grass the last time he was here?"

"Well *somebody's* been here recently. We need to see what we can find."

"We? Unless you got a mouse in your pocket, you're referring to you and me, the two of us?" The sheriff rolled his eyes and headed out the door. Outside in the dappled sunlight, Rileigh pointed toward the west where the sun was hanging just above the mountaintop.

"How about I go this way, you go that?"

"Check fifty, seventy-five yards out, maybe. Give me a holler if you find anything."

He turned to leave, then turned back.

"And if you do find anything, don't touch it," the sheriff said.

"You mean, 'don't pick up the gun to see if it's loaded', stuff like that? Gosh, I wouldn't have thought of that," Rileigh said.

The sheriff didn't respond, just headed out through the woods east of the cabin. Rileigh turned and headed out in the opposite direction.

Chapter Nine

RILEIGH HEADED off into the woods and until she came to the bed of "special weed" Ian grew for Daisy. It wasn't far from the grass hut. Then she began to systematically search the area. She walked a full seventy-five yards, searching the underbrush as she walked, looking for anything out of the ordinary. Then she made another sweep across the same area, but about five feet from where she'd been walking before. Back and forth, like mowing a lawn, Rileigh searched the tangle of brush and weeds and bushes on the forest floor. She scared a couple of squirrels and received a stern talking to from some blue jays. That was about it.

She was within sight of the hut, almost done with her circuit, when something off to her left caught her eye. Wrong color. Pink. Nothing in the woods this time of year was pink.

She moved carefully toward the splash of color, making sure not to step on ... anything. There was something at the base of an oak tree twenty or so feet to the right, a lump mostly covered in leaves. When she got closer, she could make out the shape of the lump.

Another couple of steps and she could see what the pink color was. The body lying face up in the pile of leaves, partially covered in them, was wearing a hot pink shirt.

Her gasp was involuntary. Rileigh staggered back a step. so shocked at finding anything at all, she couldn't catch her breath for a couple of seconds.

Watching where she put every step, she drew closer to the body. She didn't see anything more in the nearby loam of the forest floor, no footprints or drag marks, but she was meticulously careful not to step on anything that might be either.

The sight that was revealed when she got close enough to get a good look, was horrifying. A dead body.

It certainly wasn't the first one she'd ever seen, and some part of her mind pointed out that at least this one wasn't missing any arms or legs. Staring at where the feet poked up out of the leaves, Rileigh concentrated on taking in every detail in the same way she'd made a grid out of the search area. Sweeping her eyes back and forth, she noted the details.

One shoe, one bare foot. She'd lost the other shoe somewhere.

The toenails on the bare foot were painted a bright cherry red.

The legs and the bottom portion of the torso were covered in fallen leaves, someone's inadequate attempt to conceal the body. It would have taken more than a pile of leaves to conceal the gory wound in the girl's belly that showed through the hot pink shirt she wore.

She'd been more than stabbed — her belly had been

ripped open, a gaping wound from a big knife, maybe a butcher knife.

Rileigh's mind ping-ponged.

"DON'T you touch my sharp knife," Aunt Daisy says, though Rileigh is sitting quietly at the table making no effort to touch anything on it — particularly not the knife, with its blade that shines bright, sharpened to a razor's edge.

"You think people get cut with sharp knives but that ain't the case at all. You get cut with knives that's dull, because they won't cut through whatever it is you're trying to carve and you have to push down harder and it slips … next thing you know it's sewing thread and a darning needle, putting stitches in your thumb."

Mama had told Rileigh that when she was a little girl, they didn't go to town to see a doctor for something as ordinary as a cut open hand or foot. Grandma just got out her sewing kit and some thread and sewed the wound shut herself. That's why Rileigh is careful not to get anywhere near Aunt Daisy's prized knife. She didn't know which would hurt worse, getting her hand sliced open by the knife, or feeling the needle go in and out of her flesh to sew the wound shut.

RILEIGH'S EYES continued their upward sweep, back and forth across the body. The area just above the knife wound was clear of leaves. Not like they had gotten knocked off somehow, or blew away. it was clear that whoever'd put the leaves on top of the body had intentionally left the top portion visible.

Why would that be? Either you hide the body so nobody can find it, or you leave it out for all to see. Either one of those choices made sense, but covering up half of it and leaving the rest clean made no sense.

It was then that Rileigh swept her eyes over the face. Suddenly, she couldn't breathe, the air as thick as pudding around her.

She felt her knees connect with the leaves below her. She floated down to the ground in slow motion, because time had stopped when she got a good look at the face of the very dead Tina Montgomery.

The world had stopped spinning in its orbit and ceased revolving around the sun. The whole solar system, the whole universe froze rock solid in that instant.

The only thing moving in that frozen universe, the only thing that could still move were Rileigh's eyes and they traveled up the face, slid up to the top of the girl's head where her black hair was a tangle in dirt and leaves. She looked at the eyes—closed, so you could see the false eyelashes. False eyelash. One of the falsies had gone the way of her shoe. But there were still rhinestones affixed to the top of her eyelids and Rileigh wondered yet again how she kept them there.

Only yesterday she had watched this girl — alive and vibrant and full of life — come barreling out of the women's bathroom at the Rusty Nail ... shouting at somebody on her cell phone.

That part was significant, the yelling at somebody on the cell phone part. Obviously the girl who lay here partially buried in leaves had been killed only a few hours after that argument.

Then Rileigh looked — had to, tried not to, but the universe was frozen in place, suspended in eternity like an insect in amber, and only her eyes were still alive and functioning. Able to transmit images to her brain, which was also still functioning. And her brain was able to interpret those images, make sense of them even though the horror made no sense at all.

The reality that Rileigh's eyes revealed to her as the world stood still and her body collapsed onto the leaves was too awful to countenance, but too vivid not to be real.

Tina Montgomery lay on her back in a pile of leaves on the forest floor, her mouth open as if in one final shriek of horror.

And her tongue had been cut out.

Rileigh Bishop began to scream.

Chapter Ten

It's the perfect thing to do. Rileigh knows it the moment the idea comes to her and even though her heart is full to bursting with sorrow that her sister will be leaving tomorrow, she thinks doing this thing, this perfect thing, will make her feel better somehow.

She gets up out of the bed her mother tucked her snug into, turns on the desk lamp, gets out a sheet of lined paper and carefully prints a letter on it. The paper only has the small lines, not the great big ones, with dots between them, so you know how how high to make the bottom of a b or d, or how big to make the letter e. She gets half way through with her first attempt, reads and realizes she has misspelled. She made the e's in the note backwards.

Disgusted, she wads the piece of paper up in a ball and throws it away.

Finally, she has all the words right and the letters are all front-wards. She sets down the pencil and whispers the words out loud as she reads them. "Please don't forget me." She had put a period at the end of the sentence, but she goes back now and puts a line above it, making it an exclamation point. "Your sister, Rileigh."

She has no trouble locating a picture of herself to include in the envelope with the note because the school pictures that were taken in

59

the fall came in last week and she has sheets of wallet-sized pictures to choose from. There is the eight-by-ten, the two five-by-sevens, and the twelve wallet-sized in the package her mother bought. Mama kept the eight-by-ten for herself, and gave one of the five-by-sevens to Jillian and another to Aunt Daisy.

Rileigh has one of the two sheets of wallet-sized photos. She has to be careful with the scissors cutting them apart, but when she has a single wallet-sized photo of herself, she's ready. She will have to get a paper clip out of the top drawer in Jillian's desk to attach her picture to the note. Then she will place the note under Jillian's things that she packed in the the new suitcase somebody gave her at her bridal shower.

She sits for a moment, examining the face in the picture. Dark hair, hazel eyes and missing teeth in front. She searches the face for the image of her sister. Rileigh wants nothing else in life as much as she wants to look like Jillian. Well, except for her sister not moving out. She wants that more than she has ever wanted anything, but she knows she won't get what she wants, knows that after they do the wedding thing, Jillian will get into David Hicks' car in her big white dress and they'll drive away and Rileigh will be alone in her bedroom without Jillian for comfort.

She swallows a sob, folds the note in half, and tiptoes out into the hallway with the picture and the note clutched tight in her hand.

As soon as she gets near the door to Jillian's room, she hears voices. It's late, like really late, maybe even midnight or something like that. Who could Jillian be talking to at that hour of the night? Well, doesn't matter who it is, Rileigh can't hide the note in her sister's suitcase until whoever is in her room leaves. So she goes back into her bedroom and curls up in a blanket beside the door.

She has left her door open a crack, and she will listen carefully until the person who's been talking to Jillian leaves.

The next time she opens her eyes she knows it is very late indeed and she has slept longer than she intended to. She gets out of bed again and tiptoes down the hallway to listen at Jillian's door, but there are no voices now.

Turning the knob slowly so it won't creak, she steps into the room. It's dark except for the spill of moonlight through the big window on the wall on the other side of the bed. Her eyes get accustomed to the darkness, so she can see well in the full moonlight. What she sees is that Jillian isn't in her bed. But it's not made up. So Jillian must have gone to bed and then got up later and went … downstairs to get something to eat, maybe. Sometimes Jillie got up in the middle of the night to get a sweet roll or make herself cinnamon toast.

Rileigh stares at the unmade bed where Jillian isn't sleeping, and there's something wrong. Even in the dim moonlight, she can see that the bed is unmade, and there's some dark substance smeared on the sheets, on the bedspread, and on the pillow. She edges around the bed, trying to get a closer look, and she sees a splash of something dark on the little bead things on the front of Jillie's wedding dress, which is lying in a heap on the floor beside the bed.

What in the world?

Closer now, Rileigh reaches out a finger and touches the black substance … whatever it is that's been spilled on the sheets on the bed. She looks at it wet on her fingertip, and up close it doesn't look black. It looks … red.

Suddenly, Rileigh is afraid. So afraid she can't get her breath. Because she thinks she knows what it is that's spilled on Jillie's bed.

In two steps she reaches the lamp with the lacy shade that Mama gave Jillian, the one Jillie put smiley faces on and Mama got mad.

Light floods the room and Rileigh freezes in place, as stiff as a statue, looking at the small blotch of red on her fingertip so she won't have to look at the blood-stained sheets beyond it.

The sheets are hanging off the bed on the floor, and there is a huge stain of blood, like, how could there be that much blood. It's more blood than there is in anybody's veins, it's splattered everywhere.

She tries not to think the thought, but she can't banish it. She tries not to know what she knows, but you can't unsee a thing after you've seen it and you can't unknow the truth about something once you know it. The blood on the sheets on Jillian's bed is Jillian's blood.

So where is Jillian?

Rileigh wants to look for her, to cry out her name in a shriek that will wake up mama and daddy and Aunt Daisy … but she can't make her mouth form words or her voice form a sound. She is frozen there in her bare feet. The note and picture she planned to hide in the bottom of Jillian's suitcase slip out of her hand to the floor. She feels them, but can't hold on because her fingers don't work anymore.

That's when she sees it, and wishes then that it was her eyes that didn't work so she wouldn't have to look. It's right there in the center of the pillowcase, the white one next to the one covered it blood. It's like a cherry on the top of vanilla ice cream, a red thing you can't miss on the white sheet.

What is it?

And as soon as she sees it, it seems like the thing gets bigger and bigger until it's bigger than the pillow it's lying on — blue and purple and red and bloody, it is the single most horrible thing Rileigh has ever seen in her life.

She doesn't want to know what it is, but she can see it. It's right there, lying on the white pillowcase, obviously placed carefully there so it wouldn't soil the pillowcase, on display on the white background so you can't miss it.

Rileigh stares at it, uncomprehending, trying not to see it, trying not to know that lying on the white pillowcase in the bloody sheets of her sister Jillian's bed is a tongue. A human tongue, cut out of somebody's mouth.

Chapter Eleven

MITCH MOVED AWAY from the little cabin in the woods in the opposite direction than Rileigh Bishop had gone. He forced himself to concentrate on the search, to drain all the irritation and frustration out of his thoughts so he could put all his mental resources to the task at hand — locating anything that might lead him to find Tina Montgomery.

Yeah, it was a stretch. But she'd gone *somewhere* after she got off work at the Rusty Nail yesterday. Maybe it was here to meet the mysterious secret boyfriend.

Rileigh Bishop had thrown a large monkey wrench into this investigation, and he tried to hold onto that, because if he didn't, he'd have to accept some uncomfortable realities he'd rather not face.

No, not happening. Self delusion was a non-refundable, one way ticket to failure … in the middle seat with no leg-room.

She had said out loud what everybody else was thinking, what he knew to be true before she said it, but since she had tacked words onto the concept, he couldn't ignore it anymore. Mitch was an outsider here. He was … what had she called it … oh yeah, he was from Away From Here. He didn't belong. Oh sure, he was a southerner, a fellow Tennessean. But growing up in Nashville was a world and culture away from growing up in Black Bear Forge.

He knew how hostile the mountain people could be to outside strangers, knew it intellectually, the way you know the periodic table or the recipe for bean dip. But he had never experienced it until he had taken the job here. And in the beginning, the natural courtesy and friendliness of the people in Yarmouth County had masked the truth for awhile. Now it was unavoidable.

He was the sheriff, at least for the time being and who knew for how long, in a place whose residents wouldn't give him the time of day because he wasn't one of them, didn't wear a team jersey, didn't know the secret handshake or the magic code word.

A thing like that would only be mildly annoying under other circumstances, but you couldn't keep the peace, really keep the peace, for long in any community if they didn't trust you. If they wouldn't open up to you and give you the information a law enforcement officer had to have. The maybe-missing, maybe-not Tina Montgomery had simply flushed the pheasants out of the bush. Her mother had gone elsewhere looking for help because she didn't trust the Away From Here Sheriff to do the job. Not that he'd given her any reason to trust him.

But Rileigh didn't invent that reality. She'd just shone a floodlight on it so he couldn't ignore it anymore.

Rileigh Bishop.

Her face formed in his mind when he thought of her and he was taken aback, only just now registering how pretty she was. She was slender. Okay, thin, almost delicate, but her fragility was of those Steel Magnolias kind, the kind that would still be standing after a Category Five hurricane blew through. Hazel eyes, chestnut colored hair with copper highlights that sparkled in the sun.

Copper highlights that sparkled in the sun?

Seriously. He definitely had to get a better grip on his professional persona if he was taking note of a thing like that.

Coming to a stand of bushes at the edge of a steep incline, he stepped closer to peer over the bushes. He needed to walk it back, establish more distance between him and the woman who —

Suddenly his feet slid out from under him. One second he was upright, walking through the woods, and the next he was sliding on his butt down a steep embankment, struggling not to pitch over and roll all the way to the bottom.

He ended on his butt with a bone-jarring thump on something painfully solid in the leaf cover at the bottom of a ravine, then rocked backward into the dirt he'd just plowed a path through. So jarred, he barely noticed the little avalanche of dirt that had chased him down the embankment and landed on him— in his hair— sliding down the collar of his shirt in the back. And he'd lost his hat.

He tasted blood in his mouth and realized he'd landed so abruptly he'd bitten his tongue.

What the …?

He sat where he was, jarred and disoriented, trying to piece together what had just happened. He'd just been walking through the woods, had gotten close to the edge of an embankment. Tried to look over it and the ground beneath him had given way.

When he shook his head to clear it, dirt flew out of his hair in ever direction like water off a dog.

Getting slowly to his feet, he searched the area and spotted his hat a few feet away, half buried in the mini avalanche. He picked it up, beat the dirt off it on his leg, and set it on his head. Then he tried to get the dirt/leaf mixture off his shirt — and out of his shirt. It was a useless effort.

He unbuttoned the brown shirt and took it off, shook it out, groaning at the smear of damp dirt/almost mud up the whole back of it, turning to see that the smear extended down his pants to his butt and —

The sound of a scream froze him in place. A woman's voice, some distance away, a cry of horror and terror that set his teeth on edge.

Rileigh.

He was moving before he willed it, clawing his way back up the side of the embankment, digging his fingers and boot toes into the soft dirt. He crashed through the bushes that had obscured the crevice from view and ran through the woods back toward the grass hut. There were no more screams, just the one that'd risen higher in pitch and volume, then cut off abruptly.

He drew his service revolver from its holster with muddy fingers, pointed the muzzle toward the ground as the building came into sight in the trees ahead. Slowing, he moved from tree to tree as he approached it, his head on a swivel, looking all around, his eyes searching the tangle of forest around him.

Perhaps he should call her name, holler out to see if she was okay, but immediately jettisoned the consideration. The scream he'd heard hadn't come from a woman who'd happened upon a snake in the woods. It was a cry of horror and revulsion that'd been ripped from the throat of someone in trouble.

Running from a tree to the hut, he peered in a window

and saw that it was deserted. Down the side of the house with his back to the wall, then he peered around the corner. Nothing. He moved carefully into the woods, tree to tree, beyond the cabin where Rileigh had gone to search for—

There she was. About fifty feet away, he could see her outline through the brush. Approaching cautiously, he stopped at the last tree between them.

Rileigh Bishop sat on her knees beside a pile of leaves, and from his vantage point, Mitch could see a human foot sticking up out of the pile.

Chapter Twelve

"RILEIGH." The sound of her name came from behind her as if from a great distance, and she couldn't seem to assign a person to the voice that'd spoken it.

But the sound pulled her back from the edge of some lonely place above a black, empty, bottomless void and an awareness of her surroundings returned slowly to her.

She felt the leaves under her knees where she knelt, could hear the approach of footsteps. Then a man was standing beside her, but it was all wrong and the sight of him confused her. He was wearing a brown cowboy hat but had no shirt on. He held a pistol in a double-hand grip, pointed at the ground.

"Rileigh," he said again, as he holstered his weapon with dirty fingers, and the pieces fell into place. It was Sheriff Webster. Why had he taken off his shirt?

"Are you all right?" He took a step toward her, but made no effort to touch her, which was a good thing because she didn't want to be touched. She felt a sudden revulsion at the thought, because it would reengage her to the world, hook her back up to reality and she wasn't quite ready …

Her eyes went again to the face of the girl buried in leaves. Not to her eyes with rhinestones on the lids, but to her mouth, the open bloody hole in her face below her nose.

She got unsteadily to her feet, and the sheriff made no effort to help her. That was good.

"Tina Montgomery," he said, his voice level, dispassionate, almost businesslike.

No, not businesslike. Professional. He was a professional, doing his job here, just like she was. Like she was *supposed* to be. Gritting her teeth, she grabbed hold of her emotions and managed to answer the unasked question with a voice that didn't shake or quaver.

"Yes, that's Tina."

"Did you touch anything?"

The question landed like a drop of water in hot grease.

"No, Sheriff Webster, I didn't touch anything." There was acid in her voice and she was glad of it. She was glad of the surge of anger that rushed through her veins because it was empowering, giving her back the strength that'd drained out of her when she saw …

Own it. Own the reality, no shying away.

When she saw the dead body of Tina Montgomery — with her tongue cut out.

Pointing to the ground at her feet. "Those two marks in the leaves — my knee prints. You can have forensic make casts of my knees so you can eliminate those knee prints from any other knee prints you might find."

He either didn't pick up on the sarcasm in her words or didn't care, because he was all business.

"Back away from the body, please."

If he tells me this is a crime scene, I'll punch him in the face.

"This is a crime scene."

Her fury cleared her vision.

"What happened to your shirt?"

He looked down at his own bare chest as if he'd just realized he had no shirt on.

"Fell in some mud." He tried to keep that professional tone in the statement, but his face flushed and rather than feeling triumphant at the gotcha, she relaxed just a little at the display of humanity. When he repeated the request — "Please, step back from the body," the cold tone was gone and it became merely a reasonable request.

Rileigh retreated from the pile of leaves, walked back through the leaves and stopped about twenty feet away.

"That pink shirt she's wearing, a work shirt, like she was wearing yesterday at the Rusty Nail."

The sheriff merely nodded, stood where he was examining "the crime scene" without approaching closer. Then he took his cell phone from his pocket, wiped his muddy fingers on the leg of his pants, and punched an icon on the screen. The phone was set to "speaker" so Rileigh could hear the dispatcher at the sheriff's office answer.

"I need Rawlings, Crawford and Mullins to report Code 10-38 to Shady Creek Road, about two miles from the bridge..." he paused, turned to Rileigh, "What's that river?"

The bridge didn't span a river. It spanned a creek, and if every creek in the mountains had a name...

"Just tell her it's the second bridge past where the guard rail's out on Cutter's Branch. Another quarter of a mile on the right."

"It's the second–" he began but the dispatcher cut him off.

"I heard. Rawlings, Crawford and Mullins, Code 10-38."

Rileigh wasn't completely certain — different munici-palities embellished standard signs with some of their own — but she was relatively certain Code 10-38 meant, "lights, no siren."

"Ten-four," the sheriff said and ended the call.

There was silence then. She could see the sheriff considering.

"I need you to go, now. This is an official police matter and–" He held up his hand to ward off her protest. "I need to protect the integrity of the crime scene until I can get a forensics team from Gatlinburg in here."

She opened her mouth and he cut her off again before she could speak.

"But you could ... if you would." Then he gestured down at his bare torso. "I dropped my shirt when ..." he paused for a beat. "I heard you scream." There was no condemnation in the words, no judgement, but she read into the words reactions she was sure weren't there anyway, and her face colored.

Should she try to explain? She couldn't let him think she was some kind of hysteric, that she didn't have the stomach for the kind of work she was in. She needed to make him understand that this was different, that it hadn't been the dead body that had ripped the cry out of her soul. Lord knows she'd seen more dead bodies than a lot of morticians. It had been... the image of Tina's savaged mouth flashed in front of her eyes and took her breath away. She couldn't explain, couldn't go there, certainly not with this man, a stranger.

"I can't leave now," he continued. "I have to stay with the body. Could ... would...?"

"You want me to go get your shirt?" she was incredu-lous, bit back an acerbic response —*You want me to make coffee while I'm at it? How do you take yours, one lump or two?*

Instead, she gritted her teeth.

"Where'd you leave it?"

He told her, described sliding down the embankment and she made herself do as he asked. Heading back into the woods in the direction from which he'd come, she thought she'd ask if he'd left anything else at the site she should look for, turned around to ask …

But she didn't. The sheriff was facing the body, had his back to her. She stared at it. His broad, muscular back was criss-crossed with scars slashing all the way across his body from his shoulders to his belt. Dozens of them. Too many to count. Some were thin, white lines, like a mesh of vines. Others were big, thick ones, half an inch across. What in the world…?

But she knew. She knew what would make marks like that.

A bullwhip.

Chapter Thirteen

MAYBE IT WAS HER IMAGINATION, but it seemed to Rileigh when she brought the sheriff's shirt back to him, that he was careful to keep his back to her as he put it on. She'd used a piece of bark to scrape off the worst of the mud from the shirt, and he'd obviously used something —- not from the crime scene, of course!— to scrape the rest of the mud off his pants. And he'd obviously gone into the grass hut and pumped water on his hands because they were clean.

Maybe she'd imagined that he didn't want her to see his scars, but she had definitely been careful to make it appear she'd noticed nothing.

"Thanks," he said.

She grunted, then left without protest as soon as she'd done what he'd sent her to do.

Driving home, she was slower than usual on the winding mountain roads, thoughts chasing themselves around and around in her head so fast it was a wonder her hair didn't catch on fire from the friction.

Tina Montgomery had been murdered. Wasn't just

missing. Hadn't been at some girlfriend's house sleeping off a drunk or shacked up somewhere with her secret boyfriend. She was dead. Somebody had murdered her. In fact, Rileigh herself was likely on the short list of people who'd seen her last. She hadn't bothered to go home to change clothes after she left work at the Rusty Nail. She'd died in the shirt she was wearing when Rileigh saw her there.

And the rest of it. Her ... mouth. Rileigh allowed her mind to skip over that part for the time being, until she could get her emotional ducks in a row enough to think about it rationally.

Then ... there were the scars. And that was absolutely none of Rileigh Bishop's business. But dang— scars like that. Mitchell Webster had been whipped. More than once. When could ... but she didn't know, realized she knew almost nothing about the background of the new sheriff in town. He'd come from Nashville, that's all. Had he been in the military? Maybe... captured by, well, depends on what war. But captured and whipped? There was no other explanation she could think of — and it was none of her business.

She'd do some digging around, though. Couldn't help doing something to scratch the itch of her curiosity about the man. And she needed to find out who he was, who he really was, because it was likely she'd be bumping into him, that they'd be locking horns, now and then in her line of work.

That was a big fat stinky excuse, but she let it go.

When she got out of her car, she saw movement and turned in time to catch a glimpse of one of the Houlihan boys, Burt or Sid, disappearing up the trail into the trees. The Houlihans — hooligans — were their nearest as-the-crow-flies neighbors. They lived on the other side of

Tucker Mountain, only a couple of miles away. Of course, it'd take twenty minutes, maybe half an hour, by way of the winding mountain roads from her front door to theirs.

Rileigh ground her teeth. Her mother and aunt sometimes got the Houlihans to do odd jobs like fixing the fence in back after Daisy drove into it. (Rileigh dreaded the taking-the-car-keys conversation she could see in the near future.) Burt was good with his hands and Sid was a master mechanic, could get any car running. But Rileigh didn't trust either one of them any farther than she could throw a sperm whale and she didn't like them hanging around the house. She'd said as much. Several times. And the old ladies had nodded dutifully, though neither one of them was likely to remember the warning half an hour later.

When Rileigh opened the door, the smell wafted out to her. Pinto beans and cornbread. One of her absolute favorite meals, which was, of course, why her mother'd made it. Her mother and her aunt had seen it as a divine calling to put some pounds on Rileigh, and the two of them had been preparing one glorious dish after another for weeks. Daisy had worked for years in different confectionary shops in Pigeon Forge, making fudge and taffy and funnel cakes. Nobody could whip up a more mouth-watering, calorie-packed dessert. Rileigh had no appetite then. But she did tonight. Tonight she was actually starving.

She paused to consider that, to wonder if it was because she was involved in something like police work, something that felt normal. Who knew?

"I waited to start the cornbread until I seen you was home," her mother said as she stirred the pale yellow cornmeal mixture in a bowl. Mama's back was to Rileigh, but she was certain that when she turned around, she'd be what she called, "all fixed up." She'd have on makeup — not a whole lot, some eyebrow pencil to draw on too-thin eyebrows, mascara, a little powder and blush and just a touch of lipstick. Rileigh's mother had worked all her life. When Rileigh's father committed suicide after Jillian vanished, she'd had no other choice. It was a good job, too. She'd started to work at the Cade's Cove Visitor's Center at the Great Smoky Mountains National Park right after she got out of high school, and over the years she'd worked at each of the other three visitors' centers —Oconaluftee, Clingmans Dome and finally at the biggest one, Sugarlands, until she'd run the Backcountry Information Office there, which issued permits for all manner of activities. If you wanted to get married in the park, or scatter Uncle Herbert's ashes there, go fishing or spelunking or stage a war protest there, Lily Bishop had been the one to issue a permit for it. Working a lifetime for Uncle Sam had its perks, and she'd retired a few years ago on a fat, juicy government pension.

Lily was by far the prettiest of the six girls born to Elmer and Frances Gillespie. The bouquet of girls, everyone called them, because every one was named for flowers — Lily, Iris, Daisy, Rose, Jasmine and Della. Della was really delphinium. Mama and Daisy were the only ones left of the bouquet.

"Hand me that canister of flour, will you dear?" She said, turning around and smiling a lipsticked smile.

Rileigh handed her the flour. No cornbread out of a box for Mama. Everything was from scratch. She doubted that either her mother or her aunt had eaten more than half a dozen prepared meals in their whole lives. "These beans been cooking all day. Put almost a pound of bacon in—"

"A pound of bacon! No wonder it smells so good!" Mama picked up on her enthusiasm.

"You can go on ahead and have a bowl, don't have to wait until the cornbread's–"

Rileigh held up her hand. "I'm good, Mama. I won't lose my appetite if I wait half an hour."

Mama turned back to the cornbread and asked over her shoulder.

"You find Tina Montgomery?"

The question stopped her and she sat down heavily at the table.

"Yeah, we found her."

"We who?"

"The sheriff and I."

"I thought Mum–"

"The new one, the deputy from Nashville who's in charge now."

"Where'd you find her?"

Rileigh took a breath.

"Tina's dead, Mama."

Rileigh's mother dropped the stirring spoon into the cornbread batter.

"Dead? What? … She wasn't but what? Sixteen? Seventeen?"

"She was eighteen, and … she was murdered."

Mama's hands flew to her mouth.

"Oh dear god, no. Who would want to hurt—?"

The same question had been asked of Jillian when she was — nope, couldn't say murdered. Not allowed. Jillian had merely *vanished*. The sacrosanct family delusion, so let it be written, so let it be done. Why, Jillian was still alive out there somewhere, just hadn't never gotten in touch with her family in almost three decades because …no one knew. But Jillie obviously had a good reason for it.

Except Jillian wasn't out there "somewhere'. She was dead. Rileigh knew it. But nobody would believe her, and after years of nightmares images got tangled up with her memories, Rileigh wasn't sure anymore what had happened to her.

RILEIGH RUNS.

Out of Jillian's bedroom and down the hall. Down the stairs, out the back door, and into the night. No plan for where she is running to, just running away.

She runs off blindly into the woods, tripping, falling, skinning her knee, ripping her nightgown, just running and running and running...

When she can't run any more, she crawls to a windfall, and squirms into the tangle of branches and leaves. Then huddles in a ball in the cold dark, shaking so hard that surely the bad guy will see the limbs of the tree moving, the man who killed Jillian will find her there. He'll kill her, too, and cut out her tongue. Or maybe cut out her tongue first, then he wouldn't have to kill her, because without a tongue, she couldn't tell what she'd seen.

What happens after that is particularly sketchy. None of her memories of that time are clear, but it's possible she crawled so far down into herself in terror as she hid in the forest, that she really doesn't see clearly what came after that.

Mostly her memories are snapshots, frozen scenes where the people aren't moving, just caught like with a flashbulb, maybe with their mouths open or their eyes closed or with funny looks on their faces.

They find her, of course. The screen door slamming when she ran out into the night would have cracked like a rifle shot, awakened the whole household. It's her Aunt Daisy who spots her huddled in the among the dead tree limbs.

Snap!

Aunt Daisy's face is frozen as she peers into the darkness at her. There are too many emotions on her features to say what she's feeling. Relief. Anger. Surprise. And other emotions Rileigh doesn't recognize.

And then she's in the kitchen, sitting at the table wrapped up in a quilt, with her mother trying to get her to drink a cup of hot chocolate, and her aunt washing the dirt off her face and hands with a cold cloth. Why not warm? Why hadn't she bothered to wait until the water in the tap got warm ...

Snap!

Her aunt's face isn't caring and concerned. There's more. Other emotions are there, too. But not the right ones.

Why is everybody acting like her running away is the catastrophe when they ought to be ... what? What emotion should they be feeling after seeing the blood and the ...? Whatever it was — horror — she didn't see it in their faces. Was it possible ... they didn't know what'd happened to Jillian?

She's shaking so hard, she can't speak words, can't form them in her mouth, and so she bursts into tears, gut-wrenching sobs ripping out of her chest, and when her mother tries to comfort her, tells her "everything's all right," the words tear down the dam holding back her own words.

"She's dead ... all the blood ... killed her ... and ... cut out her tongue!"

She shrieks the last part into stunned silence, then leaps out of the chair, shrugs out of the quilt, bolts upstairs to her sister's room and throws open the door, trailing a keening cry of horror and loss and fear behind her like the tail on a kite.

Snap!

Jillian's room is ... fine.

Her bed is made. All the smiley face pillows are piled on it just the way she likes them. There are no bloody sheets, no ripped-up wedding veil. Her wedding dress is laid out on the back of a chair. The note and picture Rileigh dropped on the floor are gone.

Now that they know Jillian isn't asleep in her bed, Rileigh can't get anybody to listen to her story. She is just upset because her sister is gone, has run away somewhere, has vanished, they say. She's just a little girl with a big imagination.

And later, after they find her father's body hanging from a garage *rafter with an extension cord dug so far into the flesh of his neck you can't even see it, they tell her to hush … can't she see something terrible has happened.*

Her father is dead! Since he's ignored her all her life, Rileigh doesn't care. She doesn't find out for years about the suicide note Aunt Daisy found and threw into the fire. The words on charred pieces pulled from the flames explain nothing. "Sorry" and "Jillian" and "forgive." Everyone's frantic to find Jillian before the funeral so she can tell her father goodbye. Rileigh knows Jillian won't be coming home for anybody's funeral, not even her own.

"LOTTIE MONTGOMERY PAID you to help find Tina that day when she come over here, didn't she?" Her mother's words jar Rileigh back to the present. Rileigh had been foolish to think her mother hadn't been eavesdropping on her conversation with Lottie. "So you're gonna help find out who killed her, aren't you?"

Before Rileigh could answer, Daisy came into the kitchen and saw the horrified look on Mama's face.

"What—?"

"Tina Montgomery's been murdered!" Mama said. "Rileigh's going to find out who did it."

"I never said any such–"

"Go sticking your nose in other people's business, you could get it bit off so don't nothing stick out on your face farther than your upper lip," Daisy said, not looking at Rileigh when she said it. And when she did turn toward her, Daisy's face registered shock … and then anger.

"What are *you* doing here?"

"Uh … I live here, Aunt Daisy, you know–"

"You ain't supposed to be here, Jillian! You're supposed to be *dead.*"

The words shocked Rileigh so profoundly she couldn't find her breath.

"This ain't Jillian, Daisy," Mama said. "This here's Rileigh. You 'member her doncha?"

"You'll be sorry!" Aunt Daisy screamed at Rileigh. "You think you can just come walking in here pretty as you please, and everybody's gonna fawn all over you." She sneered. "You think J.R. cares? Well, he don't. He stopped caring about you a long—"

"That's enough!" Mama cried. "I ain't gonna let you say mean things about my girls' daddy. He loved his baby girls."

At that, Daisy growled something unintelligible, turned and strode out of the room. Rileigh and her mother stood in shocked silence.

"You think she can't get any worse, and then ..." Mama sighed out the words.

"Just when you thought it was safe to go back in the water," Rileigh said.

"Huh?"

"Nothing. Never mind." Rileigh stood and went to her mother's side, fished the spoon out of the cornbread batter and began to stir it.

"She's mad most all the time now," Mama said. "And I don't never understand what it is ... who it is ... she's mad at. Or why. But sometimes she gets so angry ... I'm 'fraid she might hurt somebody."

The thought of her crotchety aunt getting into a fight with someone — though the old woman was big and strong as a bull — was ridiculous. But it reminded her of yesterday when Tina had been *fighting* with somebody on the phone. That's where the sheriff needed to start looking. Rileigh wondered if he was smart enough to figure that out.

She also wondered if Tina's mother had heard anything yet. You couldn't keep a thing like that quiet in Yarmouth County and she hoped Lottie hadn't heard it through the rumor mill. No telling what story was out there now. And the ugly part—that'd get out, too. Try all you want to hush it up, but people would find out about Tina's tongue.

Daisy reappeared in the doorway. "You get me that rat trap like I asked, Rileigh?"

Apparently, she now knew Rileigh wasn't Jillian.

"It's in the car."

"Well it ain't doing no good in the car now, is it? Set it up in the storage room. Them rats was having a party in there last night after I went to bed, scratching around and squeaking."

Daisy's room was on the second floor on the back of the house. From there, she couldn't have heard the Marine Band and Bugle Corps marching through the storage room attached to the garage.

"On it," Rileigh said, gave her mother the spoon, and went out to her car to retrieve the rat trap.

Chapter Fourteen

MITCH PULLED his cruiser to a stop in front of the big old house set back from the road at the end of an impossibly steep driveway. Couldn't imagine how anybody could negotiate it in the wintertime when it was covered in snow and ice. The house sat on a little more land than most of the places around here. It was old, though, which explained it. The first settlers here claimed the biggest pieces of flat real estate they could find, leaving the smaller stuck-up-against-a-rock-wall homesteads for those who came later.

He supposed that had been the biggest surprise for him when he took the job in Yarmouth County three months ago. That people had somehow managed to build homes up in the mountains. Not in the hanging valleys, like the one where Black Bear Forge nested amongst the trees beside Cat Gut River.

It was a *river* and he knew its name. He'd asked. People had perched houses so precariously on the steep inclines that he wondered sometimes, often, how many of them finally slipped off the side, got blown off in a storm, or washed off in a heavy rain. How often did the neighbors come driving down the road and find somebody's house sitting in the middle of it, when it'd been sitting a hundred feet above the road the day before?

He didn't ask that question, though. It was on an ever-growing list of questions he didn't ask because he realized it made him look like one of the tourists getting their picture taken beside the Great Smoky Mountains National Park sign. The only way to get information was to ask questions, but he had self-censored himself so often, that he really didn't have much more idea of what the place and the people were like now than he did the day he drove into town.

Which is what had sent him out to the home of Lily Bishop on Bent Twig Road, about a mile north of where Bent Twig crossed Shallow Rock Lane. Those were the directions he'd been given and he'd actually found it on the first try. *Give the man a Kewpie doll.*

He switched off the engine and sat for a moment, pretending to be studying his cell phone in front of the audience observing him from the porch. Rileigh and two old women sat together there, Rileigh on the swing and the other women facing her in rockers.

He used the cell phone ruse to draw a steadying breath. This wasn't going to be easy, but he absolutely had to do it and … what was it his grandfather used to say? If you have to eat a frog, don't look at it, too long. So he got out of the car and walked with purpose up the stone walkway to the bottom of the porch steps, where he paused and tipped his hat.

"Evenin' ladies," he said.

"What makes you think we're ladies?" asked one of the old women, the one whose white hair looked like she'd just gotten out of bed. "Ladies is prim and proper, and the women in this family got cajones big as yours."

He saw Rileigh roll her eyes at the remark and the gesture relaxed him, provided a sort of bond between them — keeper of the asylum, rather than one of the inmates.

"Sheriff Webster, I'd like you to meet my mother, Lily Bishop," Rileigh said, rising and walking his way, past a plump old lady with a sweet face who was probably quite a looker in her day. "And this is my aunt, Daisy Gillespie."

Lily said, "Glad to meet you, Sheriff."

Daisy scowled at him and said nothing.

"I'd like to speak to you for a minute," he said to Rileigh, "if I'm not disturbing you." He paused and added, "Privately."

Rileigh's mother got the message and rose from her rocker. Casting a smile his way, she started into the house. "It was good to make your acquaintance, Sheriff."

The other old lady stayed seated until Rileigh's mother passed her chair and grabbed her arm, hauling her up with surprising ease. Steel Magnolia fragile.

When the front door closed behind them, Rileigh turned and walked back to the swing. "Come on up and sit a spell," she said, gesturing to the rocker across from the swing. "See you got cleaned up."

He was wearing a clean, starched and pressed uniform — brown, with a big gold badge on the front that he did not shine every day, but that was so glossy, he feared others would think he had.

Settling into the rocker he started to speak, then paused. "Wait a minute. Something's not right here."

"If you're holding your breath waiting for the porch swing to squeak you may return to your regularly scheduled exhalations. It's mute."

"What'd you do to it? My grandmother tried everything — WD 40 and–"

"It never squeaked. One of the eight wonders of the world, right up there with the other seven, or eight, or however many."

He smiled, then rearranged his face.

Just say it, flat out.

"I …" He didn't mean to pause there, but the other words took a little longer to get moving after the engine pulled out."…would like to ask for your help."

To her credit, she didn't react in any way other than a slight tightening around her eyes.

He pushed ahead, able to talk now that he'd moved those first words down the track.

"You said it and you were right. I didn't want to admit it, but … I had a grandmother who really was the fount of all wisdom. She's the one who told me, 'You can't un-know the truth. Once you know it, you're obligated to do something about it.'"

"Wise indeed."

"You told me that people don't want to open up to me because I'm–" he almost said *from Away-From-Here*, but caught himself, "not local. I get it. Mountain people don't cozy up to strangers. Actually, it's been apparent since I got here, but I wouldn't own it until now. It didn't matter before, but now it does. This is a murder investigation, not a cat in a tree or a stolen bicycle. I want to find out who killed Tina Montgomery. But … it appears I'll need your help to do that."

There, he'd said it. That should have been the hard part. But as soon as the words left his lips he realized the really hard part was after. Waiting for Rileigh to respond.

In the elongated moment before she spoke, he could have second-guessed his decision to ask, to actually be that vulnerable. He could have, but he didn't, because finding out who'd killed Tina Montgomery *really was* more important than his ego.

And he wouldn't botch this investigation. Not this time. He wouldn't watch a murderer walk free because he didn't do his job. He would find out who killed Tina Montgomery, arrest the son of a bitch, and sit in a courtroom listening to the jury foreman return the verdict — guilty. There was no other single thing in Mitch's life more important than that.

"No," Rileigh said firmly. "I'm afraid I can't."

Chapter Fifteen

WELL IT APPEARED Sheriff Webster had a pair after all, brass ones. It took some serious hutzpah to come out here to her house and ask for help.

Then she watched the muscles in his jaw clench and she realized he hadn't received the message she'd intended to send.

"I mean, I won't become your deputy or go to work for the sheriff's office or anything like that. I won't put on a badge."

She said that last part too forcefully, too emphatically, but she couldn't help it. She would not become a law enforcement officer. End of discussion.

Besides, she didn't need a badge to enforce the law. She had clocked in her ten years, plus a couple of months extra, in the Memphis Police Department, which entitled her to certain privileges under LEOSA, the federal Law Enforcement Officer Safety Act. The law had been part of the old Patriot Act passed shortly after 9-11. The powers-that-be at that time determined that the retirement of police officers meant fewer guns in the hands of people trained to use them. And in the political climate in America at that time, that was not a good thing.

"But I will help you any way I can." She watched him relax. A little. Imperceptibly. Given how much it had cost him to ask for help, she knew a lot was riding on her response. She was impressed that he managed to hold onto his own response as well as he had.

"I didn't mean … I wasn't going to ask you to do anything 'official'."

"And why me?" she blurted out the words before she could catch hold of them. So she plunged ahead. "You have deputies. Jeb Rawlings was in my kindergarten class at Black Bear Forge Elementary school. He used to terrorize Georgia with bugs — my best friend is arachnophobic and it doesn't have to have eight legs to send her up a tree. Six, four, ten— she never pauses to count, just freaks out at anything creepy crawly. And Tony Hadley's lived here his whole life. Billy Crawford is from Knox County, but he's been here since he got out of high school and he married local. Can't they help you?"

He looked uncomfortable.

"Spill it. If you want my help, start shooting straight with me right now."

"The men who serve as deputies here are fine men. They're loyal, good guys—"

"But not the sharpest knives in the drawer."

"I'm just going by what Sheriff Mumford told me when he asked me to take his place. He said…"

He didn't finish.

"Go on. What'd he say."

"Not a one of them could pour water out of a boot if the instructions were on the heel."

Rileigh burst out laughing and her laughter seemed to surprise the sheriff, maybe unnerved him a bit.

"He's right. There are brighter bulbs … but how do you know I'm not a fifteen-watt too?"

"I don't."

That surprised her.

"Look, I'm going for full disclosure here, so please don't be offended. I don't know that you're any more on the ball than the deputies, but you don't work for me. If it turns out you're not as … as competent as you seem to be, I can say thanks for the help, I got this and move on."

"And…?"

"Look, I've been here for three months and I've got a list as long as my leg of things I'd like to know about this place or the people or the history. I didn't ask because… I'm an outsider and it's not likely any of the locals will cut me any slack. And that grandmother of mine, she also said it was better to keep your mouth shut and have somebody wonder if you're stupid than to open it and prove that you are."

"So basically, you're willing to look like a dumbshit with me, but not with them."

"Yeah, pretty much."

She found herself smiling at that and she wasn't even sure why. In his convoluted way, he was right. If he had come in here asking all kinds of dumb questions, word would have gotten around. So instead, he kept his mouth shut, and as a result, the people she'd talked to about him didn't have anything good to say about him, but they didn't say anything bad either. He kind of had a blank slate. And that wasn't a bad place to start.

"Deal, then. And even though you didn't ask, I'll place myself under my own personal NDA." She made a zipper gesture across her mouth.

"Thanks." It wasn't effusive. Dignified, if she'd had to

describe it. He got points for that. "So I'd like to start right now."

"Okay."

"I'd like you to come with me to deliver the news of Tina's death to her family."

That surprised her.

"You think they don't know yet?"

They'd found Tina's body hours ago. And she was sure the grapevine had started humming as soon as the dispatcher sent out three deputies with lights but no sirens. Maybe she didn't call up her best girlfriend breathless, "Guess what just happened?" The dispatcher was likely more professional than that. But who'd been standing in earshot when she did it? What had the officers said to disengage themselves? And when the sheriff called for the forensics team from Gatlinburg …

"I was hoping you could come along to help me read the response."

It took a moment for that to land home.

He wanted somebody who knew the family members to watch their responses to the news of Tina's death, to listen to what they said and read their body language for what they didn't say.

That was a smart move, but surely he didn't think what he was going to tell them was going to shock anybody?

"Please tell me you don't believe they really don't know yet."

"Well, I'm sure they know something, but–"

"It's been hours. They not only know by now that she's dead, but where her body was found, and maybe the apparent cause of death. That knife wound in her belly."

She could tell that surprised him.

"Have you ever heard of the hundredth monkey?"

The look on his face answered the question. "Ok, so

there's this theory, that if ninety-nine monkeys discover a thing, the one hundredth monkey will know without having to figure it out himself. It's not quite that bad in Yarmouth County, but close."

"I will find out which one of my officers—"

"Save your effort for something that matters. People talk. And in this county, the grapevine is made of fiber optic cable. All we can do is hope all the gory details aren't floating around out there."

She looked him in the eye.

"Let's hope it's not common knowledge — yet—that whoever killed her cut her tongue out. That part will get out eventually, too. It always does."

He said nothing, just nodded. Rileigh forced herself to ask, "Did you find it— the tongue?"

"We found it."

A wave of relief flooded over Rileigh. "So they can bury her — all of her together."

The emotion packed in her words seemed to surprise him.

Which meant he likely didn't know what Rileigh had seen the night Jillian disappeared.

Chapter Sixteen

RILEIGH HAD to park down the road a ways because the area around the old trailer house next to the wide creek where Tina's family lived was already full of cars. There wasn't much space, but people had jammed half a dozen cars into the cleared area and the sheriff had to park on the roadside. He turned on his light bar and flashers — couldn't miss seeing them — and waited beside the cruiser for Rileigh to catch up.

"We found Tina's car on the other side of the mountain by a creek," he told her once she had.

Rileigh almost smiled. "Yeah, dope growers are like cats. They won't stay anywhere that doesn't have at least three exits. It's farther to the grass hut from that spot, but the incline's not as steep."

She didn't bother to ask if he'd found any tire tracks beside Tina's car. That space there was solid granite. A tank wouldn't have left a mark on it.

Tina's mother was sitting on the porch with some other family members, and when she saw Rileigh, she came running down the porch steps and flung herself into Rileigh's arms.

"They tell me you found her, Rileigh girl. She was at Jeanie's, wasn't she? I bet they was doing them drugs that come in baggies. She thinks I don't know about that, but I do. Them drugs'll knock you on your ass for hours. She was probably just waking up when you–"

"I didn't find Tina at Jeanie's–"

"G.G. Masterson's then," Her mother hurried on, using her words to hold back the truth she could read in Rileigh's eyes. "You found her with G.G. and they was–"

"Tina isn't at Sue Ellen's or G.G. Masterson's." Rileigh held up her hand and finally Tina's mother fell silent. She was about to continue when Sheriff Webster spoke beside her.

"I'm sorry to have to inform you, ma'am, but your daughter Tina Marie Montgomery was found dead this afternoon–"

Lottie Montgomery leaned her head back and screamed. It was almost a howl, a feral, animal sound of pain. Rileigh had heard the sound before, but it was a sound you'd never get used to no matter how many times you heard it.

Lottie's sons, Chad and Joel rushed forward—everyone gathering around. They took both her arms as her knees collapsed out from under her. She would have fallen if they hadn't carried her to the porch steps and set her there.

She was sobbing then, great wrenching sobs that sent tears shooting out of her eyes to smear her black mascara in twin tracks down her cheeks.

"What'd you find? Did she wreck her car?" Aubrey Tucker, Tina's boyfriend stepped forward. "Where's my Tina?"

Rileigh wanted to say that it was likely Tina was not his Tina at all, but somebody else's. But she held her tongue.

Sheriff Webster took over then, answering Aubrey's questions in as much detail as he could. Most of the people here probably knew all of it— and other things about the incident that weren't true as well. But hearing the words from the sheriff brought sufficient gravity to the pronouncements. Didn't matter what you've heard on the phone or somebody said they'd seen when they were driving. When a man in a uniform tells you a family member is dead, the reality of it is usually stunning.

Several women — Tina had no sisters, but maybe friends of hers, her brother's girlfriends maybe — started to cry, and the scene quickly degenerated into a wake.

Rileigh looked from one mourner to the next, trying to get a read on their reactions, how genuine they were. She was a pretty good judge of people and she didn't see anything that was demonstrably out of place.

The family wanted to know what had been done with Tina's body. The sheriff told them it had been transported to Gatlinburg, where the coroner there would do an autopsy to determine the official cause of death.

Aubrey cleared his throat. "I heard that there was … you know… pieces of Tina—"

The sheriff cut him off before he could continue. "When the coroner has completed his autopsy, he will provide a report on his findings to sheriff's department and Tina's family."

He emphasized the word *family*, because clearly the young man who'd asked the question wasn't one of them.

Rileigh heard part of a whispered conversation behind her.

"… one of her fingers was cut off is what I heard."

"Wasn't no finger, something else. I heard it was both her ears."

Rileigh whirled around on the people engaged in the gruesome game of *can you top this*.

"I don't know what you heard, but I am here to tell you that none of that shit is true," she said.

"How do you know—"

"I was there. I saw Tina's body." Yeah, she'd been mutilated. But at least her corpse would look decent in a casket for the funeral, and around here, a thing like that mattered. "You need to shut your mouths and stop spreading that around." She leaned closer. "You want Lottie to hear her little girl's been cut into pieces?"

The men looked properly chastised, but it wasn't a rebuke that would last. Until the whole story was out, the rumors of horror would continue to spread and intensify, because that's just how people were.

The sheriff stepped close to Rileigh.

"I'm leaving now. Can we talk tomorrow?"

"Sure, I can come by your office after the pancake breakfast."

"Pancake breakfast?"

"The Black Bear Forge Fire and Rescue Department puts on a pancake breakfast every summer to raise money for St. Jude's hospital in Memphis. Mama and Aunt Daisy will be helping with the cooking. The whole town will file through the fire house at some time or another tomorrow. You probably ought to show up, give people a look at you."

He nodded, and went back to his cruiser and drove away.

Rileigh was about to follow when Joel took her arm and told her, "Mama wants to talk to you, please."

The boys had gotten their mother inside the house and

into the parlor, where she sat in what was probably "her spot on the couch" in front of the big television set.

Rileigh went inside, and when Lottie saw her she tried to rise, but Rileigh went to her. Lottie cocked a thumb at the crying woman seated beside her, who was probably her sister Edna, to move out of the way. When she had shuffled along, Rileigh sat beside Lottie.

"I want you to find out who kilt my Tina."

"The sheriff and his department—"

"I don't give a tinker's damn what the sheriff's department is going to do, I want you to find out."

"I told you before that—"

"I'll pay you. I'll give you five hundred—"

"No!" Rileigh protested too loud and she lowered her voice. "I don't want your money."

"You keep that three hundred. You earned it. You found her, didn't you?"

Actually, she had.

"I will help Sheriff Webster find out who killed her," Rileigh said. "He's a whole lot more on the ball than you give him credit for. But I won't take your money."

Lottie grabbed her hand, squeezed it hard. Her hands had been cold and sweaty before. Now they were hot and surprisingly strong.

"You find out. You hear me? Find out who kilt my baby girl."

It occurred to Rileigh that she could start the investigation right now, here in Tina's house.

"Do you mind if I take a look at Tina's room?"

"You go look wherever you want. You do whatever you have to do, but find out who done it."

She lost it again and began to cry. Rileigh gave up her spot on the couch beside Lottie and walked away, wandering around the cramped trailer, while mourners consoled each other. Nobody paid any attention to her and where she went.

Tina's room was the smaller bedroom, down a short hallway from the living room full of people. This was a three-bedroom trailer, and it must have been crowded when Tina's father was alive and her brothers were still home.

Closing the door to the bedroom softly behind her, Rileigh wandered around the bedroom, aimlessly opening drawers and peering into the closet. It was small, but tidy. Tina's belongings were neat — even with her closet jammed with so many clothes the doors wouldn't close over them.

Wouldn't it be wonderful if Tina'd kept a diary? Rileigh looked for one without any hope of finding it. She hadn't thought to ask the sheriff if they'd found Tina's phone on her. Lots of girls didn't carry purses anymore, but they all had cell phones.

There was no purse anywhere that Rileigh could see. She sat at the vanity, where a brush and comb set were arranged neatly on the top of a mirror. The drawers of the vanity were filled with makeup and other girl things like fingernail polish, small jars of perfume, makeup remover. The top drawer on the other side contained underwear — not frilly and lacy, just cotton briefs, and she rifled through it, looking for…

Her hand fell on something in the back of the drawer and she drew it out and looked at it. A flat cylinder about six inches long with a display window in the center. Slowing prominently a plus sign in bold face.

It was a pregnancy test. Positive.

Tina Montgomery was pregnant.

Chapter Seventeen

RILEIGH HAD PASSED the big pink building on Danny Thomas Place in Memphis many times. It was special to her, for many reasons, but the most important was the little boy named Danny Thomas... Danny Thomas Mozaroffski. He liked to be called D. T. because it sounded like E.T., which was the kid's favorite movie. She'd bet he'd seen it fifty times.

Well, not seen. He'd probably seen it only the one time, the first time, when he was five and could still see.

But you could look at that kid's face when he was describing a scene from the movie... "And the bikes went up in the sky. E.T. was in the basket and all three of the bikes just started flying. Don't you wish you'd been there to see it? Don't you wish you'd been there, one of the kids, riding along on your bike and then, Shazam, you're flying."

She'd met the little boy the first time when neighbors called police to report a bad smell coming from the apartment next door. What they found when they forced the door was horrifying. A woman lay dead on the floor —

and not recently dead, either — and a little boy was snuggled up beside the stinking corpse, sucking his thumb.

He mother had overdosed, died, and left the little boy in his diaper crawling around on the floor. He was maybe eighteen months old — old enough to climb up onto the table to get food. Even pushed a chair to the counter, so he could climb up and get chips out of the cabinets above it.

She was the officer who'd had to remove him, and that kid had fought, kicked and screamed and scratched and bit her, determined to stay with his mommy.

When she next crossed paths with D.T. six years later, she was providing security for a St. Jude's Children's Hospital fundraising event, and he was still fighting for his life. But this time, he had people in his corner. His adopted parents adored him, and had done everything they could to help him survive the cancer that had begun in his right eye and spread to the other, and then to his brain.

She didn't mean for it to happen, but she let herself fall in love with the tough little boy who'd been dealt so many bad cards in his life. She'd watched him struggle, fight, and ultimately die, as she had any of the soldiers she served with in Iraq and Afghanistan.

That's why Rileigh Bishop suited up and showed up at anything that benefitted St. Jude's Children's hospital. That included the annual pancake breakfast put on by the Yarmouth County Fire and Rescue Squad as its annual fund-raiser. She had worked the early shift — getting to the fire house to start mixing the batter at 3 a.m., and was just getting off when her mother and her aunt showed up to flip pancakes.

She stepped out of the kitchen into the big bays that normally housed fire trucks but today were fitted out with row upon row of folding tables and folding chairs, where volunteers hurried to fill the "all you can eat" orders of the people seated there.

"You have something in your hair … what is that…?" someone said from behind her and she turned to see the sheriff, picking a piece of goo off the top of her head.

"Pancake batter. Lift the mixer out of that bowl too quick and it sprays everybody for twenty feet in every direction," she said.

He looked wound tight and she smiled, then realized Derby was sitting beside her, licking the batter off the side of her pants.

Pointing to the black mutt — so old almost his whole face was white — she told the sheriff, "One of these days, that dog is going to eat pancake droppings until it puts him in a coma. Derby lives at the fire house, and they never have to mop the floor after one of these. Derby cleans up after everybody."

She led the sheriff to a spot down from the table containing rows of coffee pots, and sat down. It was a small table, but with a full sized checkered plastic table cloth, which reached all the way to the floor. Derby padded along happily beside her, licking her pants.

"I found something last night in Tina's room you need to know about."

That's as far as she got before Daisy saw her from the kitchen door and made a beeline toward her with a plate piled high with pancakes.

"I've been waiting for you to take a break, made these especially for you, Jillian, your favorite kind — put blueberries in them." She placed the plate on the table in front of Rileigh, along with a bottle of maple syrup. "Couldn't find no blueberry syrup though." She squirted a gob of syrup on top of the pancake. "Eat up."

"*Rileigh*, Aunt Daisy… remember?"

Her aunt blew her off. "Whatever. Now eat your pancakes."

"My mother and my aunt are on a mission to fatten me up on pancakes with lots of syrup–"

There was a loud thump from outside, a sickening sound, the crunch of metal and breaking glass of a collision.

The sheriff leapt to his feet and headed for the door as the crowd surged out of the building to see what had happened. Rileigh followed.

Apparently, Joe Davenport had pulled his old white Chevy out of the parking lot, right into the path of Hank Crankhauer's pickup truck— which center-punched the old Chevy, caving in the passenger side door and shoving the vehicle up against the wall of the fire house.

Joe appeared to be unharmed. Hank appeared to be drunk, likely was, but the small bump on his head gave him license to say he was groggy — not staggering — and half an hour later he was on the way to get a couple of stitches, when he should have been on his way to jail.

Rileigh walked back inside with the sheriff.

"Before we were interrupted, I was telling you that I found something at Tina's …"

Her voice trailed off as she saw the look on his face and followed his line of sight. Derby was up on his hind legs with his front paws on their table. He grabbed the pile of pancakes off Rileigh's plate, dropped back down to the floor and scooted under the table with his prize.

"That little rascal," Rileigh said.

"Must have gotten tired of waiting for food to be dropped on the floor and took matters into his own hands," the sheriff said.

"Paws," she corrected.

They crossed the room to the table and Rileigh got

down on one knee and lifted the too big table cloth. Derby lay on his belly under the table with his face sticky from the syrup and the remains of the last pancake hanging out his mouth.

"I'll have you know that was *my* pan—." The dog's head dropped to the floor and he closed his eyes. "If you're going to steal it, the least you could do is eat the whole thing."

He didn't move.

She reached out and shook his shoulder. He lay still, didn't open his eyes.

"Derby?" She shook him hard. He was limp. She put her hand in front of his nose, but could feel no breath.

"He's not …" She looked up into the sheriff's face.

Rileigh looked around, picking out faces from the crowd, then pointed to a small gray haired man in a plaid shirt at the end of the row of coffee pots.

"That's Dr. Plumby. He's a vet. Maybe he can do something …"

The sheriff turned on his heel and headed in the direction of the coffee tables. Meanwhile, people continued to stream past Rileigh's table, to get a cup of coffee in a styrofoam cup at the coffee table. Rileigh let the tablecloth fall back to the floor to cover the dog under it.

The sheriff returned with the vet, who got down on one knee and did a cursory examination of Derby. Nobody had yet noticed the dog, mostly hidden beneath the too-large tablecloth, but Rileigh had to consider what they should do with … face it, you don't want to have to remove a sick dog from a place where hundreds of people were eating.

Dr. Plumby got to his feet, shaking his head at Rileigh.

"He's gone."

"It's my fault," she said. "I left my plate here and he got it — eating all those pancakes—"

"He didn't die from eating too much. Something he ate instantly shut down his respiratory system."

"What does that mean?—"

"If I had to guess, I'd say he got into some fentanyl. I've treated several dogs and a cat that got into their owners' stash. If it's the good stuff, just one good noseful and it's over."

That was a conversation stopper.

"But he was right here. Where'd he get into fentanyl?" Rileigh asked.

"Maybe somebody's got some hidden in the back of the building and he dug into it this morning when they were unloading supplies from the storage room," the sheriff said.

"If he had, we'd have found him dead in the storage room. If there's enough of it, fentanyl is fatal almost instantly."

The three of them looked down at the poor dog, his face sticky from the syrup on Rileigh's plate.

The sheriff stepped away from the table, went to the coffee table and got a styrofoam cup. Then he knelt down and carefully scooped up the remains of the pancake the dog didn't eat. He picked up the bottle of pancake syrup off the table, too.

"What are you doing?" Rileigh asked.

"Getting it tested."

"What for?"

"Fentanyl."

"You'd don't think somehow the pancake batter got contaminated?" She looked wildly around at the room full of chattering adults and children.

"No, I'm not suggesting anything like that. If the batter

was laced with fentanyl, people would be dropping like flies." He turned back to the vet. "If you don't mind, I'd rather you didn't mention what you've seen here to anybody."

The vet nodded agreement, then turned to take his place again in the coffee line.

"Whoa, whoa," Rileigh said to the sheriff. "Wait a minute. Are you saying that there was only fentanyl in *my* pancake ... but not in anybody else's? That's crazy. How could somebody have–"

"Everybody was outside for fifteen minutes and your plate was just sitting here." He gestured at the crowd. "No fewer than three hundred people were milling around in this room. Any one of them could have–"

"Could have what? Deliberately poisoned my pancake? That's crazy."

The sheriff said nothing. Rileigh was so confused and flabbergasted she couldn't seem to organize her thoughts.

"We'd best leave the dog where it is until the crowd's gone," the sheriff said.

All Rileigh could do was nod, dumbly. Then she remembered.

"I've been waiting to tell you. I searched Tina's room last night and found a pregnancy test. She was pregnant."

That was another conversation stopper.

Chapter Eighteen

RILEIGH SPENT the afternoon after the pancake breakfast talking to the list of Tina's friends that Tina's mother had given her. She hoped they'd be willing to open up now that Tina was dead. She'd merely told the sheriff where she was going, didn't bother to "ask" if he thought that was a good idea. It seemed like the right next step in the investigation of a missing person. She knew he wouldn't oppose her asking the questions because he had sense enough to know that Tina's friends would be a whole lot more willing to tell Rileigh their deceased friends deepest buried secrets than they would to divulge an embarrassing truth to … well, a former resident of Away From Here.

By the time she showed up at Sheriff Webster's office late that afternoon, she had gleaned a few gems of information that might be helpful.

From Gloria Gale — G.G. Masterson — she'd learned that Tina used to have a drug problem. Past tense.

"She was real into the pink lady, you know. I told her she hadn't ought to try that stuff, shouldn't be experimenting with something like that that could kill you. You know it can, doesn't take but a little bitty bit and you go to sleep and never wake up."

Rileigh had stumbled over that remark, but went on. GG was the only one of Tina's friends who hadn't known she was dead when Rileigh arrived, and she had taken the news hard, cried uncontrollably for ten minutes before she could get her emotions in check enough to talk. And then she opened up like a faucet, gushing information about Tina, and about the things she and Tina had done together.

"I wouldn't do any of that shit with her and that made her mad at first, but then she said she understood and to each his own, you know, and if I didn't want to have my mind expanded, that was fine with her." She stopped, wrinkled her brow.

"I told her I was real happy with my mind the size it was, thank you very much." The girl looked horrified. "That was a terrible snotty thing for me to say. And now Tina's dead and I can't tell her I'm sorry." That led to another session of crying. When she was finally able to answer questions, she wasn't much help. No, she didn't know who had introduced Tina to drugs. No she didn't know who her dealer was. No, she didn't know if she was seeing somebody secretly, someone her mother and boyfriend didn't know about.

But yes, she did know that Tina was pregnant, said that was the reason Tina's drug use was in the "past tense."

"Soon's she found out she was knocked up, she cleaned up her act. I thought it was really hard to get off drugs like that, you know, why people have to go to those rehab places for help because they can't do it on their own. But Tina did. She just quit. Cold turkey, or so she said. She said she wasn't about to take drugs that might hurt the baby.

"So she intended to keep it, didn't plan to get—"

"An abortion! Lord no, she wouldn't never have considered such a thing. She went with her mother to church every Sunday, never missed. Catholic, she was." She pronounced the word Cath-o-lic. "Most everybody around here's Protestant, Baptist or Pentecostal."

She pronounced it *penny-costal*.

G.G. continued: "Well, actually, nobody I know's much of anything anymore, might be their parents and grandparents are, but I don't know people who go to church. Oh, Tina did but, not because she wanted to. Because her mother made her. But even though she'd had her nose rubbed in church her whole life, when push come to shove, she believed what that priest said on Sundays. She believed that getting an abortion was killing a baby, she was real adamant about that, and it wasn't a popular opinion, I can tell you. I didn't agree with her, wasn't hardly anybody who did, but Tina didn't care what other people thought. She believed that getting an abortion was a mortal sin, the kind you get sent to hell for, and she wouldn't have done a thing like that."

"Uh, you didn't answer my question," Rileigh was finally able to squeeze the question into the avalanche of verbiage. "Did Tina intend to keep the baby?"

"Oh, I wouldn't know about that. She never said. All's I know is she got off drugs because she was pregnant, and I think she was getting her life ducks in a row in other ways, too."

"What makes you think that?"

"Oh, it wasn't nothing she said. Just, you know, she looked better, didn't look so strung out all the time, so tired, with circles under her eyes. She looked good."

The girl heard her own words and burst into tears. "She looked good … and now she's dead!"

Two other of Tina's friends mostly confirmed what G.G. had said — that Tina had been looking better in the past couple of months than she had for a long time before that. But one of them said Tina was still using, said she'd seen her with her dealer recently, but she flat out would not tell Rileigh his name.

Skyler Ross, who had been in Tina's class at the Forge high school but dropped out before graduation, didn't see much of Tina after that. Skyler had moved into an old trailer house with her boyfriend, up the dirt road from Aspen Pike. Rileigh had a hard time finding the place, and when she knocked on the door, Skyler told her to go away, that she wasn't expecting company and her house was a wreck.

How could the interior of your house be a source of embarrassment, when the exterior was such a disaster? It was littered with trash that'd apparently blown out of a barrel and nobody'd bothered to pick it up. And yes, there was an old car up on blocks in the side yard with all four of the wheels missing.

When Rileigh said she'd come to ask her some questions about Tina, Skyler had opened the front door a crack and peeked out. When she did, it was clear that it wasn't the interior of her house she was trying to conceal, it was the bruises on her face. Her eye was black, her lip split, and an ugly greenish purple bruise showed on her right cheek.

"I fell down the stairs," she said, answering the question Rileigh hadn't asked. Which was odd, because it was glaringly apparent that the house was a single story. "I heard Tina's dead. Is that true? Is she ... did somebody murder her?"

If she'd asked the sheriff that question, Rileigh was sure he'd have responded with some noncommittal answer about "a continuing investigation" and "no official cause of death," and other weasel words. Rileigh just told her the truth.

"Yes, she was murdered. I'm helping the sheriff to find the killer."

"Tina was a nice girl. she didn't never hurt nobody. I don't know why anybody'd … well, maybe …"

"Maybe what?"

"Oh, nothing, I don't know nothing."

"Somebody cut Tina open, so if you know something …"

"I done said I don't know nothing." Skyler jutted out her jaw in determination. Then she faltered. "I just …"

She leaned close to the small opening between the door and the jamb, then whispered the rest. Maybe somebody was inside the trailer with her and she didn't want them to hear, but there was no vehicle — other than the one up on concrete blocks — in the front yard to indicate anybody else was home.

"I heard from … well, it don't matter where I heard it, but I did hear that she owed a right smart chunk of change. I think she borrowed it to use as a down payment on a car, but then she spent it on drugs and … he wasn't happy."

"Who wasn't happy? Who loaned her the money?"

The girl gave her a disparaging look. "You know well's I do who's the money man 'round here." She looked fearfully over her shoulder, so there must have been somebody else inside after all, because she said, "I don't think that truck's still for sale. The sign was gone out of the window last time I passed. But that's all I know about it. Now I got to get back to fixing supper."

Skyler closed the door in Rileigh's face.

As she returned to her little Ford, Rileigh saw the

curtains in the front window move, like somebody was peeking out at her as she drove away.

The final two girls Rileigh talked to gave her no new information, but did confirm what she already know, or at least suspected.

"Tina was running around on Aubrey," said Connie Pruitt, before Rileigh even got sat down at her kitchen table. "I don't know how many people know it, but it's true."

"Who was the new boyfriend?"

"That I couldn't tell you. When you'd ask, she get all evasive, got this little *I've got a secret* look on he face and wouldn't say."

"Why not? Do you know why she didn't want you to know who he was?"

"Oh, I don't think it was Tina didn't want word to get out. If it had been, I couldn't have wheedled his name out of her sooner or later. It was him, the boyfriend. He's the one didn't want her telling."

Sheriff Webster listened in silence as Rileigh delivered her report on her conversations with Tina's friends. When he didn't celebrate, or show any emotion whatsoever at the revelations, she was miffed.

"So now we know she was pregnant, a user, maybe quit, maybe didn't, owed money, and had a secret sweetie. That's a whole lot more than we knew this time yesterday. "

"Not all of it's new information. The coroner's report says she was pregnant." He tapped some papers on the top of his desk.

"How far along?"

"Almost five months ... getting to the point she couldn't hide it much longer."

Rileigh shook her head.

"No way would I have guessed she was pregnant, much less going on five months, when I saw her at the Rusty Nail. She had on tight jeans and … well, maybe a little bit of a belly. And now that I think of it, her chest was stretching her shirt tight."

"He didn't find any trace of drugs in her, so the part about her quitting rings true."

"When I came in here yesterday, it was to look at public records because Smitty said he thought—"

"Checked all the police reports. She was never busted for anything, but she was in the car with a known drug dealer named—"

"Chigger."

"Yeah, Chigger. Once when he was arrested and charged with possession of a controlled substance with the intent to sell. Charges were dropped. And she was listed as a "person of interest' in a couple of penny-ante burglaries. Maybe when she was using, she needed the money."

"Apparently she was into a loan shark from some serious cash, or so Skyler said. And the only shark cruising the waters in Yarmouth County is Charlie Hayden."

"Hayden? The guy who runs Blarney Stone Real Estate? I thought he was an upstanding citizen—"

"Which is why you need me along to keep you between the fence posts here."

"The man I want to talk to is Ian McGinnis. I don't know where the boundary lines are out there, but his property is next to the grass hut — which, by the way, is likely sitting on property owned by the county because the last owner never paid his taxes. So it's possible Tina's body was found on Ian's land."

"He's the only person I know who spends any time at the grass hut, keeping Aunt Daisy supplied."

"That little patch of weed in the clearing not far from the house? Ian is growing it for your aunt?"

"You didn't hear that from me. And if you're looking for witnesses, you're welcome to talk to my aunt about it. I'm sure she'll cooperate. Unless she decides you're Custer and she's Sitting Bull, in which case she might try to scalp you with a meat cleaver. Not a witness that'd impress a jury."

"I'm not looking to prosecute anybody for growing weed in the woods. Maybe he's seen something."

Rileigh rose to leave.

"Might want to sit back down," the sheriff said. "The coroner's report isn't the only thing I got from Gatlinburg today."

"Tina's phone records? It's about time." Tina's phone was missing. He had been wrangling with the stupid phone company trying to get the records so they could find out who Tina was fighting with when Rileigh overheard her conversation at the Rusty Nail."

"Not yet," he said. "Working on it. What I got is the results on the piece of pancake and bottle of syrup I had analyzed."

He paused and she ground her teeth. Was he going to drag it out —

"There was fentanyl in the piece of pancake slathered in syrup, but none in the bottle of syrup. The drug could have been inside the pancake itself, I suppose, but what makes sense is that somebody sprinkled fentanyl on the top of the pancake after your aunt poured syrup on it, while everybody was outside ogling the wreck. It would have looked like powdered sugar."

Somebody had tried to poison Rileigh? Who? And why?

The sheriff read her mind.

"Maybe somebody doesn't want you sniffing around Tina's murder?"

"*You're* sniffing around her murder. Have you found any strychnine in your oatmeal?"

She managed to hold onto the next thought and not say it out loud, but from the look on the sheriff's face, he was likely thinking the same thing— the murderer was going after Rileigh because he thought *she* might be able to catch him … and he didn't think the sheriff had a chance.

Chapter Nineteen

RILEIGH WENT ALONE to talk to Chigger and the sheriff probably wouldn't like that, so she decided not to give him a choice. Maybe Tina was getting her drugs from some other dealer, but Chigger was as good a place to start as any, and given the line of work Chigger was in, the presence of "real" law enforcement would rattle him. This wasn't his first rodeo. If you weren't careful, he'd lawyer up and you wouldn't find out anything at all.

The rattle and clack of bowling balls hitting pins assaulted Rileigh's ears as she stepped into the I Got a Spare Bowling Alley that sat down in Mud Creek Valley below the Forge. She couldn't very well talk to Chigger when he was at home. She'd checked a couple of his other known haunts and if he wasn't here —

He was. Four men were bowling on the last lane on the far side of the building and Chigger was one of them. He was tall and thin, all arms and legs, a good basketball player in high school who never seemed to fill out as he got older. He said something and the other men laughed. He was a charmer, smooth without being slick, had a contagious laugh and a wide, toothy smile.

She made her way through the little coffee shop and down the aisle with racks of bowling balls to the last row. Chigger was waiting beside the ball return when Rileigh approached.

"I need to talk to you, Chig."

"Not now. Can't you see I'm busy here?"

He gestured down the bowling lane where a lone pin stood upright on the back end, the number four pin, then pointed at the score card on the monitor above the lane.

"If I get this spare, we win the game."

His ball popped up out of the ball return and Rileigh grabbed it before he had a chance.

"Hey, what the—?"

She turned, took a four-step approach, released the ball low on the right with a handshake grip so it would curve back left—

Whack! The ball struck the pin and knocked it backwards into the pit.

The other bowlers with Chigger immediately exploded in an argument about the score. Chigger turned on Rileigh, but she leaned in close before he could cut loose on her. "You really *need* to talk to me Chig — *privately.*"

He took a beat to think about it. "Fine, come on."

Then he called over his shoulder to his friends and teammates, "You guys work this out. I won't be long."

He led the way to the side entrance to the building and they stepped out into an area where the ground was littered with cigarette butts. The stench of spoiled cheese and marinara sauce wafted to them from the nearby dumpsters.

"Look, if Georgia put you up to this, you're wasting

your breath. It's a 'no', full stop. We ain't getting a new double-wide–"

"GEORGIA DIDN'T SEND me and I don't want to talk about trailers. I want to talk about Tina Montgomery."

He looked like she'd landed one in the solar plexus. But he recovered quickly, shrugging it off.

"Shame what happened to her. I heard she–"

"How about we skip this part, okay? The part where you say you don't know Tina, and I say you were selling her drugs, and you get all outraged and claim you don't sell drugs, and I tell you even your six-year-old knows what daddy does for a living and … well, we won't do that part, we'll just say we did. So tell me, what you were selling her?"

"How's this any business of yours? You're not a cop. At least not anymore." The last part was slathered with venom and erased the small measure of slack she'd been willing to cut him because he was married to her best friend.

"You don't want to talk to me about it, fine. Sheriff Webster will be around shortly to ask you all kinda uncomfortable personal questions about your drop site at the Dairy Delite, which, by the way, is less than a thousand feet from the Tiny Tots Daycare, placing you in violation of Tennessee's Drug Free School Zone statutes, which enhance the penalties–"

"Okay, okay. Tina was … one of my customers. But that's old news now, she got clean, stopped using two or three months ago."

"How come?"

Clearly the question made him uncomfortable.

He shrugged. "How would I know?"

"So you didn't know she was pregnant?"

He feigned surprise, but he wasn't very good at it. His eyes had narrowed and he kept blinking. That was a more subtle sign than hopping from one foot to the other, but they both indicated the same thing. She was hitting nerves.

"Why would I know a thing like that? Look, she stopped buying. I don't go chasing down all the people who used to buy from me and ask them to fill out some customer satisfaction survey."

"So, you're saying you didn't know she cleaned up her act because she was pregnant?"

"You need to back off and let it go. Just a friendly warning, 'cause you and Georgia are friends."

"What does that mean?"

He actually looked around, like maybe somebody was hiding in the dumpster recording their conversation. Then he hissed the words.

"What I mean is that Tina wasn't buying from me, and I didn't go around hassling her about why not because I enjoy breathing in and out on a regular basis."

"I'm a little slow on the uptake here, Chig. Draw me a picture. What are you saying about Tina and–"

"Tina was mixed up with some big, bad dudes. Nothing local. I cut a wide path around those guys because they play for keeps."

"She was buying drugs from–"

"I don't know that she was buying anything, and I don't think she was using anything. But she was doing some kind of business with the bad guys and I don't want nothing to do with that."

He set his jaw.

"That's all I got to say about it and you can send the sheriff around to talk to me if you want, but I'll tell him the same thing." His face softened, just a little. "You need to let this go, Rileigh. You been good to Georgia over the years, and I'd hate to see you get hurt. You need to listen to what I'm telling you. *Back. Off.*"

He turned on his heel without another word and went back into the building.

Rileigh stood where she was for a moment, ignoring the stench of rotted food to process what he'd just said.

I'd hate to see you get hurt.

Well, if she'd eaten that pancake at the St. Jude's breakfast, she would have been in what Aunt Daisy liked to call a world of hurt.

Poison wasn't usually the weapon of choice for drug dealers. They were more into bullets in the back of the head or slashed throats, things like that. She flat out couldn't conjure up a scenario where some bad ass drug kingpin came to the St. Jude Children's Hospital pancake breakfast and sprinkled a lethal dose of fentanyl on top of her blueberry pancake.

Besides, Chigger said these guys weren't local, and a stranger would have stuck out like a dog in a duck parade.

Except minions.

Every organized crime operation or drug gang she'd ever encountered had guys at the bottom of the food chain who'd blend into the community. Strangers couldn't start a big business in Yarmouth County, or anywhere else in the Smokies, without go-betweens to grease the skids. People like the guys who worked in the back, cleaning up plates and utensils at the breakfast — men doing that to meet some kind of "community service" sentence slapped on them by a judge. Any one of them could have doctored Rileigh's plate of pancakes when Aunt Daisy wasn't look-ing. Shoot, even if she had been looking, she might not have noticed. She'd been looking right at Rileigh and called her Jillian that morning, so the synapses definitely weren't connecting.

Was it possible that Tina had got involved with the wrong people, maybe wanted out because she was pregnant, and they weren't amenable to her early retirement so she threatened to go to the police?

She'd been threatening "to tell" somebody something when Rileigh overheard the cell phone conversation the day she was killed.

Is it possible those "wrong people" had targeted Rileigh — she tried to keep her mind from completing the sentence but couldn't — and Rileigh's life was in danger?

It wouldn't be the first time. And on every one of those other occasions, she'd eliminated the danger before it could eliminate her.

Even that last time. She'd been in danger. That's why she'd fired her gun. And maybe she shouldn't have. Maybe she shouldn't have taken the shot. How many times had she played that particular three or four seconds of her life over and over in her mind? Could she have done something different? Should she have done something different?

No matter how many times she chased that weasel, she always ended at the same place.

Round and round the mulberry bush, the monkey chased the weasel.

The monkey stopped to pull up his sock.

Pop goes the weasel.

The weasel had fired on her. She had returned fire. If she hadn't, she'd be dead. But in some ways, maybe that would've better than what did happen.

Chapter Twenty

"You used lethal force, didn't you Sergeant Bishop?"

Well, duh, that's why we're all here, right?

"Yes, sir."

"Will you please explain why you believed the circumstance warranted such an extreme measure."

You mean, why did I decide to shoot the man who had a gun pointed at me, the guy who'd just shot two civilians and my partner?

That particular interrogation was what always came back to Rileigh when she thought about the three or four seconds that changed her world, destroyed everything she had once believed to be true, and pretty much fucked up the rest of her life.

But when the internal affairs officer had asked her that question, she'd still been operating under the totally erroneous assumption that the facts in the case mattered. That what had really happened mattered. That the outcome was in some intrinsic way linked to reality.

And so she had parroted to him what her instructor at

the police academy had told her more than a decade before, that three things must all exist at the same time to justify the use of deadly force — ability, opportunity and jeopardy.

Which meant that somebody actually possessed the ability to pull the trigger on a pistol, and at that particular moment in time, that person had a pistol aimed at you, ready to fire. But the third one, jeopardy was trickier.

"Let's say you are having an argument at a softball game with the batter," the instructor had said, "and he pokes you in the chest with his bat. At that moment, he certainly would have the ability to beat you to death with the bat, and the opportunity to do so. But unless it is his clear and indisputable intent to attack you violently with the bat, you could not use deadly force to protect yourself."

The man who'd pointed a 9mm Glock at her that bright spring morning when the jasmine was in full bloom in Memphis and she could hear the distant calliope on a riverboat on the Mississippi, had satisfied all three criteria.

But in the end, it flat ass didn't matter.

IT'S SPRINGTIME. Somehow, after it's all over, Rileigh is offended by that fact. It seemed an affront from the universe that Rileigh's life was totally destroyed on such a beautiful sunshiny day. It's fundamentally wrong, like finding a cigarette butt in a little girl's music box.

She and Patrolman Tyrell Crocker, her partner, are out to do a well check on an apartment house near the river. Some elderly person, a Mrs. Pearl VanDyke has suddenly gone off the radar. Nobody's seen her in four or five days. Her out-of-state children have tried to call her and she doesn't answer the phone. Finally the superintendent of her building got in touch with the police and Rileigh decided to do a ride-along with Crocker to check it out.

She knows what they're going to find. This isn't her first rodeo.

The old lady has died, hopefully had a heart attack and died instantly, but maybe not as rosy a story. Rileigh once did a well-check on an old man who had fallen and broken his leg. He couldn't get to a phone. Surely he'd cried out for help, but nobody was near enough to hear him. He did not die an easy death.

That's the reason Rileigh has come along. This is Crocker's first rodeo, as a new recruit. Not exactly fresh out of the academy, but he's only worked patrol for six or seven months. Finding a dead body, particularly one that might not be recently dead, is gruesome. She wants to be there for support, but also to get a look at how Crocker handles himself. As a sergeant, Rileigh is in charge of twelve officers. She makes assignments. She has to decide in a pinch which officers can handle themselves and which can't. And those kind of command decisions are borne out of a wealth of conscious and unconscious impressions.

If they'd just driven on by ... but they couldn't have done that. That's like saying if a car had been a few seconds later or earlier going into an intersection, the wreck wouldn't have happened. You could what-if a situation to death, but it wouldn't change anything.

It only takes seconds for Rileigh's gaze to sweep the building, but Rileigh has good instincts and she listens to her gut. And when she sees the liquor store with cars in the parking lot but no customers visible inside and no proprietor at the counter, all her alarms start going ding, ding, ding.

"Pull in here," she tells Crocker, checking her duty weapon, a Sigg Sauer .40 caliber pistol, as she does so. "Something hinky about this place. Park down at the end so you can't see the car from inside the building."

Crocker does as instructed, pulls in and parks beside a white SUV with tinted windows which totally blocks their cruiser from view. Rileigh doesn't draw her weapon. Just gets out the passenger side and sidles along the side of the SUV toward the door of the store.

Suddenly, there's screaming from inside the building. Shrieking. A woman's voice cries, "No, please, do—"

The rest of the word is cut off by the sound of a gunshot.

A man's voice tumbles on top of the words.

"Help me, please, somebody. My wife's—"

Two more gunshots silence the voice.

Rileigh only has time to draw her weapon and take one step around the SUV before the door of the store bursts open and a young man in a tee shirt comes running out. He has something in his hand. It could be a bottle of beer. It could be a gun.

Rileigh pivots, draws down on the man running across the parking lot, her pistol in a two-hand grip, arms straight, feet spread apart.

"This is the police. Stop where you are and drop that gun."

After that, time melts into slow motion. It was always that way in a firefight. And usually the sound wasn't quite hooked up to what made it, so a hole would appear in the side of the truck three inches from your face, but the thwuck of it smashing into the metal was a beat or two late.

It's the adrenaline dump that causes the phenomenon. The medulla in the adrenal gland kicks into action to fuel your fight or flight instinct by dumping a load of it into your bloodstream. The adrenaline narrows your vision, removes your peripheral vision altogether so it looks like the whole world is at the end of a long, dark pipe. It increases your heart rate, makes your hearing more acute, and compresses or expands time.

A moment takes an hour. An hour-long battle is over in seconds.

The blond man whirls around and lifts the hand holding what could be a beer bottle and Rileigh hesitates a second, checking. No cars in the street beyond him, nothing but a hedge on the other side of it. During that second, the man fires the not-beer-bottle blindly in Rileigh's direction and she hears a grunt from Crocker as he goes down.

Rileigh pulls off three shots in rapid succession, the sounds so close together it might have been a single round. The young man lurches backward as the first shot— the kill shot— slams into his chest. The second bullet catches him in the groin. The third bullet misses, hits the asphalt in the parking lot and ricochets with a pinging sound.

The gun flies out of his hand and Rileigh sees it, watches it float in slow motion up into the air and then down again, hitting the parking lot and sliding away under a parked car.

Then it is over. There is silence.

The blond man lies unmoving.

Rileigh grabs the microphone clamped to her shoulder, pushes the button and cries, "Officer down, repeat officer down. Need assistance at..." she tries to read the words of the sign in the liquor store window, but she can't make the letters form a word in her head. "The liquor store on Haymarket street. I need a bus, multiple victims."

And then perhaps she went into a loop, at least briefly. It happened sometimes when danger is suddenly over. You just keep repeating the same things. She'd once watched an officer keep telling a dead man not to move or she'd shoot him.

If she does go into a loop, it doesn't last long. It is only then that Rileigh becomes aware of the passers by, the people on the sidewalk, a woman walking her dog half way down the block, the sudden burst of screaming. It doesn't come from inside the building, where later Rileigh will find one woman dead, shot in the face, and her husband barely alive. He survives, but he is paralyzed from the waist down.

Crocker took one in the belly. An inch higher and it would have been deflected by his kevlar vest. Rileigh acts quickly, grabbing a towel she'd left in the backseat of the cruiser after she cleaned graffiti off the hood that was probably supposed to say "Die pigs," but which was smeared to become "dipi-gs." She uses the towel as a pressure bandage to keep Crocker from bleeding out.

How long the unnatural silence lasts she doesn't know. One second there is not a sound in the world and the next there is a cacophony of noise and movement all around.

But the screaming that's not in the store. Somehow she hears that even when she can't seem to hear anything else. The sound rises up out of the general hubbub to become like a siren, the wailing of a siren, but it doesn't get closer and closer as the other sirens do, as the cruisers and ambulances and the whole world descends on the scene. It never gets any closer. It is a constant sound at a constant distance and it is recognizable and memorable because it is in the wrong place.

It started when she shot the young man. And it never stops.

EVEN NOW SOMETIMES, when she was in a quiet place, she could hear that voice, the shrieking of that voice. The voice that ripped open a bright spring morning and ate up Rileigh Bishop's whole world in a single bite.

Chapter Twenty-One

THE LITTLE BELL on the door of the Blarney Stone Realty Company dinged when Rileigh stepped inside, and the buxom receptionist looked up from her telephone and hung a smile on her face.

"Good afternoon. How may I help you today?"

Squeaky voice. God, how Rileigh hated that squeaky voice so many women affected these days. And surely it was an affectation. Rileigh hadn't known a single girl in her high school who talked like she'd just inhaled helium, but now every third woman she met sounded like Minnie Mouse.

"I need to speak to Charlie," she said, instinctively deepening her own voice to compensate.

"May I ask if you looking to purchase or sell a property, or are you looking for a rental of some kind. We have—"

"I just want to talk to Charlie. Please tell him Rileigh Bishop would like to see him."

Saying that felt like she was trading on her name and on their past relationship, or lack thereof. She wasn't.

Theirs hadn't been a relationship you could trade in for favors afterward. For starters, Rileigh didn't drop her name around town as if she thought she was famous somehow. Local girl goes to the big city, has a great career, screws up her career and her life and comes home in disgrace wasn't a likely lead story for the WMMM– "Mountains! Mountains! Mountains!"—News. Film at eleven.

The receptionist punched a button and told the man on the receiving end that Rileigh Bishop wanted to see him. There was no response, but a few seconds later, Charlie came striding into the reception area from a hallway leading to the back.

"Rileigh," he cried, as if he were sitting under a palm tree in rags on a desert island and she'd just pulled up in a yacht to offer him a beer.

He looked way too tan for it to be natural. Spray on, she was sure. He whipped off the sunglasses that he wore for affect and advanced on her as if he intended to hug her.

She cut him off at the pass by sticking out her hand.

"Good to see you Charlie. I promise I won't take up too much of your time."

He took her hand and shook it, then held on. His hand was soft, almost like a woman's hand, and his fingernails had seen a manicure in the past three days. Rileigh had never had a manicure, and she took ridiculous pride in that statement.

"It's so good to see you, my dear. I didn't know you were back in town."

The hell he didn't. Charlie Hayden didn't miss a trick. He knew who was where and what they were doing when it came to Black Bear Forge, probably better than the sheriff and all his deputies put together.

"If we could just talk in your office ..."

Bad move. What she'd been trying to do was get him moving toward his office so they could sit down and get this over with. But he had misinterpreted, clearly thinking that she was itching to be alone with him. Charlie Hayden was a pickle shy of a full barrel in the self awareness category.

He'd been a heartthrob high school football player. Handsome, with broad shoulders and a head of thick blond curls. Now, a couple of decades down the road from high school, he was still good looking. But he had to work at it, and his blond curls had given way to a very, very short haircut, designed to hide the fact that male pattern baldness was slowly eating his hairline.

His teeth were too white — caps, new ones it looked like. And the dark tan was definitely trying too hard.

"Certainly, of course, please come right in. Would you like something to drink, a soft drink, or— Sylvia, could you make a fresh pot of—"

"I don't drink coffee and I'm not thirsty," Rileigh said, then turned and walked ahead of him down the hallway that she assumed terminated in his office.

It did. The door was solid oak. The office, like Charlie, tried too hard.

One whole wall was a gigantic topographic map of the region. On it you could see Black Bear Forge, a big star out of proportion to the town's size. Its star was bigger than Pigeon Forge's or Gatlinburg's— both with three or four times the population. Bigger than Sevierville, even, where Dolly Parton had built more than just Dollywood. She'd also built Dollywood's Splash Country, Dollywood's DreamMore Resort and Dollywood's Smoky Mountain Cabins.

Dolly Parton had brought the whole world to the Smoky Mountains of Tennessee— and not everybody thought that was a good thing at all. The tsunami of tourists now threatened to overwhelm everything and everyone who called the beautiful mountains home. Even the occasional Famous Person sightings, or Almost Famous Person sightings, didn't make up for the snarled traffic and the infestation of housing developments and resorts.

Charlie Hayden had been responsible for some of that blight and was working night and day to be responsible for a whole lot more of it.

The Smoky Mountains had the misfortune of being located less than five hours drive from more than a dozen metropolitan areas — some of them big cities like Nashville and Atlanta, some smaller cities like Louisville, Cincinnati, Knoxville and Birmingham.

At some point in the past while Rileigh had been gone, at least half the residents of all those cities had purchased property to make a get-away vacation cabin in the mountains, bringing grandma and the kids and half the people on their block with them to spend a week in the Smokies. Which, of course, was a boon for the crapola stores in Pigeon Forge and Gatlinburg and Sevierville but a nightmare for the local residents, who had to fight the traffic on mountain roads that could *not* be widened.

On the map were dozens of little signs that featured Hayden's trademark— the Blarney Stone. He needed a new logo. Though you'd think he'd planted a lip-lock on the stone, given his gifts of gab and flattery, it was clear from the shape of his rock that Charlie Hayden had never laid eyes on the real thing — a piece of limestone built into the battlements of Blarney Castle near Cork. Well, Rileigh had seen it and the one on his signs looked like a slab of concrete off the side of a collapsed building.

There was a time, years ago, that she remembered he'd had a Blarney Stone out front of his office, but that had been painted and repainted and re-repainted by every graduating class at the Forge high school until he'd finally hauled it off somewhere and put out a sign with a flower bed around it.

Charlie had picked out the perfect spot on a mountainside to perch his office so that the huge floor-to-ceiling windows offered a breathtaking panoramic view of the virgin forests in Gum Tree Valley — just about the only pristine, undefiled-by-development valley left — with mountains marching off toward the horizon, and the signature wisps of mists that had given the Smoky Mountains its name clinging to the mountaintops.

She couldn't help stepping to the window to stare out at the view. It still took her breath away. Even after all these years, she had to hold onto her emotions when she came upon a sight like the one that rested below Charlie Hayden's Real Estate Office windows.

With that view as a draw, it was no wonder Charlie had made a killing in the real estate business. Which, of course, begged the question of why he side-jobbed as a loan shark. Everybody knew the answer to that question, of course. Gambling. Charlie had likely won and lost ten fortunes in his life, and would likely win and lose as many more before he was done. If there was a game, he bet on it. A horse race, he'd put a thousand dollars on the nose of the 80-1 long shot. He went to Vegas, Atlantic City, and was probably on a first-name basis with the concierge of every river boat casino in the country.

His financial needs were bottomless. He couldn't make enough money to throw away on slow horses and fast women, so he'd figured out a way to augment his income. Loan Sharking. Was loan shark a verb? He had let it be known he could get you a thousand dollars, no questions asked, if you were in a pinch. Or ten thousand. Or fifty thousand. But the interest rates would eat you alive.

Charlie came up behind Rileigh as she stood looking out the window, got too close, which was his style, and she was forced to recall the single date she'd had with him years ago, where he wined and dined her, drank way too much and, of course, expected payment in full in her bed. Turning him down had gotten … ugly. It had to be demoralizing for a man to be dumped on his backside by a woman half his size, but if he'd really put it together that she was in the military, he might have kept his hands to himself. As it was, they hadn't parted company as friends.

Clearly, Charlie was willing to set all that aside and start over with a clean slate. He was too vain to realize that ship had sailed a long time ago.

"How have you been, Rileigh?" he said into her hair, because he was standing that close.

"If I was any better, I'd be twins," she said, quoting Daisy. She turned away from the windows, had to elbow him aside to do it, and sat down in one of the chairs facing his desk. Charlie perched on the corner of it— probably thought that was a sexy look.

"Let me cut to the chase, Charlie. I'm here to ask about a loan you made to Tina Montgomery."

His face froze.

"That's right, the Tina Montgomery whose dead body was found in the woods Tuesday afternoon. She was murdered."

He was genuinely surprised and shocked. Not that he didn't know what had happened to Tina. There wasn't anybody in Yarmouth County who didn't know that by now. He was surprised that Rileigh was asking questions about it, though, and appeared to be surprised she knew anything about his loan operation. Because he tried to bluster his way out of an answer.

"What loan …?"

"Please. I know you loaned money to Tina Montgomery. That's a fact, not a guess, and now she's dead and–"

"Why on earth would you think … I mean, what does a loan have to do with her murder?" He'd stepped down off his perch on the desk as he spoke and went around and sat in his huge chair behind it. That offered him the throne position that was supposed to cow subordinates.

"Oh come on, Charlie. Like the whole town doesn't know you're a loan shark."

"Loan shark!" He tried to look offended but couldn't pull it off.

"Unlicensed money lender, then. You pick the title."

"I don't know what you're talking about. Why would you say a thing like that–"

She decided to try the tack that'd worked with Chigger earlier.

"You talk to me or you talk to the sheriff. You don't know this guy. He's a bulldog." She figured she could say whatever she wanted about Sheriff Webster, since nobody in town knew him. "He'll come after you, look under every rock, put your whole business under a microscope and–"

"Ok, I loaned her five thousand dollars. She was in a bad way then, *needed* money for … you know. But that was months ago."

"And when she couldn't pay you back the —what, *fifteen* thousand she eventually owed, counting interest–"

"No, not fifteen. It was just ten."

"Right. It was *just* double what she borrowed. And when she couldn't pay, you started leaning on her."

He looked uncomfortable. "Like I said, that was

133

months ago. And then she paid up. She walked in here a couple of months ago and handed me every dime she owed me in one payment. Cash."

Of course, Charlie could be lying. But it fit. Tina was trying to get her ducks beak to tail feathers because she was pregnant. She'd stopped using, or so Chigger said. So she didn't have a gaping maw of addiction sucking every resource she had. It made sense.

What didn't make sense was the "one time, in cash." Where did Tina get ten thousand dollars in cash? Maybe that's how she got hooked up with those "big bad guys" Chigger warned Rileigh about. Unless she was robbing Peter to pay Paul, borrowing from one loan shark to pay another.

But why would a shadowy organization selling drugs (and who knew what else) give Tina Montgomery ten thousand dollars?

Except for the "give" part. They didn't give her anything. If she got money from them, she'd earned it.

The question was, doing what?

Chapter Twenty-Two

RILEIGH PERFORMED the well-practiced maneuver necessary to make it up her driveway. She had to gather speed coming down the hill on Bent Twig Road that transversed Tucker Mountain, whip a U-turn into the drive and give the old Ford the gas right before the spot where the rocks were loose, then bounce up over the rock protrusion halfway and come to an easy stop at the top of the grade in front of the fence.

She'd waited until she stopped to call the Sheriff's office. He wasn't in, so she left him a detailed message about what she'd found out from talking to Chigger and Charlie. She hoped he'd call her back to report in whatever he'd learned today, but she didn't really expect it.

When she stepped into the house she had to smile. It smelled like a bakery. Was that … was that the smell of fresh bread? Brownies, definitely brownies. And pot roast maybe.

If she'd had any appetite at all, she'd be the size of a small-sized rental car. As it was, she could tell that the conspiracy to fatten up Rileigh was succeeding somewhat.

She'd gained a little weight. More important to the even-
tual success of the mission her aunt and her mother had
signed on for, she was beginning to regain her appetite.
Well, some of it. Enough that the smell of whatever culi-
nary delights the two old ladies had whipped up for her
didn't make her nauseous.

Made her hungry, actually.

A little.

The combined old lady babble turned on as depend-
ably as a movement-sensitive security light as soon as
Rileigh stepped into the kitchen.

"Been wondering when you'd get home," Mama said.

"… made brownies and they're special!" Daisy said.

"… homemade bread will be out of the oven in ten
minutes …"

"… and a strawberry rhubarb pie, and if you think it
was easy to come by rhubarb …

"… got the makings for sweet potato pie, too …

"… make you french toast in the morning to eat with
that," Daisy paused. "That stuff that's kinda like coffee
that comes out of that machine of yours."

Rileigh had brought home her Keurig and the two
women in the household had looked at it with all the awe,
wonder and *suspicion* of cave men peeking over a rock at
the first fire. She'd given them samples — one was apple
cinnamon and the other was black cherry — but they had
both pronounced the liquid undrinkable. Daisy spit hers in
the sink.

In this house's 's'posta book — the book that laid out
how things were s'posta be to preserve life as we know it on
this planet — coffee must taste like, well, duh, coffee. Milk
or cream and sugar were optional, but the coffee itself
must be actual coffee.

Those in violation of the tenets of the s'posta Book were witches and should be burned at the stake.

Rileigh leaned back against the door frame, closed her eyes and let the babbling sounds flow around her like the water in a brook.

" ... Tina Montgomery ..."

Those words hung on a nail in her mind as the babble flowed through it.

She opened her eyes. "I'm sorry, I missed what you said about Tina."

"I asked you if you'd found out yet who kilt her," her mother said.

If Daisy said, "who'd want to kill a sweet girl like that?" Rileigh would—

"Who'd want to kill a nice girl like that?" Daisy asked.

Close enough. The words yanked the knot back in her belly that the smells and sounds had loosened.

"Can we wait until after supper to talk about it? I'm actually hungry..."

The women exploded into action, ushering her to her chair at the table, like mother ducks paddling around their gosling. And soon her plate was piled high with with enough food to fill the bellies of two, perhaps three people her size. Then Mama and Daisy filled their own plates and sat down to eat.

She managed to get her mother talking about the flowers she was planting in the garden, knew she could run along that track for half an hour with no more encouragement than a nod, or a you-don't-say, leaving Rileigh in peace to wolf down cut-it-with-a-fork roast beef, potatoes, carrots, onions in a light brown gravy.

The sun was setting and Rileigh was feeling more relaxed — and certainly more full — than she had in weeks when Aunt Daisy asked, "Would you pass me the green beans, please, Jillian?"

The words stabbed into her chest, though her mother didn't appear to notice.

"*Rileigh*, Aunt Daisy. Remember? Rileigh?"

"I bet them flower girl dresses is as itchy as wearing a burlap bag full of mosquitoes," Daisy continued. "You shoulda thought about putting a satin lining in 'em so the girls won't be wiggling and squirming'"

Her mother had caught the drift of the conversation. She didn't engage it, just picked up the ball and ran for an entirely different set of goalposts.

"Remember when you was a little girl, Rileigh, and you knocked over that wasp nest and–"

"Who's Rileigh?" Daisy asked.

Her mother pointed to her.

"Rileigh. Right here. My daughter. Your niece."

Daisy made a humph sound in her throat.

"I ain't never met anybody named Rileigh — girl or boy, cause that name could go either way."

"Girl. Me. Rileigh. Look at me, Aunt Daisy, *I'm Rileigh.*"

It was no use trying to make a woman with dementia see reality. And if she'd gone off on any other tangent, Rileigh would merely have smiled indulgently. But this was different. It hurt.

"I know you don't want to marry that boy, that David Hicks," she held up her hand to forestall Rileigh's beginning protest, "and I'm saying I don't blame you. That receding chin of his" — David didn't have a receding chin — "runs in the family and you don't want a bunch of chinless children–"

Rileigh thought of Cat on a Hot Tin Roof, the part

where Maggie called the children of her husband's brother, "little no-neck monsters."

"… but you leave him standing' at the altar and that boy ain't gonna take it well. He done told me if you don't say the I-do's to suit him, he's gonna cut out your tongue."

She said the words as casually as "pass the salt."

Cut out your tongue.

Suddenly, Rileigh lost her appetite, knew if she sat there another second looking at all that food, she'd vomit her dinner back out on her plate. Scooting almost violently away from the table, she stood and ran out of the room, didn't say a word to anybody.

Why had her aunt suddenly decided she was Jillian? Why right now?

Words followed her up the stairs and into her room.

"Jillian Bishop, you get your skinny butt back down here and help me with these dishes. If you think I'm—"

Closing her bedroom door behind her, she could still hear the voice but not the word. She leaned against it, dragging lungfuls of air into her chest as if she were choking.

Cut out your tongue.

Why had that phrase bobbed to the top of the stormy sea of her aunt's brain right now?

The image of Tina's mouth, full of blood, was briefly superimposed in her mind on the image of the thing that'd been lying on the white pillowcase in Jillian's bedroom all those years ago, and she gritted her teeth to keep from throwing up.

Rileigh was certain she wouldn't sleep a wink tonight.

Chapter Twenty-Three

IN RILEIGH'S NIGHTMARE, a man in a black hood pulled up over his face stood over her holding sticky-looking balls of some kind in one hand and a knife dripping blood in the other. She awoke in Jillian's bed instead of her own, her white cotton nightgown was soaked through with her sister's blood.

"Your turn now," the man said as he began to lean down toward her. She shrank away from him, pressing herself into the pillow. That smell, wet pennies. Blood. It make her stomach roil, but fear had clamped such a tight hold on her stomach, she couldn't have vomited if she tried.

The closer the man got, the more stench rose off him. It was the smell of old dead things, a cat flattened on the highway with fat green flies buzzing around it, or the bloated carcass of cow, lying by the fence line, its eyes glazed over and bugs crawling around on them.

"Please don't." She heard her little girl voice cry, but it didn't come out her mouth. The cry stuck in her throat, hurting like she'd swallowed a piece of glass.

Then she saw what the sticky things were in the man's hand. They were eyeballs. Blue irises, the exact color of Jillian's eyes.

"I cut out her eyes so she couldn't see, and I'll cut out your tongue so you can't tell anybody what you saw."

He laughed then, plunged the knife down toward her face. Rileigh turned her head to the side, so that he missed her right eye and plunged the blade into her temple. When pain exploded in her head, it freed the scream stuck in her throat and the sound filled the room. But Rileigh couldn't hear it because she was dead.

You can't breathe when you're dead, so she stopped breathing.

Rileigh awoke gasping. She felt like she'd been holding her breath. She couldn't seem to get enough air into her lungs. Her heart hammered in her chest, a lunatic woodpecker whacking away, and each beat pulsed in her temple.

She reached up and touched the spot where the knife had gone in, where her heart's pounding —

"You gonna sleep until noon, girl?" The voice was Daisy, shouting from the foot of the stairs.

Rileigh looked at the glowing numbers on her alarm clock. It was seven o'clock.

"I made you something special for breakfast." The old woman actually giggled. "Whipped cream!"

Last night she had threatened french toast with strawberries, and apparently she hadn't used all the whipped cream on the brownies she'd made last night. Rileigh was certain she wouldn't be able to force a bite into her mouth, but she got up and put on slippers and a robe, avoiding the mirror, not wanting to see her sheet-creased face and bed head in the mirror.

"Where's Mama?" Rileigh asked.

"She's coming down with one of them migraine

headaches so she took some medicine, hoping to head it off."

Rileigh's mother had been plagued with debilitating headaches her whole life and had tried dozens of remedies to no effect. Maybe whatever medicine she had now would work.

"Well?" her Daisy said expectantly, gesturing toward the plate where a pile of French toast lay soaking up the juice from the clump of … it looked like still-frozen strawberries on top.

"Surely you don't think I can eat all that?"

"Why would I have made them if I didn't think you'd eat them?"

Rileigh sat down, picked up her fork and cut off a piece of french toast.

"You don't want any syrup?"

"I take mine straight up." She put the piece of toast in her mouth and forced herself to chew and swallow it. Then cut another piece. Her aunt turned to the sink, where she was washing a mixing bowl.

"You gonna go looking for that killer again today?" Daisy didn't turn when she said it.

"I'm going to help the sheriff, if he needs me."

Daisy turned around, told her to "Go on, take another bite."

She watched the fork as it left the plate and carried the bite up into Rileigh's mouth.

Even with her aunt cheering her on, she barely finished half of the french toast, even after the strawberries melted. To mollify her, Rileigh plucked up a couple of last night's brownies and took them upstairs with her to eat as she showered and dressed.

The shower was glorious. She loved the feel of hot needles on her skin. When she stepped out of the shower, she was amazed at the lacy pattern of shadow and light on the floor where the sun was shining through the leaves. She'd eaten one brownie before her shower and now she gobbled down the other greedily. They tasted divine.

Grabbing her purse and car keys off the sideboard in the hallway, she stepped outside into the summer morning that smelled of pine trees and cedar, and the roses growing beside the porch and she inhaled deeply.

She'd parked facing out last night, and when she got into it and put the key in the ignition. She missed. Missed the hole with the key. Had to stab it twice more to fit it into the ignition. That struck her as hilariously funny, and her startled belly laugh filled the interior of her old Ford.

That laugh should have told her something. It didn't.

She turned the key in the ignition, the little engine sprang to life and Rileigh hit the accelerator to head down her torturous driveway to the road. When she put her foot on the brake to ease over the big bump at the top of the hill, the pedal went all the way to the floor. The car didn't slow. That took way too long to process, but when it did, the shock of fear that shot up through her body definitely got her attention.

Rileigh hit the brake pedal again. Again and again, but the car continued to roll faster and faster down the steep incline toward Bent Twig Road below. She couldn't stop it, couldn't even slow it down.

She had no brakes.

Chapter Twenty-Four

THE WORDS of her driving instructor at the Tennessee Police Academy shouted in her head as if the burly man were still sitting in the seat beside her.

"A brake failure transforms a vehicle into a missile on wheels."

And now Rileigh was riding a missile down a mountainside. *That* definitely got her attention.

She shook her head and her vision blurred for an instant, then became clear. Everything seemed to take way too long. Her thoughts were sluggish, thicker than syrup.

Pump the brakes! Pump the brakes!

She pumped the brakes, almost stuck her foot and the brake pedal through the floorboard, but to no avail. Pumping the brakes would only work to stop a car if there were still brake fluid in the lines. Obviously there was no fluid in hers.

Commands tumbled through her mind like the numbered balls in the cylinder when they spun it at bingo during a church social.

Downshift.

Turn off the engine.

Use the emergency brake.

The imperatives rang in her head, bounced off the inside walls of her skull. But the words of Sergeant Jefferson spoke into the cacophony.

"Downshift too quickly and you'll go into a skid."

Turn off the engine and it also turns off the power steering and freezes the steering wheel.

"Yank on the emergency brake and you'll definitely skid."

Rileigh passed over the gravel at the base of the driveway and kept going. Turn right toward Shallow Rock Lane, left toward Pine Bluff Road, or don't turn at all and plunge down the side of Tucker Mountain, pinballing off trees on the way to the bottom.

Left, right, straight, which?

Yanking the steering wheel to the right, she pointed her missile north on Bent Twig Road and realized as soon as she committed to the move that it was the wrong one. North was *down*hill.

Now her missile was heading toward the intersection of Shallow Rock Lane at the bottom of the hill.

By the time she thought all those thoughts, however, she was flying down Bent Twig Road, mindlessly pumping brakes that didn't work and totally freaking out.

WhatdoIdowhatdoIdowhatdoIdo? Her mind was scrambled and she needed all her concentration to grab hold of a single one of the spinning thoughts and hold onto it long enough to think it.

Lucille Davenport passed going up the hill and waved. Rileigh didn't wave back. Crap. What time was it ? Please dear Mary, Joseph and baby Jesus, let it be after nine o'clock. Before nine, there'd be school buses on the road.

No, summertime. School's out. She breathed a sigh of

relief as if that solved all her problems, but struggling to hold the car on the road forced her to concentrate there.

Around the first hairpin turn. Made it. Around the second. Made it. But she was going faster and faster.

"There's a difference between managing a problem and solving it." One of her academy instructors had said that, or was it Lieutenant Hitchcock in her tactics class after boot camp?

What difference did it make who said it? She was keeping the car on the road, hadn't hit anything yet, but she was doing nothing to solve the problem of no brakes.

The alternatives turned over in her head again and she was able to select one.

Downshift.

Okay, her little Ford had an automatic transmission, so it wasn't like she could downshift through gears, five, four, three until she hit first gear. But it did have a L on the gear selection screen. Low gear.

But she did notice the P on that shift-selection bar. Park. What if she just threw the car in Park. Or R. Couldn't she throw the car in reverse? Surely to God that'd slow it down.

Yeah, and rip out the transmission on a car that was already under water—meaning she still owed money on it, more than the car was worth.

She slid into the gentle curve where, if you looked to the right, there was a break in the trees and you could see the base of Clingman's Dome and the valley below it. She didn't look right.

Park and reverse, yeah they were options. But she hadn't yet tried the emergency break, which wouldn't rip out her transmission but which would surely burn up and have to be replaced.

She reached her left hand down and felt for the brake

handle. It wasn't there. She fumbled around for it, frantically, couldn't take her eyes off the road to look. Where could … no, the emergency brake on her old car was a handle on the side of the front seat. The emergency brake on this one was a little pedal on the floor board, high up under the dashboard. She felt around with her left foot, found it, resisted the urge to jam the pedal all the way to the door, just put steady pressure on it.

The car slowed. Not enough. Not nearly enough, but it slowed. Then the pedal hit the floorboard. the emergency brake was fully engaged and she was still flying down the hill, gaining speed, probably half a mile from the intersection.

Martha Kirkpatrick passed and waved.

Some tourists passed and didn't wave.

Please don't let me come up behind somebody going toward the intersection. She didn't want to jam into the back of somebody's car.

Then she realized the likelihood that she was going to hit somebody was growing by leaps and bounds as she approached the intersection. There was a traffic light, and if her lane was red and she just sailed through it, she would t-bone whatever car had the green light.

A CRV passed, full of tourists, the kids in the back whacking each other over the head with rubber tomahawks.

Dwindling options, and though the drag of the emergency brake was slowing her descent it was too little too late. She turned the final corner before the intersection and could see a red light ahead in her lane. The light must have just changed because cars from the other sides hadn't yet pulled full into the intersection.

She couldn't thread that needle, though, couldn't wind between them and come out on the other side.

Options.

There were no more options. As a white CRV pulled into the crosshairs of her hood ornament, she threw out all the stops.

Slamming the car into park, she struggled with all her strength to control the resulting skid, directing it toward the shoulder of the road on the opposite side. She flew in front of a big double-wheeled truck of some kind and plunged over the embankment and down the mountain-side. More trees here and not as steep. It was her only shot.

Then her car clipped a pine tree with the left front bumper, throwing the car sideways, and she saw the trees rushing at her through the passenger side window.

Rileigh Bishop closed her eyes and the world went black.

Chapter Twenty-Five

THE RADIO in Mitch's cruiser crackled to life.

"Be advised there is an 11-83 on Tucker Mountain at the intersection of Bent Twig Road and Shallow Rock Lane."

An 11-83 was a traffic accident, no details. An accident with minor injuries was an 11-81, major injuries was an 11-80 and an accident where an ambulance had been dispatched was an 11-79.

Though there was some standardization in police call signs between jurisdictions, the reality was that every agency had their own unique codes. Some had more, some less.

It had appeared to Mitch that whoever designed the code system for Black Bear Forge had had way too much time on his hands, or was smoking weed. Most were the standard, but there were also codes on the sheet — numbers he had to memorize and be able to repeat in his sleep, for "officer being followed by auto containing dangerous persons." That kind of situation arose so frequently you needed a special code for it. Really? Or a

"horse on the road." Or his favorite catch all, 10-30—
"does not conform to regulations."

Mitch was in the area — he thought. He knew where
he was and knew where the intersection was, but didn't
know the specific route to reach it quickly. And if there was
a mountain in between, it could be one of those "you can't
get there from here" trips

Clicking off the mic attached to his shoulder, he spoke
into his Apple Watch. "Siri, give me directions to the intersection of Bent Twig Road and Shallow Rock Lane."

As he followed her directions, he recalled that Rileigh
Bishop lived on Bent Twig Road and he drove faster, took
the corners without slowing.

Rileigh was a complete conundrum. A total pain in the
ass ... who had helped him find out things he'd never have
found out on his own. She was smart, knowledgable, and
with the one exception of going completely to pieces when
she found Tina Montgomery's dead body, she worked
professionally. She'd been a cop — in Memphis, he
thought — but he hadn't gotten around to digging up her
background, so he didn't know why she'd left that job.

But it was easy to guess. Her Aunt Daisy was deep in
the throes of dementia and her mother wasn't far behind
— though he wasn't sure Rileigh had picked up on that
yet. The woman certainly seemed sane in comparison to
her sister. Before long, both of the old ladies would be
unable to look after themselves.

His radio crackled again and the dispatcher's voice
said, "The 11-83 on Bent Twig Road is now an 11-79."

That meant an ambulance had been sent. Somebody
had been hurt. Mitch concentrated on watching the curves
and drove a little faster.

When he got to the scene, the Rescue Squad was just
getting Rileigh out of the vehicle. Her car had crossed the

center line, left the road and plunged into the woods, bending around an oak tree so tight the squad had to use the Jaws of Life to extract her.

The sight of her, lying unconscious on the ambulance gurney with her face covered in blood from the wound on her scalp, did things to his insides he didn't like at all. If she was seriously hurt ...

"You smell that?" asked Jeb Rawlings, one of his deputies who'd worked the wreck.

"What?"

"Burnt out brake pads, can't you smell it?"

Now that the smell was identified, Mitch did, indeed, smell that distinctive burned-rubber stench.

"Witnesses said she was coming down the hill like a bat outta hell, then her car lurched and started skidding, and she managed to hit the trees instead of the cars in the intersection."

"The car lurched and then went into a skid," Mitch repeated the deputy's words, considering, and concluded, "She wouldn't have burned up the emergency brake in just a few hundred feet."

Jeb nodded. "She'd probably been riding it all the way down the hill."

"Her brakes went out." Mitch said the words with none of the emotion churning around inside him.

That wasn't a common occurrence by any means. In the mid-1960s, car manufactures divided the brake lines in the cars they built, ran them through two different sets of lines to prevent a catastrophic failure of both at the same time. On most cars, the left front wheel and the right back wheel were serviced by brake fluid through one line and the other two wheels got fluid through another. So a brake fluid leak ought to affect only two of the four brakes.

If Rileigh was coming down the hill so fast her car flew

over the embankment and into the trees beyond, she obviously had no brakes at all. A failure of both brake systems. You didn't see one of those every day.

He recalled reading the toxicology report from Gatlinburg the day before, surprised even though he'd been prepared for the result. A lethal level of fentanyl.

Yesterday, somebody had poisoned Rileigh's pancakes, and today, her brakes had failed.

Mitchell didn't believe in coincidences. He walked back to his cruiser and headed for the hospital.

10-40 — lights, no siren.

Chapter Twenty-Six

RILEIGH OPENED her eyes and didn't like how the world was spinning, so she closed them again.

"Miss Bishop, can you hear me?"

It was a man's voice. What man would be in her bedroom first thing in the morning to wake her up?

She opened her eyes, still spinning. She shut them again.

"Miss Bishop, I need you to open your eyes. Can you talk to me?"

Rileigh opened her eyes, blinked, and the world settled. She was looking at the face of a young man in a white lab coat. She knew the face, but couldn't place it.

"How many fingers am I holding up?" he asked and held up a finger.

"One finger, but not a particularly interesting one. If you're going to display only one finger, the proper one–"

The man looked back over his shoulder and spoke to somebody standing behind him.

"She's awake and clearly aware."

Awake and aware. What the ...

Then it came back to her, flooded back into Rileigh's mind with a little wash of residual terror that put goose-flesh on her arms. Her brakes had failed and she'd gone barreling down the mountainside trying to figure out how to stop.

The last images played through her mind— the traffic light, on red, the white CRV pulling into the intersection in her path, slamming the shift handle into park and yanking the wheel hard to the left as it skidded. You were supposed to turn into a skid, not out of it, but getting out of the skid was less important than not center-punching the white CRV.

That's when reality settled around her and she realized that she was in the hospital. She looked down at her body, didn't see any spots where she was missing pieces.

The few times she'd been knocked unconscious in combat, she had always done a body-part check first thing when she woke up, couldn't breathe until she was sure she was there — with some of her parts injured sometimes, but all of them still firmly attached to her body.

Pieces all accounted for, so where did she hurt? That was more an internal assessment than just what she could see. The systems all checked off: hands, arms, torso, legs, feet, head.

Ouch. She wrinkled her brow and felt a prickly feeling on her scalp. She'd obviously suffered a head wound — thus the how-many-fingers quiz — but it couldn't have been a serious one. Head wounds alway looked worse than they really were anyway, the scalp bled like a faucet.

And her effort to move had revealed some kind of issue with the index finger of her right hand. She looked down at it, saw it was splinted, sticking straight out from her knuckle.

Okay, a lump and a broken finger. Could have been a whole lot worse.

She looked at the man in the white lab coat and didn't know whether to laugh or cry. Sitting all starched and perfect at her bedside was Alexander Dowling, the little red-headed kid she'd babysat for whose parents had decided he would only fulfill his potential in life if he were not restricted in any way. Translate that, they didn't discipline the kid and he was a holy terror.

They'd stopped asking her to babysit him after the night he decided he needed to freely express his rage at an outage in the tv cable by throwing a bowling ball through the television screen. When his parents got home, they found their unrepentant and still pissed as hell son, securely duct taped to a chair.

"Doctor Alexander Dowling now, I see," she said to him.

"Still in training," he said. It should have been a self effacing remark, but somehow it sounded more like a boast, made in the typical I-made-it-through-med-school-so-you-can-kiss-my-ass tone.

"If she's awake, can I talk to her now?" came a voice over Zander's shoulder. A male voice.

"Sure, just don't tire her out."

Those words had a possessive sound Rileigh didn't like.

"I'm good to make tiring out decisions for myself now, if you don't mind. Would somebody please bring me my clothes so I can—"

"We're keeping you overnight for observation."

"The hell you are! I'm going home."

The doctor leaned back in his chair and spread his hands expansively.

"You're welcome to do whatever you want, Miss Bishop, but if you leave it will be A.D.O."

Like she was supposed to know what that meant. But she refused to ask and after allowing it to dangle out there in the air, he obliged by translating it.

"That's against doctor's orders. You'll have to sign papers releasing me and the hospital of all responsibility for what happens, should your condition worsen."

"I'll chance it." Then he played his trump card.

"And if you leave without a proper official discharge, your insurance company could deny payment of your hospital bill."

That got her attention.

"A form of legal kidnapping," she said. "Which is defined as holding someone against their will. That's a felony, which carries a pretty stiff prison sentence out there in there real world."

"I'm merely looking after your welfare."

Actually, he was milking her insurance to cover an overnight stay in the hospital, and she could hear the cha-ching dinging in the distance.

Settling back on the pillows, she reached up and felt her head. There was a goose egg with a bandage on it right above her left eye. She winced when she touched it.

"Fine then. I'll stay. It's not like I have a choice." She fixed the doctor with what she hoped was a withering look. "You were a little shit when you were a kid, always demanding to get your own way. I see you haven't changed a bit."

He favored her with his own dirty look. "Hey, I'm not duct taping you to the bed."

They exchanged glares and the young man got up. His seat was immediately taken by Sheriff Webster.

It was only then that it occurred to Rileigh that she hadn't seen her aunt or her mother, both of whom had likely suffered coronaries when they were told Rileigh was in the hospital.

It was, again, as if the sheriff read her mind.

"Your mother and your aunt are in the waiting room and have been assured, reassured, and re-reassured that you are not badly injured and that they can see you in a few minutes." He paused. "But before they distract you, I'd like to ask you some questions."

"I get it. You got an accident report to fill out. Well, the story's short…"

She told it to him, how she'd started out of her driveway and realized she didn't have any brakes, and thus ensued a wild ride down a mountainside that terminated with her car in the trees.

Totaled, of course. Her car was totaled. She'd be making payments for the next five months on a vehicle that would soon be reduced to a block of scrap metal in a junkyard.

She was thinking about how she was going to get from point A to Point B from now on and missed the first part of what the sheriff said.

"I'm sorry, could you say that again."

"I said your blood tests indicate a pretty high level of THC."

That was marijuana

"What? Are you kidding me? I haven't had any weed. There must be a mistake."

But was there a mistake? She recalled then how foggy she'd felt, how she'd had trouble concentrating. The whole thing had started when she couldn't even fit the key into the ignition.

She looked at the sheriff in wonder.

"I was *high*. Crap, that's why the shower felt so good

and the air smelled so fresh and the brownie tasted ..."
She let the sentence trail off.

Brownie. She had eaten several of Daisy's brownies
that morning. What had the old lady put in them?

"I was drugged," she admitted, and he seemed taken
aback by the words. "Oh, not intentionally. You know I
told you that my aunt and Ian McGinnis have a little
garden out by the grass hut. It started out as a treatment
for the nausea of her chemotherapy. Now she's just your
basic garden variety pothead. She must have put weed in
her brownies and I ate some of them." She paused.
"There was no harm intended."

"Well, there was harm intended when somebody cut
the brake lines on your car."

Talk about a conversation stopper. Rileigh couldn't
wrap her mind around the concept. "You can't be serious."

"I suspected that you had no brakes when I was at the
accident site."

He had come to the accident site. Ok, no problem, he
was the sheriff. But did he show up at every wreck in
Yarmouth County?

Probably not.

"I smelled the burnt rubber smell of failed brakes.
That was from you riding your emergency brake. The only
reason for somebody to ride an emergency brake all the
way down a mountain is that they can't stop the car any
other way."

Her mind was still reeling, but she could think a whole
lot more clearly now than she'd been able to think when
she got in her car to come to town.

"The lines were cut," Mitchell added. "Not a brake
fluid leak."

Cut. Deliberately.

"Somebody snipped both the brake lines, so all the

brake fluid going to both sets of brakes drained out. Total
brake failure."

She couldn't form words for a moment.

"First somebody tried to poison you. Then somebody
cut the brake lines on your car. What part of *somebody's
trying to kill you* don't you understand?"

Rileigh wanted to tilt her head back and scream: *slow
down.* Not at the sheriff, but at the world, at reality. It was
all coming at her faster than she could process it.

Then she thought of what Chigger had told her about
Tina Montgomery yesterday.

"Chigger said that Tina'd gotten mixed up with some
really bad people, some kind of drug operation that was
way more sophisticated than his little penny ante drug
sales."

"I've heard of them from other sources." If he needed
her in his pocket to get anybody to talk to him, how had he
found about the existence of some deep, dark secret drug
ring? She wouldn't ask. If he wanted to tell her—

"I talked to some friends who work in narcotics in
Nashville. The way fentanyl is flooding the whole country,
there's a lot of money in distribution systems. They're
springing up from Bangor to Bakersfield."

Riliegh tried to think. The bad dudes had access to
enough fentanyl to kill everybody in the county. Probably
everybody in the state. But thinking about that led her to
an inescapable conclusion that she didn't like. There was
no other reasonable explanation, though.

For some reason, whoever killed Tina Montgomery
was afraid that Rileigh was going to figure out who the
murderer was.

Why?

Why was the killer so sure *Rileigh* was going to find
him?

The sheriff was talking again, so she concentrated on what he was saying.

"You said Tina was selling some kind of vitamin supplement, and she had to go to Knoxville three times a week to pick up supplies," the sheriff said thoughtfully.

She nodded.

"Think about that for a minute. That would mean she was selling enough of that stuff every week to fill up her car three times?"

That one had blown right by Rileigh.

"If Tina was mixed up with some big bad druggies, I'm betting she was a mule," he continued. "That would explain the trips to Knoxville."

"Pays pretty good, from what I hear. Benefits suck. But with expendable income, she'd have been able to pay off her debt to Charlie Hayden."

"In cash."

"And when she told her bosses she wanted out because she was pregnant, they told her the employment door only swings in one direction. She didn't like it, threatened to go to the police, which would violate the non-disclosure agreement in her contract, so their personnel director had her 'terminated.'"

The sheriff sat back in his chair and looked at her.

"So why would that drug cartel believe that *you* — and apparently *only* you — will smoke them out, unless…"

She bit. "Unless…?"

"Unless you know something you don't know you know," the sheriff said. "There's a killer out there who is so convinced you're going to catch him that he has to kill you to prevent it. He must believe you know something that will point the finger at him. That's the only reason I can come up with."

"So I know something about Tina Montgomery's

murder that will point the finger at her killer... but I don't know what that something is. That what you're telling me?"

"You got a better explanation?"

She didn't.

"So how do we find out what I know that I don't know I know?"

He shrugged. "I don't know."

That pulled a small smile out from the corners of her mouth. He got to his feet. "Oh, I forgot to tell you. I got the handgun out of the console of your wrecked car. It's in my office. You can come by and get it anytime." He paused. "Might want to keep it handy."

She held up her hand with the broken index finger. The broken *trigger* finger.

"Fat lot of good it'll do me."

He turned toward the door to go. Then he turned back.

"Think about it. Is there anything about this murder, even a little detail, that made some kind of connection with you?"

Rileigh froze.

Oh, you mean like, the killer cut out Tina's tongue, just like somebody did to my sister thirty years ago?

Chapter Twenty-Seven

RILEIGH WAS glad that Sheriff Webster had offered to come by the hospital and take her home. She had no desire to ride in the car with her aunt behind the wheel, and now the taking-the-keys-away conversation was about to get way more complicated.

Daisy shouldn't be driving. Besides the fact that she didn't see very well, or hear very well, was the fact that her dementia made every car ride an adventure. About a month before, she'd gotten in the car to go the the grocery store. She was determined to make lemon meringue pies for the bake sale at the church and she needed lemons, concentrated lemon juice, and a can of Eagle Brand condensed milk, which she also needed to stock up on. Oh, she'd had enough for a couple of pies, but Eagle Brand came and went on store shelves, so she grabbed as many cans as she could whenever she found it.

She didn't come home by lunchtime. She didn't come home by midafternoon. By six o'clock, Rileigh had scoured the Forge and all the surrounding little towns, had gone to the homes of all her aunt's friends, which didn't take long, and was about to call the state police, when her old gray Honda Accord pulled up in front of the house.

Daisy hadn't been able to find Eagle Brand in Gatlinburg, so she'd gone all the way to Knoxville.

Rileigh had been apoplectic, knew then that she'd have to take the keys away and that would be ugly. Now that she had totaled her own car, Daisy would claim that Rileigh was taking her keys away so she'd have something to drive herself.

Clutching the discharge papers in her hand, she got into the front seat of the sheriff's cruiser and yanked the plastic identification bracelet off her arm.

"Not going to ask how getting checked out went," he said. "Just gonna drive."

For some reason, the fact that he'd recognized her frame of mind and had wisely chosen not to poke the bear was comforting. She liked that about him, and it also proved he was a much more astute judge of people than she'd previously thought.

Her mother and her aunt were both seated on the porch when he stopped the car in front of the fence. He'd said nothing about the big bump in the driveway or how steep it was, but she watched him take note of it and saw the gears turning. He was considering how hard it'd be to stop a car with that kind of a kick start.

"Let me fix you a glass of lemonade and you sit a spell," her mother offered.

"It's okay, Mama, the sheriff's real busy right now."

"Best lemonade in the Smoky Mountains," claimed Daisy. "Make it myself from fresh lemons ... and lemon concentrate."

Which meant she'd soon run out of both and then she'd decide she needed to go restock. If she couldn't find what she was looking for, she might go all the way to Nashville this time. Rileigh gritted her teeth.

Tonight. She had to take Daisy's keys tonight, no matter how big a stink she raised.

"I used to make big jugs of it for the the funnel cake store where I worked in Pigeon Forge," Daisy continued.

"I love funnel cakes," the sheriff admitted. "My secret guilty pleasure."

"Well, then I'll whip you up–"

"Not now, Aunt Daisy. Like I said, he's busy–"

"But I'll take a raincheck."

"Then I insist on the lemonade," she said, and literally shoved him toward the rocker. He sat down and she turned and marched into the house.

Rileigh's mother smiled. "My Jillian loves funnel cakes, too. That's why we always keep the ingredients handy, so we'll have them when–"

"Jillian's not coming home, Mama," Rileigh said, wondering if she was somehow transmitting out Jillian vibes of some kind. She had thought of nothing except Jillian as she lay in the bleach smelling sheets in the hospital. But Mama hadn't mentioned her in months. Why today? Why now? "We've talked about this, remember."

"Why don't be ridiculous, sweetie pie. Of course, she's coming home. I talked to her on the phone just the other day–"

That was a new one. Both old ladies now and then claimed to have heard from Jillian, but it was never as specific as a phone call. And this was her mother who was claiming the Elvis sighting. She was getting as bad as Daisy.

"No you didn't. Jillian didn't call and she's never going to call. You know that."

"What I know is that you don't know everything,

Missy!" Her mother was suddenly near tears. "Jillie could come driving up that driveway any minute now. When she does, you'll be eating your words."

Mama didn't cry, but came close to it. She got up from her chair and went into the house, let the screen door slam shut behind her.

There was an awkward silence.

"You do know about Jillian, right?" Rileigh finally said, feeling a black hole open up in her belly.

She didn't want to go there, but this did give her an opening she needed to tell the sheriff that "little detail" about Tina Montgomery's murder that had connected with her.

"I have heard you had an older sister who ... disappeared."

She let out a long breath. "My sister Jillian was eighteen, and on the night before her wedding thirty years ago, she vanished."

She didn't go on, tried to think how to frame the rest of it.

"The next day must have been incredibly hard on your family." It was an empathetic thing for him to say, but she couldn't keep the edge out of her voice when she replied. It was such a raw nerve. Even after three decades, the pain was right there.

"Hard? Yeah, pretty much, what with Jillian disappearing and my father hanging himself by an extension cord from a rafter in the garage."

Stunned silence.

"I didn't know that part."

"It was a neat trick, too, the hanging part. He'd had shoulder surgery and there were complications. He could barely move his right arm, couldn't lift either arm above shoulder high without excruciating pain. But I don't guess it matters to you if your arm hurts when you're about to be dead."

The sheriff said nothing. What was there to say?

"Mama and Aunt Daisy never mention his name, never say a word about him. But Jillian ... her name's likely to drop into any conversation even after three decades. They still believe she's coming home."

"And you don't?"

"I know she's not."

"How do you know?"

There it was. The door to the dungeon where all the monsters were kicked wide open, letting the light from above shone down the stone steps into the darkness below.

"She's not coming home because she's dead. Only nobody believes that but me."

The rest was a whisper. "I'm the only one who ... *saw.*"

Chapter Twenty-Eight

WHEN RILEIGH HAD THOUGHT about telling the sheriff about Jillian, she'd expected it would be hard. It wasn't. It was easy. All she had to do was open her mouth and the words came tumbling out so fast that they tripped over each other — like a jailbreak where all the prisoners make for the open door at once and some of them get trampled in the stampede.

She told him about discovering the morning before the wedding that Jillian would be moving out of the house after she got married, and how she'd tried to derail the whole thing by hiding.

"No flower girl, no wedding. Like every other six year old in the world, I assumed the planet revolved around me. That's the morning when I found out it didn't."

She told him about lying in bed that night, unable to sleep with the knowledge that it would be the last night Jillian would be in her room down the hall, how she was so desperate for her older sister to stay in her life that she'd come up with a plan.

"I was going to hide something in the bottom of

Jillian's suitcase, so she'd see it when she unpacked. I cut out one of my school pictures and wrote a note to go with it."

"What'd the note say?"

"Please don't forget me."

But when Rileigh finally went to deliver the note, she heard voices coming from Jillian's room. So she'd curled up in a blanket beside the door to her own bedroom — open a crack so she could hear when Jillian was alone again. And she'd fallen asleep, slept a long time apparently, because the whole house was quiet and there was no light coming out from under Jillian's door.

"I tiptoed into her room … but something was wrong. I didn't know what, but I could smell … wet pennies."

She'd poured the story out, her body animated, her voice strong. But when she got to that part, she suddenly felt all the energy drain out of her. She felt weak, and completed the tale in something like a monotone — no inflection, like an automated attendant announcing that you could pick up your checked bags at Carousel Number Three.

When she got to the part about the thing lying on the white pillow on the bed, she flat out didn't have enough air to say the words. There was a silence while she gathered herself.

"Six years old," the sheriff said, shaking his head. "How does a six-year-old child deal with—?"

"She runs away, that's how. That's what I did."

Rileigh had never told anybody the whole story like she was doing now, not from beginning to end. She began to tremble. By the time she'd described how Jillian's room was untouched, her sheets not covered in blood, the floor not splattered with it, she was shaking all over.

"They said I imagined it. Said I had a nightmare about Jillian leaving and I dreamed it."

She drew a great shuddering breath, and said in a small voice: "And sometimes … I think I did. I thought I saw bloody sheets, blood on the floor and little brown specks of it on the pearls on her wedding dress. But the bed and floor were clean …"

She drew a breath, tried to stop shaking. "In the years since, I've … there have been so many nightmares, twisted horrible images, seas of blood … and when I wake up, for a few seconds I still believe they're real, so maybe I *did* dream it. I …"

She needed to tell him the rest of it, the thing so strange a little girl would never have dreamed it. She tried, and the words wouldn't come out.

"I *think* I went back into her room later that day, and there were spots on her dress. And I *think* I crawled under the bed and found brown stains in between the floor slats in the floor, like something had dripped. But I don't know now if I really did those things or not. I do know I never showed them to anybody. By then nobody cared about Jillian's disappearance anymore. The family had bigger fish to fry."

About five o'clock that afternoon — after all the friends and family had been convinced to leave, after Ellie Hicks, the mother of the groom, finally managed to drag her son away and Sue-Sue Ragland, one of the bridesmaids, had asked Jillian's mother if she was going to refund the money Sue-Sue had spent on her dress — that's when everyone noticed that her father was missing.

"Nobody will talk about it now, so I've never known if anybody suspected what was about to happen, if he was there for part of the day and then left, if he'd said anything or left any clues, or … I never saw my father that night or the next day. I don't know where he was."

He'd tied extension cords together and hanged himself from a rafter in the garage ceiling, Rileigh told the sheriff. Daisy found his body.

"I heard her scream. I was in my room, curled up in a ball in a corner with my teddy bear because I was so traumatized." She stopped. "Over the years … in the military and … after… I've heard the sounds people make when they're confronted with death, right in their face, unavoidable. But I have never in my life heard a cry like that. It was a banshee shriek, a wail, so gut-tearing it was feral sounding."

"After that, the house was pandemonium. All the friends and family who'd left, came running back, filled the place up with hysterical people. I didn't see this part, only heard about it, but I was told that Aunt Daisy was the one who found his suicide note, and she tried to burn it. Set the paper ablaze and somebody stopped her, but there was nothing left of the note but a couple of charred bits of paper with words on them. 'Jillian … forgive … sorry.'"

The sheriff didn't speak, then finally said, "Why was your father so upset over Jillian if nobody believed your story? If they all thought she just ran off the night before her wedding day. It happens. Why—?"

"The answers to all *why* questions are I don't know. I don't know what people were thinking then, thirty years ago. But it seems obvious *something* happened to my sister *sometime*, because nobody has heard a word from her in thirty years."

"Now don't you be lying to this nice man, Miss Joseph Rileigh Bishop," came a voice from behind the screen. Daisy stood there empty-handed, apparently having forgotten all about making lemonade. No telling how long she'd stood at the screen listening. In the past few minutes, Rileigh had told the sheriff a boatload of things that were "lies" in Daisy's world. "We know that ain't true."

"Which particular statement are you referencing, Aunt Daisy?"

"Why, we have too heard from Jillian from time to time over the years." She paused. "Well, *you've* heard from her. Tell him. Tell him that part."

Rileigh was suddenly very tired and she let out a sigh.

"What my aunt is referring to is—"

"Is what's right here in this here box," Rileigh's mother said, coming to stand beside her sister behind the screen. The two of them stood there like Tweedle Dum and Tweedle Dee.

Her mother held the box Rileigh had put in the back of her underwear drawer as soon as she got home. Apparently, one or the other of the sisters had been riffling through Rileigh's things when she wasn't there. First Daisy and the box with her badge, and now Mama with this one. This one was far older than the other box, and way more precious to Rileigh.

Rileigh stood and went to the screen door, opened it, and took the box out of her mother's hand. It was a beautiful hand-carved box she'd gotten at a bazaar in Kabul years ago. She'd transferred the contents of the box she'd been keeping since she was a little girl into the new box when she got home from the war. And she would have sworn that nobody in her family even knew it existed.

Apparently, there wasn't anything private in Rileigh's life anymore.

Wordlessly, she returned to the porch swing opposite where Mitchell still sat in the rocker. Her mother and aunt both came out onto the porch then, but Daisy's belligerence was gone. Perhaps it had just occurred to her that she'd been caught taking her niece's things.

Rileigh opened the box slowly, almost reverently and picked up the most recent postcard. She'd gotten it right before Christmas last year.

Chapter Twenty-Nine

MITCH WATCHED as Rileigh took an ornate box out of her aunt's hands, returned to the porch swing, and sat down in it. She opened the box slowly and lifted a postcard from it.

It depicted a scene of snow-covered mountains and a little village in a valley.

She handed it to him.

"This one is postmarked Zurich, Switzerland. I found it in the mailbox at the foot of the driveway right after Thanksgiving."

He turned the post card over and looked on the back. There were no words written in the space for a message there. But somebody had used a red Sharpie to draw a cheerful looking smiley face.

Rileigh picked up another post card from the box. It showed a city that looked like it was out of a science fiction novel, but he recognized the skyscrapers and the huge fountain. It was Dubai. He'd never been there, but he'd always wanted to go there, had studied pictures of it as a kid. A trip there was at the very top of his bucket list.

He turned the post card over and found another smiley face, inked with thick stroke from a blue Magic Marker.

Rileigh picked up a handful of the cards and began to lay them down on the seat of the porch swing beside her, dealing them out like a blackjack dealer in Vegas.

"Paris. Rome. Lima. Johannesburg. Tokyo." She looked up from the pile. "It's only gone international in the past few years. In the beginning they were from different places in the US, different states — Phoenix, Portland, Key West, Omaha. There are thirty postcards here, from thirty different locations. About once a year, I get one. They don't all arrive on the same date, or the same month, so sometimes it's only nine months since the last one, sometimes it's fifteen or sixteen."

Rileigh's mother spoke then from where she stood beside the front door.

"Jillian's been sending one every year since she left."

"You don't know that, Mama!" Rileigh's face was set in cold, hard lines. "There's no way to prove who sent these cards."

"It was Jillian," Daisy said. "She left."

"Why didn't she come back home, then, if that's what happened? If she just left, went off to watch the swallows return to Capistrano or something, then why has she stayed gone?"

"She was supposed to stay gone," Daisy said. "And that's what she done. She left and stayed gone."

"And what does *that* mean?" Rileigh demanded. "That she was *supposed to* stay gone?"

"Who was supposed to stay gone?" Daisy asked.

"Jillian!"

"Why was Jillian supposed to stay gone?" the old lady wanted to know.

Rileigh settled back into the swing.

"Who's on first?" she said and sighed.

Before one of the ladies could ask what that meant, or worse, reply "What's on second?" Mitch asked Rileigh: "You've been getting them all these years, even when you were in the military?"

"They have not followed me from place to place through my life, if that's what you mean. They only come here, to the mailbox at the bottom of the drive, addressed to Rileigh Bishop." She held up her hand before he could continue. "No, the address isn't in Jillian's handwriting. She kept a daytime desk calendar on her desk, the big ones with white squares where you could write things. She filled it up with notes —'go to the florist shop to pick up the green tape,' or 'To Kill a Mockingbird' is due back at the library,' things like that. Mama kept it."

She looked at her mother, who nodded.

"I got it, safe and sound," she responded, as if she'd been tasked with guarding a royal treasure and she wanted the world to know she'd fulfilled her obligation.

"We had lots of handwriting to use as a comparison, but as you can see—" she turned several of the cards over to where the address was printed—" the handwriting is different on every one."

"She musta got somebody else to address them," said Rileigh's mother.

"Why? Jillian wouldn't do a thing like that. It's not her, playing some kind of stupid game with her family. Creating a mystery so we would never know for sure. That's a mean, spiteful, hateful thing to do and Jillian wasn't like that. You know she wasn't." She spewed all the words out in a single, pained stream, then added quietly. "*I* know she wasn't."

"If it wasn't Jillian, then who did send the cards?" her mother said.

"How many times have we had this conversation, Mama. We've been over and over and over …"

She turned to the sheriff, leaned over to rest her elbows on her knees, and clasped her hands together in front of her.

"The first one was from Anaheim, with a picture of Disneyland on the front." Rileigh went to the bottom of the pile and pulled it out. It was worn around the edges. They all were. Years of wear from hands touching them, maybe even fingers stroking them. "It arrived right before my seventh birthday. I always wanted to go there as a kid. Just like every other kid in America."

She sighed.

"I liked to imagine Jillian standing in front of that castle, pictured the two of us wandering around the park, eating pink cotton candy until our faces were as sticky as our hands. The next year was Hawaii." She held up a post card with a picture of a sandy beach and palm trees. "I'd dream of swimming in the ocean, the two of us …"

She stopped.

"See, that proves my point. Those post cards tore me apart. Wondering, imagining, wanting… yearning. And Jillian would never have done a thing like that to me!"

"Postmarks can be faked,' Mitch said. "It's not all that hard–"

Rileigh waved her hand. "I know. I know. I have checked every one. Most post masters will tell you that every now and then they get an envelope addressed to the post office, and inside is a letter and a request that they mail the letter with their postmark. Anybody can do it. And the international ones … businesses have sprung up all over the world in exotic places. You can log onto a website, type out a personalized note, pay ten bucks and at some point in the future, a handwritten postcard with a Timbuktu stamp will show up in your mailbox."

Rileigh gestured down the hill.

"Shoot, it's even possible that the post cards didn't actually come 'in the mail.' Anybody could stop at that mailbox by the road and drop in a card with the rest of the mail."

"But why?" Rileigh's mother asked. "Why would somebody around here do a thing like that?"

Rileigh began to gather up the postcards and put them back in the box.

"I'm not going to keep doing this. We've chased our tails around in circles over this for years and we get nowhere." She put the cards in the box and addressed the two older women. "You guys think the cards mean Jillian's still alive out there somewhere."

"She sends them to let us know she's okay," her mother put in.

"Whatever. I don't believe any of that. Jillian's not out there somewhere drawing smiley faces on the backs of post cards. It's a sick prank that somebody's been playing on this family for decades." She stopped and said the rest with quiet resolution. "Jillian is dead."

Before the others could launch a protest, she added:

"And we are done talking about this right now. Done." Rileigh turned to her aunt. "I thought you were going inside to whip up some of your famous lemonade for the sheriff."

Her aunt looked confused for a moment, then smiled and turned toward the screen door.

"Lily, you're gonna have to get the lid off that sugar canister for me," she said, holding up gnarled, arthritic hands. Rileigh's mother merely smiled sweetly, and opened the screen door with equally-gnarled hands.

Mitch felt bad about where the conversation had led, hated pulling up such awful memories for Rileigh.

"I'm sorry. I never meant for the conversation to go this way. I only—"

"That's not all of it."

Mitch was confused.

"All of what?"

"That's not the whole story. I left out a detail."

"Look, you don't owe me an explanation for—"

"This detail might be …" —she squared her shoulders and looked him square in the eye — "what I know that I don't know I know."

Chapter Thirty

RILEIGH DIDN'T WANT to go there. Absolutely did not want to finish up the whole story about what had happened to her sister three decades ago. But she had to. This was too strange to be coincidental.

She let out a breath and spoke slowly.

"Ok, so I'm six years old, standing in my sister's bedroom, and the sheets of her bed are covered in blood and there's blood all over … except one place."

She backed up.

"Jillian's bed was by the door, the headboard was against that wall." She talked with her hands, drawing a design in the air. "So when I walked into the room, I was standing by the head of the bed, looking at the bloody sheets. Her wedding dress was lying on a heap not far from the footboard. Her torn-up wedding veil beside it. I don't remember anything else. Just the bloody sheets that'd dripped on the floor and it seemed like everything I was looking at was red, covered in blood."

She shuddered, recalling all the nightmares she'd

suffered through where there were rivers of blood, a sea of blood.

"But … there was one place that wasn't bloody. The pillow on the other side — she slept in a double bed — and the pillow that wasn't hers, it was clean."

She realized she was stammering, and tried to talk slower.

"The clean pillowcase was very white. It was like it glowed. It didn't have a drop of blood on it. But … there was something on it." *Red, like a cherry on top of a sundae.* "And you could tell it'd been put there on purpose. Like … it was on display."

She stopped again and couldn't find the air to keep going.

"What was on the pillowcase, Rileigh?" The words were kind.

"A .. tongue. A human tongue. I knew it had to be Jillian's."

The sheriff sat back abruptly, like he'd taken a blow.

Then he repeated slowly, "You saw a human tongue on the bloody bed in your sister's room the night she disappeared?"

"Nobody believed me when I told them. When we went back later, none of it was there. The bloody sheets were gone, her veil was gone and there wasn't any blood on the floor. The note and picture I dropped on the floor were gone. And everybody said that I'd imagined it."

"So only your family knows about this, right? Who, specifically?"

"My mother and Aunt Daisy. Some of their sisters were there, too, I think. And maybe their husbands. I don't remember. Not my father, though. He *wasn't* there."

"Later, after that night, who did you tell?"

"Nobody. "

"Ever?"

"Okay, Georgia. My best friend, nobody else."

"When the police came to investigate Jillian's disappearance what did you tell them?"

Rileigh's temper flared.

"Police? Investigate? And who might that have been, the fine officers who showed up at my house to help my bereaved family find their missing daughter. Sheriff Mumford was there alright, but it wasn't to talk about Jillian. It was to climb up on a ladder and use his pocket knife to cut the extension cord my father used to hang himself."

"So there was never a police investigation into the disappearance of Jillian Bishop?"

"Not at the time she disappeared, there wasn't. Later, you know, when she didn't come home and didn't come home, I think Mama went to the sheriff then."

"Did he talk to you, ask what you knew about it?"

"Why would he ask a six year old?"

"Any other police ask you anything, anything at all about what you saw that night."

"Nobody ever asked me a damned thing. Nobody believed I saw anything at all. They thought I had a nightmare. So what's your point?"

He ground the words out between clinched teeth.

"My point is that if you didn't tell anybody about the tongue, then nobody outside your family knows that one minor detail. And the killer."

And her best friend Georgia, who Rileigh told everything. But there was no way Georgia was the killer, and Rileigh wasn't going to put her through more hell by pointing the sheriff in her direction.

"And yet you never bothered to tell me about it. We have a murder case where somebody cut out the victim's tongue. And the same thing happened here thirty years ago

— a girl was murdered and somebody cut out her tongue. Didn't it occur to you that such a thing might, oh I don't know, be relevant?"

Maybe it had occurred to Rileigh. Or would have if she'd let herself think about it. But the truth was, she had done everything she could to wipe the image of Tina Montgomery's bloody mouth out of her mind. She wouldn't let herself think about it. She couldn't. It just flat out hurt too bad to dredge up all that—

"I was six years old. Maybe I made the whole thing up?"

"Is that what you think? Do you think you made it up?"

His gaze was penetrating and she couldn't wiggle out of it.

"No, I don't."

"You're working on a murder case, trying to find a killer and you …"

Rileigh suddenly realized that the sheriff was grinding out his words because he was angry. Furious. So mad he could barely talk.

"Nobody knows that somebody cut out your sister's tongue but you and the person who killed her. The killer knows you're the only link between those crimes."

"But that was thirty years ago," she sputtered. "You think the same person who killed Tina Montgomery killed my sister?"

"Maybe. Maybe not. But there is a *connection* of some kind. And *that's* why your pancake was poisoned and your brake lines cut. Somebody out there is afraid you'll figure out what the connection is."

"I'm … sorry. I should have—"

"You are off this case, effective right now."

The words hit her like a blow, staggered her.

"What? Why would you —?"

182

"Because as long as you keep poking around in the murder of Tina Montgomery, you're painting a big fat bull's eye on your back. I'll make sure it gets out that you and I are no longer working together. Maybe whoever this is will back off then."

It might be as simple as that to him, but Rileigh didn't see it like that. If he asked around about her, he would find out that she hadn't exactly come home from her last stint as a police officer with a chestfuls of medals and the key to the city. She had screwed up. Screwed up bad. And until this moment, she hadn't let herself recognize that she was determined to find Tina Montgomery's killer to redeem herself. She wanted to show the community that she wasn't a screw up, that she was a damn good police officer.

That's the reason she hadn't applied to some local law enforcement agency. She believed— whether it was reality or just paranoia she didn't know, but she damned well believed it — that she would be turned down automatically, based on what'd happened in a parking lot in Memphis last year. That's why she had taken the investigator job. It was just close enough to police work that maybe — outside chance, but maybe— it would somehow provide an opportunity for her to prove herself.

But the sheriff was about to sink that ship before it ever got out of dry dock. When he "put out the word" that Rileigh was off the case, he would be sending a message loud and clear that she couldn't cut it, she wasn't good enough, that ... maybe she'd even screwed something up on *this* case.

"So basically, you're going to throw me under the bus — tell the whole town that you asked me to help you out in the case, but you figured out fast that I was no help at all. I sucked at law enforcement, so you fired me — without ever hiring me."

"Slice and dice it any way you want, Rileigh. It's over."

He got up from the rocker, strode out to his cruiser, got in and drove away. Went too fast over the rock/bump at the top of the driveway and almost went airborne, so there was some satisfaction in that.

Then he was gone.

Chapter Thirty-One

RILEIGH SUDDENLY NOTICED that the lump on the top of her head hurt, throbbing in rhythm with her heartbeat. And she noticed it because her heart was thudding, pounding her blood through her veins in a rage.

Not a blind rage, but an icy cold one.

The screen door banged shut, sliding off Daisy's butt because she'd used it to shove it open due to her hands being full. She was carrying a tray with four glasses and a big pitcher of lemonade.

"Daisy, I'd a got that door if you'd waited," her mother called from inside. Then she came out on the porch carrying a handful of napkins. Her mother closed the screen door behind her so it wouldn't bang shut.

"Where'd he go?" Daisy looked around.

"I thought the sheriff was going to stay for lemonade," Mama said.

"He had to go see a man about a dog." Rileigh spit out the phrase, meaning he had something he had to go do.

"But he wanted lemonade. He said …"

"He left, Mama. Okay? He's gone."

"You two was fighting, wasn't you?" Daisy said as she set the tray down on the coffee table in front of the swing.

"How do you know what were were doing? Were you listening? Maybe standing just inside the door so you wouldn't miss a single sordid detail?"

Rileigh spoke more harshly than she meant to. None of this was the fault of the two ladies standing on the porch. But Daisy had dug around in her personal things and found that box of police ... memorabilia she had put on the top shelf of her closet for the express purpose of keeping it private. And Mama had dug the box of post-cards out of her sock drawer. She felt justified in being mad at both of them, so she went with that.

"Didn't have to be standing by the door to hear," Mama said. "You was shouting at each other.."

"We were *not.*"

"Had your voices raised, or we couldn't have heard you."

"We did *not* raise our voices." But maybe they had, there at the end. Maybe she'd yelled at the sheriff. She didn't know or care.

"Couldn't make out what you was saying, just heard the voices. You and him fighting like that put me in mind of the argument Jillian had with that man the night she left."

Rileigh was so flabbergasted she couldn't speak. After thirty years, now her mother decided to confirm that part of Rileigh's memory?

Why in the hell did every conversation these days find its way back to Jillian? It was like those metal shavings the teacher put on the table in sixth grade science class, how they snapped instantly to the magnet when the teacher turned on the battery.

"I could hear the voices from my room. When you get

a migraine, the pain kinda…oh, I don't now … puts all your other senses on high alert."

"And your hearing was so acute, you could hear voices all the way down the hall? That what you're saying?"

"Uh huh, I could hear them."

She was pouring out lemonade into all four of the glasses even though the sheriff had left.

"Did you hear voices that night, Aunt Daisy?" Rileigh asked, but her aunt either didn't hear or chose not to answer the question.

"The voices were fighting you say, yelling at each other?"

Her mother nodded.

"Any particular reason you've waited thirty years to mention that little detail?"

"Well you don't have to get snippy about it. I ain't never said nothing because it just now come back to me. All this talk about Tina Montgomery — that poor girl. She was such a sweet thing. I seen her in church ever Sunday, sitting there with her mama. And Lottie managed to get them boys to church, too, sometimes, Chad and Joel, and that couldn't have been no easy thing."

"Yeah," Daisy said, launching the one-word non sequitur out there into the warm summer morning. She sat down in the chair recently vacated by the sheriff and began to rock slowly back and forth.

"Yeah, what?" Rileigh's mother asked.

"Yeah, I did hear voices that night in Jillian's room."

Rileigh stopped moving the swing with her foot and it grew still.

If *both* of them heard voices, neither of them was the person Jillian had been talking to.

Of course they'd just dredged that information up out of the muck at the bottom of the rivers in their minds, and

LAUREN STREET

when something lay in muck like that with more than three decades, it probably wouldn't look much like it'd looked when it sank.

"Fine, you heard voices, too. Wanna explain how come *you* never mentioned that little detail until right now."

"Didn't nobody ask me what I heard or saw that night. If don't nobody ask, then—"

"Aw, come on. A thing like that would have come up eventually in conversation. When everybody was talking about Jillian … leaving."

But those conversations didn't happen right after she left. All the conversations about Jillian the next day were about the fact that she'd bailed on her wedding, and even those conversations took a backseat to the main attraction, in the center ring of the bigtop with all the lights focused on it, J.R. Bishop's suicide.

"The only people who were talking about Jillian leaving were David and Ellie Hicks, and they were raising a fair stink about it," Rileigh's mother said.

David Hicks was the groom who'd almost literally been left standing at the altar. Ellie was his mother.

"You'd think Ellie'd have been glad Jillie took off like she done," Rileigh's mother said. "She'd been crying for weeks about losing her 'baby boy,'. She did not want that young man to get married."

Then Mama's face registered a "recognition." If she'd been a cartoon, a light bulb would have appeared above her head.

"Maybe *that's* who Jillie was fighting with. Maybe they got into a fight and that's how come Jillian left."

That would have been a reasonable assumption to make— if there had been a man in Jillian's room fighting with her that night. And there hadn't been.

But even if there had, Rileigh knew it hadn't been

188

David Hicks.

RILEIGH COMES out the back door and down the porch steps quickly so nobody'll notice she's going. She wants to be alone and nobody in the house will leave her alone. They are all fussing over her, the poor little girl whose daddy hanged himself. And everybody looked at her with sad, sympathetic eyes. She didn't need anybody's sympathy for the death of her father. She didn't love him because he didn't love her, simple as that. He had never paid the slightest attention to her in her whole life. She knew from her name that he hadn't wanted another little girl. He'd wanted a boy. And something had happened when Rileigh was born that did something to her mother. Nobody would tell her what it was, but after that her mother couldn't have any more children. Rileigh knew her father blamed her for the fact that she had somehow broke her mother by being born.

But it wasn't like Rileigh cared that her father didn't love her. She probably should have, but she didn't. She didn't like him. He looked at her funny sometimes, with an odd look on his face, and sometimes he'd come up to her and rub his hands up and down her arms, then he'd walk away. When she had asthma that time so bad they had to put her in the hospital, he had come to visit her. And she remembered cringing back into the pillow when he put his hand on her forehead, like to see if she had a fever. Everybody knew you didn't have a fever when you had asthma so he had just wanted to touch her and she didn't like his touch.

She hadn't sneaked out of the house to be alone because she was … what was that word, the big one … distraught, that's what the minister's wife had said. The word must mean "really upset," because she'd heard other people use it to describe her mother and Aunt Daisy. They were definitely distraught about what'd happened to her father.

Rileigh was distraught, too, had sneaked out of the house to be alone because she was distraught about Jillian. Every time she remembered Jillie's tongue on that pillow —

She hears a voice, a man's voice.

She'd gone out into the backyard to the woods behind the house. There were places where the ground wasn't too steep to climb in those woods and she spent every day there. But today, there's somebody else here. A man. Then she recognizes the voice. It's David Hicks. He's talking and crying at the same time.

"Jillie, why?" he sobs, and Rileigh moves quietly through the woods until she can see him. He is sitting on a fallen log, wearing black suit pants, that special suit called a lux or something, and a white shirt. No tie or coat though. And he has his face in his hands sobbing. "Why, why, why? I don't understand. I love you and you love me, at least I thought you did, so where are you? Why would you just … leave?"

Rileigh backs away from David Hicks then because she knows the answer to the questions he's asking. She knows that Jillian didn't run away. She was killed. But Mama and Aunt Daisy don't believe her, so why would would he?

"JILLIAN WASN'T FIGHTING with David the night before the wedding. Trust me on that one, I'm sure of it."

"Musta been that other man then, the one who was always hanging around."

"What other man?" Rileigh felt like she was Alice and had just slid down a rabbit hole into Wonderland. Neither her mother nor her aunt, nor anybody else, as a matter of fact, had ever once mentioned some man "hanging around" the night Jillian was murdered. Why now?"

And wouldn't Rileigh have seen him?

You know the one I'm talking about," Aunt Daisy said to Mama. "The fella who was always asking J.R. if he had any odd jobs needed doing, had any doors that wasn't hung right, or light switches that didn't work, things like that. He said he was good with his hands."

Rileigh tried not to allow herself to get dragged farther and farther into Wonderland. Do that and there's a point at which you can't find your way back out.

Daisy was certifiable. Batshit crazy. But it seemed to Rileigh that every day more and more bats had settled in to hang upside down in *her mother's* belfry. Shit, was dementia contagious?

"I think Jillian might have run off with him," Daisy continued. "He was better looking than David Hicks with, that receding chin of his."

"David Hicks does not have a receding chin," Mama said.

Rileigh grabbed hold of the conversation and yanked it back in another direction.

"The sheriff told me that I was off the case." She couldn't believe it, but the thought was top of mind right now. "So none of this matters anyway."

"Why would he do a thing like that?" Her mother asked.

"Doesn't matter why, Mama."

"And that's all it takes. One itty bitty road block and you hit it, roll over and play dead?" Daisy was indignant. "That ain't the Rileigh Bishop I know. Wouldn't stop me. If some fella said I couldn't keep trying to find out who killed a girl who never hurt nobody—"

"Went to church every Sunday with her mother and her brothers—" her mother put in.

"I'd tell that man to pound sand. He don't get to decide who does and who doesn't try to solve this murder, does he? It ain't up to him is it?"

No, it was not up to Sheriff Mitchell Webster to decide. Rileigh could jolly well keep trying to find Tina Montgomery's murderer if she jolly well pleased.

And she did jolly well please.

Chapter Thirty-Two

SINCE THERE WAS no new information about the case, this was as good a point as any to start shaking the suspects' alibi tree to see what falls out. Trouble was, there was no list of "suspects." The sheriff had said he'd checked out the whereabouts of anybody who might be involved in the case and cleared all those people — he didn't bother to tell her specifically who those people were.

So Rileigh would make her own list and do her own checking.

Its was a short list.

One, Tina's drug dealer— Chigger Stump.

Two, the man she owed money to — Charlie Hayden.

Three, her boyfriend, Aubrey Tucker.

Four, the man she was seeing on the side — unsub. Unknown subject.

Five, the man who had gotten her pregnant. Number four and number five might or might not be the same person. Shouldn't assume a thing like that.

And the big, fat number six—some spooky somebody in an organization of equally spooky bad ass drug dealers or human traffickers or who knew what else, who had been dispatched by higher-ups to terminate an employee.

And down at the bottom of the list at a distant number seven was Ian McGinnis— because the body had been found on or near his property.

Of course, none of the names had any connection whatsoever to the murder of her sister thirty years ago.

Aubrey Tucker had been seven years old.

So how Tina's murder— with its signature gory bit, the cut out tongue, was linked to her sister's death — she had no idea. Cutting out someone's tongue was sometimes a not too subtle message that the person couldn't talk, couldn't tell what they knew. That fit with Tina's murder if the scary, spooky organization operating, as the sheriff had said, under the radar in Yarmouth County did it. But what possible connection did that have to Jillie, who'd never dealt drugs or been involved with anyone like that?

Trying to find the connection was a hopeless endeavor at this point. But she would do what she could do, starting with checking out alibis. So she borrowed her Aunt Daisy's car. For today at least, the drivers in the Forge didn't have to fear for life and limb because a deaf, blind, and crazy old woman was on the loose in a battleship gray Honda.

First name on the list— Chigger Stump.

He was working on Lester Massey's car. The Massey brothers, Lester and Ben, lived in a shack on Pigeon Ridge at the top of a driveway even steeper than Rileigh's. The car was up on blocks in the front yard when Rileigh pulled up. Lester Massey was working on the engine. Ben was bent over some unidentifiable car part on a table, looking like he was performing an autopsy on a robot. Chigger was under the car. He started protesting before he even got all the way out.

"I done told you everything I know about Tina Montgomery. Asking me more questions I don't have answers for is a waste of your time and mine."

Chigger was antsy about this, touchy on the subject, and if what he'd said was true— that he wasn't even Tina's dealer anymore— he didn't have any reason to be. So what was up?

"How do you know I didn't come out here just to tell you that Georgia needs you to pick up a quart of milk on your way to home?"

"What, you think I'm stupid or something? You and I don't have nothing to say to each other. I know what you think of me. But you keep pestering me with questions about a woman I ain't sold so much as a nickel bag in months and I'll—."

"So where were you on the afternoon Tina was murdered?"

"I done told the sheriff. I was up in Gatlinburg on … business." He sneered, "You know, meeting a client who wanted to purchase some of my wares"

"So that's your alibi. You were making a drug deal? I'm not sure I'd want to bet my life and my freedom on a jury believing that line."

"There ain't gonna be no jury hearing nothing about me. I didn't do nothing. How many times do I have to tell you? And anyway, the sheriff checked it out, talked to the Gatlinburg PD. They know my client. In fact, he was more or less under surveillance when he and I talked. That would hold up in court, but it won't ever have to, so leave me alone. It's gonna take me two days to get this junker running and I ain't wasting anymore time with you. You being my wife's best friend don't mean shit to me."

He turned around and crawled back under the junker.

Rileigh got into her car. She hadn't really made an actual list of "not-suspects" to cross Chigger's name off of.

Just a mental one. And she wasn't quite ready to cross him off. Not yet. He was way too hinky when it came to talking about Tina Montgomery. There had to be some reason for that.

Next up was contestant number two, Charlie Hayden. Rileigh wrinkled her nose. Going to see the man twice in the same week, he would absolutely interpret as a come-on.

Thankfully, Charlie was out showing a house. Rileigh spoke to the squeaky-voiced, big-boobed receptionist, who looked on Charlie's calendar and advised he had been showing a house to somebody named Cecilia Smothers, a rich woman from Knoxville.

"They'll be out there a long time."

Translate that, Charlie was screwing her.

Contestant Number Three was Aubrey Tucker. Aubrey worked in a meat-packing plant outside Pigeon Forge, and it took all Rileigh's powers of persuasion to get the foreman to let him off the line for five minutes to talk to her.

He stalked up to her covered in blood.

"I done told the sheriff everything I know about Tina, so why are you here?

"I'm just going back over the statements the sheriff took," she lied, "dotting the i's and crossing the t's. So where were you between the hours of—"

"You don't have to tell me when Tina was killed. I know when she was killed."

The burley man was suddenly choked with emotion. "I was right here, doing my job, you can ask the foreman. I was standing here hacking chicken into pieces of meat while somebody was murdering my Tina. If I ever find out who did it, I'm going to be doing some hacking into him with a meat cleaver."

Rileigh tried to talk to the foreman to verify Aubrey's story, but he wasn't working today. She didn't bother to track him down because she was sure the sheriff had verified Aubrey's alibi. If the alibi hadn't panned out, the sheriff would have told her.

Or once, he would have told her, but not anymore.

She didn't like how that settled inside her, how bad it hurt. No, not how bad it hurt, but why it hurt that the sheriff was no longer working the case with her. But she would absolutely not go there.

Next up on the alibi list were the shadowy figures of numbers five and six— the secret boyfriend, and the secret business partners. As she drove her aunt's battleship to the final contestant on the list, she acknowledged that it was entirely possible, no, probably likely, that the sheriff had been bluffing. She'd been asking questions all day and hadn't run into a single person who refused to talk to her. If the sheriff really had "put the word out" that she was off the case, nobody got the memo.

That left only the distant Contestant Number Seven— Georgia's older brother Ian, who had merely had the misfortune to have a dead body found on his property.

When she pulled up in front of Ian's woodworking shop, the sheriff was already there, getting out of his cruiser.

He glared at her as she parked beside him.

Chapter Thirty-Three

"WONDERED when you'd finally show up," Ian McGinnis said as he looked up from the chair he was sanding lovingly by hand.

He wasn't a tall man, but he carried himself like one. He was built like a fireplug, but moved with the grace of an athlete.

When Rileigh stepped into the woodworking shop behind Mitch, Ian looked surprised to see her. It knocked some of the cockiness out of him.

Mitch thought guiltily that he should tell her to leave, but he'd probably get more information out of Ian with her here.

"Rileigh?" Ian greeted. "You're keeping strange company these days."

Yeah, Mitch had that going against him, too. Not only did the mountain people distrust strangers, but they were like most everybody else in the world — they didn't particularly like law enforcement officers. Cops made everybody uneasy, even in social situations. You got used to people's faces closing up as soon as they approached.

"Lottie Montgomery asked me to help find her daughter's killer," Rileigh said. "Two horses running in front of a wagon can either team up and pull the wagon, or they can trip over each other's hooves and get run over by it."

"Make that up on the spur of the moment, did you?" Ian asked with a gleam in his eye. "Because if you did, it's not bad."

"Ten points?"

"No way! When you said the little Reynolds kid was so quiet he could sneak dawn past a rooster, *that* was ten points. This is ... um, seven, maybe."

"I gave you eight when you said Mrs. Higgins was so ugly she'd make a train take a dirt road."

"That was twenty years ago!"

The two continued the banter as Mitch watched. Clearly they were old friends. All right, not necessarily friends, but they had shown up at the important events in each other's lives— first day of school, graduation, weddings, births and funerals — for so long that they seemed like family.

Ian stood up, took a red shop rag, and cleaned the sawdust off his hands, then indicated two stools that sat beside a mini bar at the far end of the shop. Mitch sat down on one of them. Rileigh didn't sit, just hopped up on a nearby countertop and dangled her legs over the edge.

It was a well-equipped woodworking shop, and Ian was obviously a master craftsman who made cabinetry from scratch, no precut pieces with numbers inscribed on the back for easy assembly.

"It's possible that Tina Montgomery's dead body was found on your property," Mitch began. "Hard to tell boundaries out there in the woods–"

"It wasn't on my land. It was on the county's. My land goes to the oak tree that got struck by lightening in the north, curves around the top of that meadow — it's mine, the one where we used to grow–" he caught himself, looked at Rileigh and grinned, "tulips, and goes from the granite outcrop on the west to the creek and back to the oak tree. So, the grass hut is on my land, but just barely. Twenty feet beyond it and it's the deadbeat's property."

"Deadbeat?"

"Julius Harrow. He owned the property until he bailed out on the the taxes seventeen years ago. Then the county took possession. But you already knew that part, didn't you Sheriff Webster?"

"I did. And I don't care. If you think I came to talk to you about some little patch of weed, you're mistaken. I came out here to ask you what you might know about the death of Tina Montgomery. Have you ever seen her out there? Either alone or with somebody else?"

"No, I've never seen her there."

Mitch started to speak but Ian wasn't finished.

"But it's possible I did hear her there, the day she was killed, as a matter of fact. That's why I said I'd been waiting for you to show up. Figured you'd come asking about it sooner or later."

What he didn't say, of course, was what he'd have done if nobody thought to come ask him questions. Would he have kept what he knew to himself if nobody asked? Mitch suspected he absolutely wouldn't talk about it if he didn't have to … to the police, that is.

"I wasn't the only one who heard her." He said that to Rileigh. "So did your Aunt Daisy."

"Aunt Daisy was at the grass hut on Monday?"

"Yeah, I dropped by the house after you left and asked if she'd like to come out with me and work in the garden." He cast a glance the sheriff's direction. "You know, where we're raising–"

"Tulips, yes, I know."

Ian grinned.

"We were outside when we heard voices coming from up in the trees, a man and a woman, sounded like they were pretty mad." He turned to Rileigh again, who was now sitting on the wide cabinet with her legs folded beneath her like a little kid. "Aunt Daisy said they were probably mad that we beat them to it, got here before they did to 'use the facilities.' Then she winked at me and pinched my butt."

"Aunt Daisy pinched your butt!"

"If I'm lyin', I'm dyin'."

They both laughed.

"What were Tina and the man arguing about?" Mitch asked.

"I don't know if it was Tina or not. I don't know her. Oh, I've seen her waiting tables at the Rusty Nail, but I wouldn't have recognized her voice. But seeing as how she obviously got killed in these woods, I figure that's who it must have been."

"Disclaimer duly noted," Mitch said. "So you and Aunt Daisy heard a man and a woman fighting in the woods. What were they fighting about? What did they say?"

"That, I couldn't tell you. You can ask Rileigh's aunt, maybe she heard something I didn't–"

"You didn't just say that, Ian. Aunt Daisy has emptied the hot water heater twice so far this week." Rileigh turned to Mitch to explain. "She turns on the tap, then walks out of the room, forgets about it, leaving it running. She can't hear the sound of the water. I don't imagine she could hear what two people up in the woods were saying."

"Did you hear any words at all? Anything that would identify who the man was who was fighting with her?"

"I could hear Tina's voice clearer than the man's because she was shouting and her voice was high and squeaky. She said she was going to tell."

"Tell what? To whom?"

"Don't know. I just heard her say she was going to tell and everybody would know. I only caught pieces of sentences."

"So you don't know what she was threatening to tell?"

"No, but he didn't want her to do it, he was pleading — not angry, pleading. They went on for quite awhile, then Daisy decided that nothing would do but that I had to cut us both big chunks of pie right that minute — like she'd die of starvation if she had to wait."

"Pie?"

"Aunt Daisy packed a picnic basket — like, a real picnic basket."

"I saw it out on the kitchen table last night." Rileigh turned to the sheriff. "I don't know where she got that basket, but she could pack enough food in it to feed every man in the Norwegian Army. Had a table cloth and napkins, salt, pepper, mustard, catsup. Everything. Whenever she had to take food somewhere — a cake to a bake sale or to somebody's house after a funeral, she always used that big old basket."

"I hauled it up from the car and set it beside the door of the grass hut, so we could get soft drinks out of it. So I went back down and got out the pie — cherry pie, with a crust that'd melt in your mouth. I took it inside on the counter to cut it, then dug around some more to find paper plates and forks. Daisy kept working in the garden. And maybe they kept yelling at each other while she was still out there, you can ask her, I don't know. I couldn't hear them from inside. When I came out to get Daisy to eat, it was quiet. And she was gone."

"Where'd she go?" Rileigh asked.

"You don't know? Weren't you home when I dropped her off?"

Rileigh shook her head.

"She wandered off and fell in the creek. I heard her squawking and went to get her out, ended up as wet as she was."

"*That's* why her hair looked so awful when I got home."

"Would your aunt talk to me, answer my questions?" the sheriff asked Rileigh. He figured she might be pissed off that he'd taken Rileigh off the case. But she hadn't stayed off. "Maybe she heard something after Ian left."

"We can ask. And I'm sure she'll answer, but she's adept at politician speak. What she says has nothing to do with the question you asked."

Mitch probed for more information from Ian, pinpointing the time that Ian and Daisy had arrived, when they heard the voices arguing, when the fighting stopped. Ian appeared to be telling the truth, and Rileigh thought so too after they left.

"I know you're thinking what I'm thinking," Rileigh said when they got to his cruiser. "Apparently Tina had an argument with a man out there right before she was killed. So, duh, we find the man, we find the killer."

Mitch nodded.

"You did catch my meaning there — right? *We* is my preferred pronoun."

Ian McGinnis wouldn't have told Mitch anything if Rileigh hadn't been there. He hated that he was endangering her life, but he needed her to solve this case. The best he could do to protect her was try to solve it fast.

Mitch nodded again.

"I think we're close …" Rileigh didn't make a big deal

out of his agreement, and he was instantly grateful for that. "I checked out everybody's alibis. They're not all airtight…but none of them's leaking enough to fall out of the sky. Yet. "

"Had any luck getting Tina's phone records?"

"I'm done farting around with the supervisor in Gatlinburg. I've got a subpoena and I'm going to serve it personally on the district manager of Verizon Wireless in Knoxville. Surely that'll knock some pigeons off the statuary."

Chapter Thirty-Four

THERE WAS a ringing noise and Rileigh couldn't tell what it was or where it was coming from. And the pounding in the knot on her head had returned with a vengeance, so what ...

She opened her eyes and it was morning. The ringing must have been her alarm clock. She felt dopey, strange. Then she remembered. She'd come home last night from Ian's, and engaged in prolonged, meandering, maddeningly tedious conversations with her aunt about the events Ian had told them about yesterday afternoon. She had finally gotten Daisy to the point she might actually have been accessing real memories instead of fantasy, and asked her about the people yelling in the woods. Daisy had gotten quiet and sober after that, reluctant to engage, but Rileigh finally dragged it out of her that she had heard no more yelling after Ian went into the house to cut the pie.

"Why'd you wander off?"

"Wander off?"

"Ian said when he went to give you a piece of the pie you were gone, and he found you in a creek."

"A creek? He said that, did he?"

"Yes, he said that. Why did you go to the creek?"

She got indignant. "Why do you think I wandered off — I needed to pee. No, come to think of it, I needed to poop, and there ain't no outhouse at the grass hut."

That was true, when the need came on you, you had to go find a convenient place in the woods to do your business.

"And how'd you fall in the creek?"

"I fell in the creek?"

"Ian said you did, said he tried to help you out and you pulled him in with you."

She got a distant look in her eye and said, "I went to the creek to wash up."

Rileigh decided not to pursue the "wash up" part.

"How'd you fall in?"

Her aunt fixed her with a withering look.

"Did your mama have any children that lived?" she snapped. "I slipped. I'd a'done a cannonball, but it wasn't deep enough."

The conversations with Daisy were punctuated by interruptions from Mama right at critical junctures that sent Daisy down some rabbit trail or another.

"Would you like some tea, dear?"

"Not thirsty."

"Coffee?"

"Too late in the day."

"A glass of ice water, then?"

The ice made her teeth throb.

Mama had offered a soda pop, but Rileigh told her the carbonation gave her indigestion.

When she was finally finished with her "interrogation" of her aunt, the bump on her head was throbbing like she'd just been clocked right there with the business end of a claw hammer.

"You'd ought to take some aspirin for that headache," Mama had said, and Rileigh eagerly agreed. She'd found none in the medicine cabinet in her bathroom, and as she was going out into the hallway, her aunt met her with two white pills in her palm.

And like an idiot, Rileigh took them.

Only after she'd swallowed them, did Daisy bother to mention that they weren't aspirin. Clearly, Rileigh needed something stronger than that for such a headache, so she gave her two Percocet she had in her medicine cabinet from when she'd had dental work done.

She and Mama had a regular pharmacy in the house, accumulated over the years for various ailments. From muscle relaxants prescribed when her mother had strained her back to Percocet and all things in between. Contrary to the instructions on the labels, her mother and aunt wouldn't have thought of throwing the remainder of a prescription away — that would be wasteful! Consequently, they had prescription medication dating back a decade, maybe longer.

Rileigh was furious, though it was her fault for not checking. But as the pain rapidly receded, she was actually grateful. She'd been able to sleep.

Unfortunately, she'd awakened with a 'narcotic hang-over," which always happened to her when she took even a mild narcotic. She was particularly sensitive to drugs and she awoke foggy and unable to concentrate.

The ringing sound started again. Apparently she hadn't bothered to turn off the alarm. But it wasn't her alarm. It was her cell phone. She picked it up and saw the sheriff's number.

She shook her head to clear it — instantly sorry when the bump on her head screamed in protest — and answered.

"I didn't mean to wake you up."

Rileigh eyed the alarm clock, which she had not even set when she went to bed last night. It said eight o'cock.

"You didn't," she lied. "I was awake."

He didn't challenge her, just told her that he had served the subpoena for Tina Montgomery's phone records at the Verizon Wireless office in Gatlinburg late yesterday afternoon.

"I was up most of the night going through them."

"And …?"

"And Tina placed more than a hundred calls to the same number in the last three weeks before her death."

A smoking gun if ever there was one.

"Don't keep me in suspense. Whose number was it? Anybody we know or some deep, dark hired gun called Scarface or—"

"She called Roger Albert Stump."

Chigger!

"She sent him dozens of texts, too. I can't see what they said in the phone records. But I sincerely doubt that she was calling him to talk about the drugs she'd stopped buying from him five months ago."

Rileigh was completely alert now, five by five.

"So you're saying …"

"I'm sorry to say it, but Tina Montgomery and the husband of your best friend appear to have kicked off the new year with a rousing round of bump and tickle and they've been at it ever since. The coroner said she was five months pregnant, so that suggests Chigger's the father of her child."

Rileigh couldn't breathe. Oh, sure, Rileigh knew Chigger was pond scum. But Georgia didn't. She loved the creep. And when she found out …

"Going to have a long talk with Mr. Stump today as soon as I can find him. Called his house and he's not home."

"You called his house?"

"Just said I needed some information, didn't alert his wife. Mullins suggested a warehouse in Gatlinburg where there's a continuous poker game every Saturday. Rawlings said he thought Chigger was working construction, helping some guy on Turkey Ridge Road put up a house. I thought we'd start there, if you'd care to come along?"

Rileigh didn't hesitate.

"I can't. I would love to but …" Think! "Zander said I had only a mild concussion, and I was absolutely fine yesterday. But last night after I got home from talking to Ian … that lump really started to hurt. And today I'm dizzy. I think I need to–"

"—go to the doctor immediately. Can your mother or your aunt drive you?"

If her head wasn't already broken, riding as a passenger with Daisy would break it for sure.

"Yeah, I'm good to go. Call me. Keep me posted."

The sheriff promised that he would, then ended the call.

She had told the sheriff she wouldn't go with him to Gatlinburg or out to Turkey Ridge Road to talk to Chigger because Chigger wasn't there. He was helping Lester Massey with his car, had said yesterday it'd take a couple of days to get it running again.

She would go to Lester's and talk to Chigger on her own. The sheriff would be annoyed, but she would get

more out of Chigger without an audience, and she owed it
to Georgia to find out what her scumbag husband was up
to.

Especially if what he might be up to was murder.

Chapter Thirty-Five

CHIGGER PEEKED out from under the car when he heard the crunch of Rileigh's tires on the gravel. But this time, he didn't roll out to talk to her, just kept working.

"We need to talk."

"The hell you say," came from under the car. Then he spoke to the greasy-fingered man leaning under the hood to peer at the engine. "Lester, get me that socket set out of the tool box, wouldja."

Lester walked to where a tool box sat in the dirt with half a dozen tools of various kinds scattered around it.

"I won't tell you that you either talk to me or you talk to the sheriff, because you're going to be spending some quality time with both of us real soon. But I got first dibs on you."

Chigger burped out an obscenity, and began to bang on something, metal on metal.

"You think I'm scared of–"

"The sheriff got Tina's cell phone records yesterday. You got any idea how many times she called your number in the past three weeks?" The banging stopped.

"Or texted you?" She decided to bluff. "Pure porn. I never saw you as the kind of man who'd say things like that to a woman. How are you planning on explaining them to Georgia?"

Chigger scooted on his back out from under the car. His face was the color of a new gym sock. "Listen, Riliegh–"

"Don't you dare say, 'It's not what you think." You didn't leave any doubt about what it was."

"Look, I–"

"Did you kill her, Chigger?"

The man leapt to his feet, took a step toward Rileigh, then thought better of it and stayed where he was.

"Good God, no! You got to believe me. I never laid a finger on her."

He began to pace, running his hands through his hair without noticing that he had grease on his fingers, which he was now smearing in his hair.

"I never meant any of this to happen. I swear I didn't. I never meant to get involved with Tina. She was at that New Year's bash they had at the firehouse. Georgia stayed home because one of the boys was running a fever, and Tina's boyfriend fell down and sprained his ankle and couldn't dance, so we were both there on our own. She was pretty drunk when I arrived, and then the two of us kept drinking."

He gave Rileigh a pleading look: *you understand, don't you?* She glared back at him.

"So we danced and... I don't know if you've ever seen Tina dance, but she's not like most girls who can't dance but get out there anyway and make fools–"

"Skip the critique."

He paused, then continued the tale, pacing as he greased up his hair.

"When they shut the dance down around 1 a.m., Tina wasn't ready to stop dancing. She was just getting warmed up, so I suggested we go to a bar I know in Gatlinburg, not a tourist place, for locals, where you can dance until dawn if you want to. And on the way there, we got to talking — Tina's smarter than folks give her credit for."

Whereas Chigger was dumber than most people knew.

"We danced until we was ready to drop. And on the way home we ... you know ..."

"Danced in the backseat?" Riliegh asked. "Now, *that* was a contortion you could charge admission to see. Screwing in the backseat of a car between two carseats."

"We went in Tina's car. And then ..." he stopped pacing. "That was it. I mean, I didn't plan to see her again."

"Just a one-night stand."

"Yeah, a one night stand," he bobbed his head, glad she'd gotten his meaning, as if a one-night stand was infinitely less vile than an affair. Probably in his mind there were degrees of unfaithfulness and a one-night stand was the bottom rung. "It wasn't like I planned to see her again. But she called me, said she'd really enjoyed talking like we done on the way to Gatlinburg and could I meet her somewhere and we could just talk."

"And, oh my, how surprised you were when you got there and she wanted more than talk."

He ignored the sarcasm, plugged doggedly ahead. "I was going to stop seeing her, tried to, went one time to meet her — just to talk, really. To tell her I wanted to break it off, but she ..."

"Overpowered you with her superhuman strength, threw you on the ground and ravished you — right?"

"Don't keep saying shit like that, like you're so high and mighty — when all the time you're the one who—"

He must have been smart enough to read the no trespassing sign on her face because he backed off.

"I wanted to break up with her but then she said she was pregnant and it was mine and she wanted me to leave Georgia. And when I said I wouldn't, she said she was gonna tell Georgia about us."

"And so you killed her."

"No, no, it's not like that."

"But you were with her the day she died, weren't you?"

He looked conflicted, like he couldn't decide whether or not to tell her the truth.

"We have witnesses, Chigger. Ian and Aunt Daisy were at the grass hut, and heard you and Tina fighting in the woods."

"That's who was—"

"Aw, you'd planned to go at it on the floor of the grass hut, but they spoiled your fun."

"We were going to meet there, but we heard voices, and then Tina just went off on me. I begged her not to tell Georgia about us. But she was hysterical, wouldn't listen to reason—"

"And so you whipped out that switchblade you're so proud of and gutted her."

"No. No, I didn't kill her. I swear on the souls of my children—"

"Don't you dare—

"Okay, on my own soul, on the Bible, on a dozen Bibles, a thousand Bibles, I did not kill Tina Montgomery. She got so hysterical there was no reasoning with her. I figured I was just making things worse, so I left. But I didn't *kill* her. I swear, Tina Montgomery was fine when I walked away from her that day in the woods."

"And somebody else just happened by and thought,

what the hell, I think I'll stick a knife in Tina Montgomery's belly."

Chigger looked like he was about to faint or vomit. Or both.

"It wasn't *me.* I swear to God it wasn't me."

Then the man actually dropped to his knees in front of her.

"Please, I'm begging you, please don't tell Georgia about this."

"Oh, that's exactly what Im going to do. I'd rather she heard from me than from somebody else that her scum of the earth husband was banging a teenage girl, got her pregnant, then murdered her."

Rileigh turned on her heel and walked away, leaving Chigger on his knees in the dirt and Lester Massey staring gap-jawed at both of them. Chigger would try to run, of course. He wouldn't get far.

Chapter Thirty-Six

RILEIGH STARTED CRYING AS SOON as she got into her car. At least the tears started running down her cheeks then. But by the time she'd gotten to the turnoff on Carter's Mill Road where Georgia lived, she was in full-bore sobbing. She loved Georgia like a sister. Yes, like a *sister!*

And Rileigh was about to destroy her whole world.

Correction. Georgia's worthless husband was the one who'd destroyed her world. Rileigh was just the messenger, bringing news of the catastrophe to the survivors.

She could hear Mayella's screams as soon as she pulled up in the yard and it only occurred to her then that she was going to have to tell Georgia the worst news of her life in front of her children. How could she do a thing like that?

If providence ever noticed Rileigh at all, it usually hocked a loogie in her direction. But today, providence smiled on her as Thelma Ritter pulled her car up beside Rileigh's in the little bit of space in front of Georgia's trailer.

Thelma was the woman in charge of "children's

services" at the Pentecostal church that sat right on the edge of Dollywood. She smiled sweetly as Rileigh got slowly out of her car.

"I've come to pick up the boys for Saturday afternoon Vacation Bible School," she said sweetly.

Rileigh paused. Wait for it ...

"And we sure would like to see you come to church some Sunday, Miss Rileigh. You'd like Brother Jackson, our new young preacher. He's such a fine man, went to Fuller Seminary, you know, graduated at the head of his class."

Rileigh didn't know Fuller Seminary had drifted Pentecostal. It had been pretty conservative the last she heard.

Thelma moved slowly, ponderously, not because she was overweight but because she had multiple sclerosis, and fought a daily battle just to move at all. Rileigh admired her courage.

She waited to walk with Rileigh to the door, and then said to her softly, conspiratorially, "the new pastor is not only a good preacher, but he's good looking — and single."

Right. Rileigh and a minister would make a great couple.

Georgia greeted Thelma at the door like a battle-weary combat soldier greets the platoon come to take over his position. She had the boys spiffed up in clean shirts and pants— sure, there were holes in the pants, but that was a fashion statement these days— and their hair combed down so it'd lay flat on their heads. All except Liam, the oldest. He had a cowlick in the back that Georgia said you couldn't have smoothed out if you nailed it to his skull with a staple gun.

She stood with Georgia in the door as Thelma drove away with the kids.

"Ahhhhh," Georgia breathed softly. "I have a *whole day!* I've been planning to get drunk this morning, smoke some weed after lunch and round out the day with some reeeeally potent magic mushrooms right before the kids get home." She slumped against the door frame. "But then I decided I'd rather take a nap. I'm so glad you stopped by. It's been ages since we had a chance to really talk."

Rileigh felt the bottom drop out of her stomach.

Mayella chimed in right on cue. The little girl titled her head back and let out a wail that was probably audible on the space station orbiting the earth, if there was still one up there now.

"You want your ba-ba?" Georgia asked the chid, and she shut her mouth in mid-scream.

To Rileigh, Georgia said. "It won't take me but a few minutes to get her down for her nap. I have to read her a story first, but I'll pick a short one. There's coffee still in the pot. I think."

Georgia snatched the little girl up into her arms and went to the refrigerator to retrieve her ba-ba, then disappeared with her into the back bedroom of the trailer.

It was so unnaturally quiet in the house then that it almost gave Rileigh the creeps. No, what the quiet did give her was time to think, at least to finish the thoughts that had been percolating in her head ever since she left Chigger on his knees beside the junker car.

She stepped over the landmines scattered on the floor — toys from movies she'd only heard about but not seen. There were superhero action figures, and broken pieces of toys she didn't recognize.

Opening the cabinet above the sink, she searched in vain for a coffee mug, settled for rinsing out the one some-body — had it been Chigger?— had used for breakfast and left abandoned among the dirty dishes not yet loaded into the dishwasher.

She filled the cup half full of dark black coffee. That

was all that was left, so she busied herself making a fresh pot as she listened to Georgia's soft voice from the bedroom: "I do not like it, Sam I Am." Green Eggs and Ham was not a short story, but she was certain Mayella had selected it and would settle for nothing else.

Leaning against the counter, she surveyed the disaster around her. It was Georgia's life, her home, and Rileigh was about to destroy everything.

"She ought to take a long nap." The words came from behind Rileigh. She hadn't heard Georgia come into the room. "She didn't sleep well last night so she's tired. If we're lucky, she'll sleep until the boys get ho–"

Her words cut off as soon as she saw Rileigh's face.

"What's wrong?" She couldn't fool Georgia. She knew Rileigh too well. "What is it?"

Rileigh literally could not force words out of her mouth.

"Tell me!"

This was it. This was the opening. Rileigh took a breath, postponed for a second or two the utter destruction of her best friend's life. She started … tried … then chickened out and veered off down another rabbit trail, blurted out the first thing that came to her.

"Mama has been remembering things about the night Jillian was killed," she said.

Where did *that* come from? It was what she'd been thinking about before the sheriff's call shoved every other thought out of her mind. And she had to say something … because she couldn't do it, couldn't say what she'd come here to say. She flat out couldn't.

"She never told me she knew anything about that night. She had a migraine, was closed up in her room with the shades drawn. I didn't know she heard a thing. But she said last night that she heard voices from Jillian's room.

There was a man in Jillian's room, and he and Jillie were arguing."

That was a bomb of its own, particularly delivered the way Rileigh had, without warning. She and Georgia never talked about that time, but the death of Rileigh's sister was the wallpaper on which the whole rest of her life was hung, and it was always there, the backdrop for everything that came after it. Georgia knew that, but it still had to be like a bucket of ice water in the face for Rileigh to bring it up like that.

"Oh." That's all Georgia said. Then, "she heard."

That was an odd thing to say and Rileigh turned to look into her face. Shock, sure, surprise and distress. But something else, too.

Georgia sank into one of the kitchen chairs and said nothing else. But her face was a study in conflict. In fact, Rileigh would bet that Georgia's face mirrored her own.

"I never ..." Georgia stopped, then started over. "I always knew I'd have this conversation someday." She tried for a smile and missed it by a mile. "I'd a whole lot rather get drunk or do mushrooms than talk about this. It'd be a whole lot more fun."

Then she fell silent again.

Beep. Beep.

The coffee pot announced that the fresh pot of coffee Rileigh had brewed was ready and Rileigh went to the counter, picked up Georgia's half-full cup of cold coffee and poured it into the sink.

Then she poured Georgia another cup, adding one cube of sugar from the box of sugar cubes in the cabinet. Georgia used sugar cubes because she said the coffee got better and better as the cube dissolved.

Setting the cup down in front of Georgia, she pulled

out the chair opposite her, swiped half a dozen Cheerios off the seat onto the floor, and sat down.

"My turn," Rileigh said." You tell *me* what's bothering *you.*"

Georgia spoke softly as she looked deep into Rileigh's eyes.

"I know who was in the room with Jillian that night, arguing with her. It was Ian. They were arguing about me."

Chapter Thirty-Seven

THE WORLD STOPPED SPINNING on its axis, just like it did when Rileigh had seen Tina Montgomery's ravaged face, her gory mouth.

"Ian? Why were they fighting about *you*?"

It wasn't astounding that Georgia's teenage brother had been at Rileigh's house that night. Rileigh and Georgia — and by extension, Ian — practically lived in each other's pockets as children. Her father even joked one time that if Georgia had dinner with their family one more night, he was going to claim her as a dependent on his income taxes. But why would Ian have come to the house to see Jillian on the night before her wedding?

"He described what happened later. He didn't come home until after dawn."

Georgia got a far away look in her eyes, what Rileigh's military buddies called "a thousand yard stare." It was how they looked when they went *there*, to that place, wherever it was — to that firefight or that explosion or that mortar attack, the one that was worse than all the others, the one that'd killed their friends, maybe blown off a limb or blinded them or burned them so bad that for the rest of their lives people would cringe at the sight of them.

When Georgia began to speak, the story she told was Ian's. And after Rileigh heard it, she understood that perhaps that kind of disassociation was the only way Georgia had to cope with what had happened.

IAN HAS NEVER IN ALL his sixteen years seen anybody as mad as Jillian Bishop was when he came into her bedroom that night. Never. It's a level of rage he can relate to, though, because he feels it too. He feels the fury in his bones and his hands ball into fists, but he fights it down, swallows it, because he doesn't have time right now to be mad. He has to get to Jillian before she does what she told Georgia she was going to do. He has to stop her.

Ian doesn't ring the bell on the front door because it would awaken the whole house and he needs to talk to Jillian and only Jillian, so he goes around to the window in the laundry room. It's stuck, hasn't shut all the way for years because it'd been painted too many times. It was always open a crack.

And he does. It was impossible to move the window in the frame, of course, it'd been stuck for years, but he does it. Like those mothers you see pick up cars off their children. It's adrenaline. It's almost like he can feel it when it happens, when the adrenaline is piped into his blood stream and he can do anything. But what he has to do won't take that kind of strength. He won't get to use that strength in a blind rage, to … no, that's not what matters now. He has to get this part right. His little sister's whole future is hanging in the balance.

He raps on Jillian's door, lightly, and she flings it open and looks like she is about to leap through it and grab him by the throat, choke the life out of him. Then she sees it's him and she falters.

"Ian?" She steps back. "What are you doing here?"

"I have to talk to you."

She burps out a bleat of laughter. "Now is really not a good time to talk. Right now—"

"Georgia told me. Everything." Ian pictured the scene in his head. The everything Georgia told him had come tumbling out as gut wrenching sobs wracked her little body. She'd sat on the bed with her arms wrapped around herself, hugging herself, and rocked back and forth as she spoke.

"She told you what that fucker did to her?"

Ian had never heard Jillian curse. Not so much as a damn or a shit. Hearing that word come out of her mouth was like getting slapped in the face. But it was the word he'd thought, too, as his little sister rocked and cried and told him the worst story any child ever tells. He'd thought the same word, and worse.

"She told me J. R. was … molesting her and you came into the room and caught him."

RILEIGH RECOILED. Would have dropped her coffee cup if she'd been holding it. Couldn't breathe or think or take her eyes off her friend as she sat wooden on the edge of a chair in her kitchen, telling a story Rileigh was certain she'd never told anybody before.

Georgia didn't seem to notice her reaction, didn't seem to be aware of her at all, just went on in a monotone, describing what her brother told her had happened in Jillian's bedroom the night she was murdered.

"MOLESTING," Jillian spits the word out like it is vile in her mouth. "That's too polite a word for what he was doing. She was kneeling on the floor in front of him and he had her pigtails in his hands — was using her pigtails to hold her head as he—"

Ian is suddenly overcome with so much emotion he discovers that

223

he is struggling to hold back tears. "She said he pulled her hair and it hurt and—"

Jillian is holding something in her hand, a piece of some kind of see-through fabric, like a veil and she suddenly makes a sound that's grunting and crying and choking, and she rips the piece of fabric apart. Claws at it with her fingernails and shreds it, then throws the shredded pieces on the floor and unexpectedly collapses on the bed in tears.

"It hurt when he pulled her pigtails," she sobs, repeating what he said as she shakes her head. "It hurt when he pulled her pigtails."

RILEIGH'S COMPOSURE broke and she jumped up, ran around the table and threw her arms around Georgia, trying to talk through wracking sobs.

"Oh, I'm so sorry, I'm so so sorry. I never dreamed. Oh, dear God what you must have gone through. And you never told me."

When Rileigh let go of her choke hold on Georgia and looked into her face, Georgia had come back. She had been there in that place, living it all over again, but now she was here in her kitchen, a grown woman who somehow survived that nightmare horror and went on with her life.

The two women looked into each other's eyes for a moment, then fell into each other's arms and sobbed.

It took a long time to come back from that, but it had been cathartic. The crying had been necessary and when their tears were dried, they could talk to each other, just like they always had.

But Rileigh wouldn't let go of Georgia's hand. She sat down in the chair beside Georgia then, and held her hand, squeezed it tight.

"Let's hear the rest of it. *All* of it."

"It gets worse."

"How could it get any worse?"

Now Georgia squeezed Rileigh's hand. "You'll see."

Then Georgia told the horror story of years of molestation. She was only six years old when Jillian came home unexpectedly and caught them, but Georgia had no memories of life that didn't include the touches that she had finally realized weren't normal, weren't the way the world was supposed to be, weren't the way men were supposed to treat little girls, but by then Rileigh's father had convinced her that it was all her fault and if she ever told anybody, she would get into terrible trouble.

"That son of a bitch!" Rileigh growled the words and ground her teeth. Rileigh had never loved her father, merely tolerated his presence, and as Georgia described what had happened to her, Rileigh felt every kind of raging emotion it was possible to feel. What she didn't feel was surprised.

"The day Jillian caught him with me … she screamed and screamed at him. At one point she ran at him with her fingers out like claws, like she wanted to rip his face off."

"He deserved it."

"He deserved more than you know."

Rileigh found her gut clinching into a knot again, the knot that sobbing had untied in her belly. This was something new, some worse horror.

She saw compassion in Georgia's face, and she squeezed Rileigh's hand as tight as Rileigh had been squeezing hers.

"Here's the worse part. Your father didn't just molest me. He molested Jillian when she was a little girl, too."

Rileigh was too staggered to speak.

Chapter Thirty-Eight

RILEIGH'S CELL phone suddenly rang. She was so stunned by what Georgia was saying that for a moment, she didn't know what the sound was. She'd picked the little "tinkle-tinkle" tone from among the ring-tone options, the one they called broken glass. To her it sounded like wind chimes on a cold winter morning.

She reached into her pocket and drew the phone out. Sheriff Mitchell Webster.

Rileigh looked at her watch. The time she spent talking to Chigger and then coming here had been long enough for the sheriff to get to the construction site and to discover he wasn't there. Maybe even time to go to Gatlinburg — no, not with Saturday traffic in Pigeon Forge. That was going to take awhile.

But maybe the sheriff hadn't gone. If somebody on the work crew happened to know that Chigger was actually helping a friend with his car, the sheriff might have already made it to Lester's house, and if he had, he had certainly learned by now that Rileigh had already been there and left. Chigger was almost certainly heading out of the county.

The tinkle chime sounded again.

"You going to answer it or just sit there staring at the name–" Georgia leaned over and read it– "oh, the sheriff. He called this morning looking for Chigger. Said he needed some information. You going to talk to him?"

No, Rileigh had no intention of talking to the sheriff, certainly not sitting here in Georgia's kitchen. She'd come here to tell Georgia that her piece of shit husband was not only running around on her, but had gotten a teenager pregnant and then killed her.

But telling Georgia would have to wait. Rileigh couldn't possibly manage it right now. She just wanted to be sure she got to Georgia before the sheriff showed up. Mr. Sensitivity wouldn't deliver the news gently or kindly. She needed to be the one to carry that terrible tale. But not now, not right now.

Rileigh pushed the button to silence the ringer on the phone and the chime stopped in mid-ding.

"I'll call him back."

She slipped the phone into her pocket, had left it on vibrate so she would at least know when he called again. And again. And again.

Then she looked into Georgia's compassionate eyes and wanted to burst out crying again. For both of them. For the little girl Georgia had been and for poor Jillian.

"Well, that certainly explains my father's suicide — getting caught molesting a six-year-old. Explains the "I'm-so-sorry" suicide note, too."

Georgia nodded. "Jillian told Ian about what her father had done to her. Said she'd kept quiet about it her whole life, but not anymore. She was going to go to the police.

That's what Ian went there to talk her out of, going to the police."

Georgia paused. "She told Ian that she had made her father swear he would never lay a finger on *you*, and she had kept her eye out, making sure never to leave you alone with him."

"Sweet Jillie. So the bastard kept his word, he didn't molest me … he molested my best friend!"

"I told Ian that I would rather die than talk to the police about what had happened," Georgia said. "I was just six years old and the thought of having to tell some policeman — I couldn't stand the thought of it, of everybody knowing … of *you* knowing. He went to Jillian to beg her not to tell the police, for my sake."

"What did she say?"

"She refused, said she had to tell, then told him to go home and take care of me."

"And so he came back home?"

"Eventually. He was gone a long time. And when he did, he gathered me up in his arms and told me everything was alright now. That I wouldn't ever have to tell anybody what your father had done to me. That I was *safe*."

Rileigh felt her skin go cold.

"What did he mean by that?"

"Well, you know, that Jillian was gone, had run off instead of going to the police."

Rileigh said nothing, just slipped her hand out of Georgia's and picked up her cup of coffee. The cup rattled on the saucer in her shaking hands and she set it back down.

"What's wrong?" Georgia asked.

"You mean like finding out my father molested my sister and my best friend, something like that?"

"It's something else. I can tell. Talk to me."

The "else" was a sense that the puzzle pieces had finally fallen into place and revealed a picture nobody working on the puzzle would ever have expected.

Ian told his little sister when he got home from begging Jillian not to go to the police that Georgia was safe, that everything was alright. He did *not* tell her that he'd been able to convince Jillian, that Jillian had changed her mind about going to the police. All he said was that Georgia would never have to talk about what'd happened to her.

How could Ian have known *then* that Jillian had "run away" instead of going to the police? Nobody was wondering about Jillian's whereabouts then. Certainly, nobody had come to the conclusion that she had left, wasn't coming home. When Ian was talking to Georgia, Jillian had only been "gone" a few hours. Jillian wasn't considered missing until days later, after she didn't show up for her father's funeral or the burial.

There was no way Ian McGinnis knew that "Jillian's not going to tell anybody" about what had happened to Georgia unless he …

"Stop this," Georgia said. "Don't hold out on me. What's wrong?"

"Georgia, I need to go. I—"

"Tell me!"

"You're the only person in the world outside my family, that I ever told what I found when I went into Jillian's room that night. The blood and … the rest. That I knew Jillian didn't run away like everybody said, she was murdered."

"Everybody said you imagined it. And maybe you did … you've never been sure, we've talked about this."

Clearly, Georgia had never put the whole thing together in her head, didn't make the connection because she didn't want to.

229

"Georgia … honey … there's no way Ian could have known when he was reassuring you *the next day* that Jillian wouldn't tell anybody unless …"

Rileigh watched realization take over Georgia's face as the color drained out of it.

"Unless he killed her, that's what you're thinking, isn't it."

"Somebody cut out her tongue … so she *couldn't tell*–"

Georgia leapt to her feet.

"No. You're wrong. That's not what happened. Ian would never do a thing like that, you know him, he wouldn't."

"I really do need to go now." Rileigh had risen and was trying to get to the door, but Georgia blocked her path.

"It's not true. It's not. You know it can't be."

"What I know is that I have to talk to Ian. Right now. Do you know where he is?"

Georgia looked uncomfortable.

"What?"

"I'm not supposed to tell."

"You sound like a third-grader. What are you not supposed to tell?"

"That he's at the Wheaton House."

"What's he doing *there?* And why is it a secret?"

"He's salvaging. You know, scavenging whatever he can find — old mantlepieces, ornate woodwork. Stuff like that."

"Why is that such a deep, dark secret?"

"Well … he's not supposed to be there. It's private property."

Right, private property where people had been freely trespassing for as long as she could remember. There was more to it.

"What's the rest of the reason it's a secret, the part you're not telling me?"

"He's … there's … I don't know for sure what's going on, but there are other people involved. It's not just Ian. I'm not supposed to know about that part, but I've heard him on the phone. Sunday dinner, sometimes he'll get up and leave the room to talk."

Georgia's family had Sunday dinner together almost every Sunday, like the Reagans in Blue Bloods, except Georgia had eight brothers and sisters, and when you put their families together, they didn't fit neatly around a table with a white tablecloth in a well-appointed dining room. Rileigh had gone with Georgia a time or two and it was a zoo.

"What have you overheard?"

"I don't know. Just pieces of things in the past couple of months. I walked in on him Sunday talking on his phone and I heard him tell somebody he'd be at the Wheaton House today. He told me not to tell anybody. He wouldn't say why."

Rileigh thought she knew why.

Suddenly, Georgia began to shove her toward the door. "You go there right now. Find Ian. Talk to him. He'll explain it, and you'll find out you're wrong."

Mayella's signature wail heralded the end of the conversation. But Rileigh wasn't wrong.

For the first time since the night she'd gawked in horrified fascination at the severed tongue on the pillowcase of her sister's bed, Rileigh knew what had happened to Jillian.

Chapter Thirty-Nine

MITCH LISTENED to the sound of the distant ring. Again and again and again. He had been calling Rileigh ever since she'd told him she wasn't feeling well, that the bump on the head she'd received when she'd rammed her car into a tree on Thursday was perhaps more of a medical issue than the doctor first believed. Mitch hadn't liked the doctor, a red-headed young man with the I-made-it-through-med-school swagger down to an art form. He wasn't particularly surprised that the guy might have missed something on Rileigh's x-ray.

Not surprised, but concerned. She'd told him she was going immediately to the emergency room in Gatlinburg for them to examine her and see why she was suffering dizziness and pain.

He'd called her on his way out to the construction site, where word had it Chigger Stump was working today. She didn't answer.

He'd called again when he got there. She still didn't answer. It wasn't like she had turned off her phone, or his call would have gone directly to voice mail. Her phone was ringing somewhere. She just wasn't answering it.

Pushing aside worries... not worries, he wasn't worried about her. Just concerned. Reasonably concerned. After all, someone had tried to kill her twice.

He concentrated on the immediate task at hand, which was finding Chigger Stump and bringing him in for questioning about the murder of Tina Montgomery.

Problem was, Chigger wasn't at the construction site. Asking around, he got four different suggestions of places he should look for Chigger.

His mother's house on Sulphur Spring Road.

The I Got a Spare Bowling Alley in Mud Creek Valley.

A warehouse poker game in Gatlinburg.

And the home of Lester Massey on Pigeon Ridge.

He started with Chigger's mother's house. Chigger wasn't there, but neither was anybody else. He'd knocked and knocked and got no answer.

The bowling alley wasn't any more revealing. Yeah, Chigger had been there Wednesday, bowling with his team on league night. But he hadn't been in since.

It never appeared to be very far between the locations in the mountains. Look on a map, and shoot, they weren't but three or four miles apart. But as the crow flies miles didn't mean beans around here. The crows might fly over the mountains, but the sheriff had to meander down the winding mountain roads that made a five mile trip into fifteen slow miles. Mountain miles. Miles of getting caught behind some terrified tourist, afraid he was about to go crashing through a guardrail and smash his CRV, wife, kids, and dog on the rocks below.

When Mitch finally pulled into the driveway of the Massey house on Pigeon Ridge, it was late and he had been beating the bushes all day. It was dismaying to discover that the driveway leading to the house was even steeper than the one leading to Rileigh's. And that was saying something.

What he found at the end of the driveway was a car up on blocks in the front yard, and two men working on it. Chigger's Chevy pickup and an equally battered old Ford sedan were parked farther up.

Mitch saw the Massey brothers exchange a look when they saw his cruiser. It was an oh-shit look if ever he'd seen one, but that kind of look could be occasioned by any number of circumstances. Maybe they were stoned, or were smoking weed, or had stolen property stashed under the bed or had outstanding warrants in four states.

Could be they knew why the sheriff had come and it was Chigger Stump who was stashed under the bed.

"Afternoon gentlemen. I'm Sheriff Mitchell Webster and I'd like to ask you some questions, if you don't mind.

"We do mind," said the bigger of the two, a round-faced man whose belly stretched out the front of his overalls. "We ain't got nothing to say to the law."

Mitchell went on as if the man had said, "Why sure, Sheriff, ask away, we'll help you any way we can."

"I'm looking for Chigger Stump. A fellow told me he might be here, helping you work on your car."

"I ain't seen Chigger in a week," said the small one, who had a punched, weasel face.

"You're Lester Massey, right?" the sheriff asked, then said to the other man, "and that'd make you Ben." He had no idea which was which, but he had a fifty fifty chance of guessing right.

"*I'm* Lester," said the big man, "And I ain't seen Chigger neither."

Neither of the men would look directly at him.

"Well, see, that's not the way I heard it. The way I hear

it, you fellas and Chigger are tight, and he came out here to get a junker car running. Got a man who says he saw Chigger turn up into your driveway earlier today."

Total bluff.

The two brothers looked at each other.

"He was here and then he left," said Lester. "That's all I know."

Now, he was getting somewhere.

"Left you to fix it all by yourselves?"

"And we ain't never gonna get it running if we stand here all day jawing with you."

"I need to talk to Chigger. You tell me where he went and I'll be on my way."

"Ain't got no idea where he was going," said Ben. He was wiping his hands on a shop rag, just kept wiping, didn't go back to what he'd been doing.

"Chigger tell you what I want to talk to him about?"

"Drugs, likely," said Lester dismissively. But he, too, had stopped working on the car.

"Not drugs, murder."

That got a rise out of them.

"We don't know nothing about that girl's murder," said Lester.

Ben's expression said he realized his brother had stepped in it, but said nothing.

"You guys like history class when you were in school?"

The curve ball confused them. Good.

"You know from history class that President Abraham Lincoln was assassinated." Best use smaller words. "Killed. Shot by a man named John Wilkes Booth. You did know that, didn't you?"

"What's Lincoln got to do with Chigger?"

"What you might not know is what happened to the killer, Mr. Booth. He got away, but he broke his ankle and

235

had to go to a doctor. The doctor fixed him up and he was on his way, with the police hot on his trail."

"I got me a car to fix. You mind getting to the point?"

"The point is this, gentlemen. When the police traced Booth to the doctor, they arrested him, charged him with accessory after the fact for the murder of the president. They put him on trial, and he spent the rest of his life in prison." No way did these guys know the real story. "If somebody commits a murder and you help them get away, you could end up in the iron house yourselves for a good long time."

"Chigger didn't kill nobody. He told that woman that Tina was still alive when he left her."

"What woman?"

"Shut your pie hole," growled the big man.

Woman? Rileigh? Had she come here and talked to Chigger?

"Did Chigger tell Rileigh Bishop he didn't kill Tina?"

Lester looked at his brother, who wasn't ready to crack yet.

"Okay, I'm done playing cat and mouse." He put his hand on the pistol in a holster at his waist. "Both of you turn around and put your hands behind your backs."

"We ain't done nothing," Weasel face said.

"Talk!"

Lester looked at his brother, who probably would have kept his mouth shut, and then back at the sheriff.

"We don't know nothing about no murder," Lester said. "Chigger was out here today working on the car when that woman showed up to talk to him, that Bishop woman. Then he left. That's all we know."

"Where did Chigger go?"

Now the big man broke.

"Swear to god, I ain't got no idea. He didn't say a word

after that woman left, just jumped in his car and went roaring down the road like a bat outta hell."

Another ten minutes of questioning revealed no more valuable information other than the color and model of the car Chigger was driving. The man had had enough time by now to be out of the county, out of the state, in fact, depending on which direction he was driving.

After Mitch called dispatch to put out a BOLO — Be On the Look Out — on Chigger, who he was sure was on the run now, he tried to call Rileigh again. No answer. She wasn't picking up.

Anger, relief and worry wrestled each other to see which one he would feel first, and anger quickly beat the shit out of the other two.

Rileigh had lied to him and tricked him. When he told her Chigger was on the other end of all Tina Montgomery's phone calls, she'd decided — for whatever reasons— that she wanted to talk to Chigger first. Obviously, she knew where to find him — information she did *not* bother to share with the sheriff.

And equally obviously, she was not suffering any lingering side effects from the concussion she had suffered in the car wreck.

Now Chigger was in the wind, headed God knows where, and that was Rileigh's fault.

A simple bring-the-dude-in-for-questioning had turned into a manhunt, and if anybody got hurt because of that ...

He ground his teeth, searched around inside for the other two emotions. Okay, yeah, he was relieved that there was nothing wrong with her that required an immediate visit to the hospital emergency room. And he was worried about her. A little.

Where had she gone after she talked to Chigger? As

god made little white bunnies, something Chigger said put
her on some other trail she decided to follow up. And what
lay at the end of the who killed Tina Montgomery trail
was somebody who had already tried to kill Rileigh and
failed. Twice.

But third time's the charm.

238

Chapter Forty

THE OLD WHEATON estate was outside Gatlinburg and the drive gave Rileigh a chance to get her emotional ducks in a row before her confrontation with Ian.

Rileigh's father had molested Georgia.

He had molested Jillian, too.

And Jillie, kind, sweet protective Jillian had made him swear he would never lay a finger on Rileigh.

So he went for Georgia instead.

There was nowhere inside her to put the tumult of feelings today's revelations had caused. How could you process that your own father was a child molester, and but for the grace of your older sister's interference, he would have molested you too?

That was the kind of thing it would take years …

Years. Georgia had been dealing with it for years, and she'd never told a soul. Surely, she was in desperate need of professional counseling, keeping a secret like that bottled up for so long.

Of course, Rileigh was a bit of an expert herself on keeping things bottled up. She didn't know a veteran who wasn't. People who'd never served had absolutely no idea the kinds of things soldiers saw and had to do.

Rileigh had become quite proficient at walling off horrible things in her mind. She would put each one in its own private room and lock the door soundly behind them. Then she never opened the doors again.

If anything ever happened, like some kind of mental earthquake that rocked buildings and tore the locks off all the doors, she would drown in the horror.

As she drove the familiar narrow roads, with hairpin turns and switchbacks, she spotted a bear almost every hundred yards. In fact, Rileigh thought she'd seen more bears this year than she ever had.

She watched it happen, watched her mind come up with the extraneous thought about bears, then busily start building a rabbit hole about bears where Rileigh could go and be safe from thinking about things like...

The image of her father standing in the hospital room doorway that time she'd had asthma and they had to put her in a hospital oxygen tent so what little air she could draw in would keep her alive. The look on his face, that was somehow just wrong. On some fundamental level, wrong. And how she didn't want him to touch her, cringed away when he reached out to put his hand on her forehead.

She pulled her thoughts back to the new information she had received today, and made herself concentrate on it only as it affected the murder of her sister.

But that wasn't the murder she'd been investigating when she got up this morning. She'd been intent on finding out who killed Tina Montgomery, had been convinced those chickens would come home to roost in Chigger Stump's henhouse. But could she be mistaken? Was it possible that Ian ...

Chigger was among a handful of people in the world who knew what Rileigh had seen in her sister's bedroom that night. Georgia had told him. And when she thought about what had happened to Tina, it made sense that Chigger had pulled the whole cut-out-her-tongue routine to throw off the investigation, to lead the investigators off on some false trail, trying to tie the two crimes together.

But that only made sense if you knew it'd be Rileigh who would do the investigation, because she knew about the tongue on Jillian's pillow.

Was Chigger really sharp enough to figure all that out, to plot and plan like that? His had been a crime of passion. He'd gone to talk to Tina, to beg her not to tell his wife about their affair, and the argument got out of hand somehow. He must have whipped out the switchblade he bragged about all the time and killed her. Could he have put together a plot to cut out her tongue on the fly like that?

But when you factored in the new information Rileigh now had about Ian, other patterns began to emerge.

What if ...

What if Ian was involved with Tina in some way? It wouldn't have been like Chigger was involved with her. Ian was gay. So what could he and Tina have connected over?

How about those shadowy figures Chigger and the sheriff kept referring to, the Big Bad Drug Organization that was apparently operating in Yarmouth County? What if he was mixed up in that?

That made some kind of sense. The organization let it be known that Tina was making noises about going to the police. Ian is suddenly presented with the opportunity to kill Tina with Daisy's butcher knife. It would have been packed in that picnic basket of hers. When Ian said he was going into the house to cut the pie, he sneaked away into

241

the woods and offed Tina. He cut out her tongue because … either as a way to confuse the investigation, because Ian *was* smart enough to know Rileigh would get involved.

Or he did it as some kind of example that the drug dudes could use to show what happened to people who went off the reservation. Then he went to the creek to wash the blood off his clothes. Hard to cut out a tongue and keep your shirt clean.

When Daisy went looking for him, she found him at the creek and ended up falling in herself.

The scenario fit. So did the two attempts on Rileigh's life. Ian had been at the pancake breakfast, along with everybody else in the county, and he knew his way around a car well enough to cut brake lines. But why would his employers have given him orders to get rid of Rileigh as well as Tina Montgomery?

She thought about it.

Maybe his employers hadn't given Ian orders to kill Rileigh. He could've been side jobbing on that assignment. The only thing that made sense was that Ian got cold feet, realized too late that trying to confuse the investigation by cutting the victim's tongue out was likely to backfire on him. He figured out that as soon as word of what had happened to Tina got out, Rileigh and Georgia would eventually end up talking about it. And when they did, his sister was likely to spill the beans about what happened that night thirty years ago.

Ian McGinnis had killed Jillian to keep her from going to the police so that his little sister wouldn't have to testify about being molested. And he killed Tina Montgomery on some kind of assignment from the drug organization they both worked for.

And he'd tried to kill Rileigh.

She bumped her head there, though. She could come

up with reasons, sure. Motive and opportunity. But could Ian actually have tried to *kill* Rileigh? Chigger, yes. That scumbag was capable of anything. But Ian? He and Jillian had been arguing, he'd been desperate to keep Jillian from going to the police, would have done anything to stop her. He'd probably killed her in a fit of anger, he'd hit her or clocked her over the head with something and then … yeah right, and then what? Why'd he cut out her tongue? Could Ian *do* that? Could Ian plot out murdering Rileigh in cold blood? She couldn't make that fit anywhere in her head, so she let it go. No puzzle ever fit together perfectly.

So how did she prove any of it?

If Chigger had been the murderer, you wouldn't have needed a whole lot of evidence because he would have caved under the sheriff's interrogation and confessed to the crime.

Ian was much older, smarter and stronger than Chigger. He couldn't be coerced into confessing. But could he be *surprised* into it?

Maybe.

It was the only card she had to play. If the sheriff got to him first, Ian absolutely would lawyer up. Jarred Kirkpatrick, who Ian was in an on-again, off-again relationship with, was an attorney, and he wouldn't let Ian say a word.

It was full on dark now deep in the mountains, even though the sun hadn't likely yet sunk below the horizon "out there on the flat," as her grandmother always said. As Rileigh negotiated the twisting, winding mountain roads, she considered her long-held belief that tourists should only be allowed to drive in the mountains at night. Headlights can be seen around a bend in the road at night — that would cut down on the head-on's when some tourist got so engrossed in the view that he crossed the center line. And at night, you couldn't see the drop-off on one side of the car that put some tourists into full bore panic attacks. If you drove off a cliff and your car plunged down one hundred feet to rocks below, your chances of walking away from the wreck were close to zero. You wouldn't be any deader if the car fell five hundred feet or a thousand. Try telling that to some guy from Lubbock who was driving two miles an hour because he was terrified.

As she approached the Wheaton Estate she thought about the time in high school when she'd gone to the old house sometime around Halloween because it was haunted. Had to be. It was a creepy old house so, duh, it was haunted. It really didn't take logic any more erudite than that to convince a sixteen-year-old.

They had taken several carloads of kids from the Forge. And they'd had a few beers on the way. More than a few, actually. Mostly, they'd smoked weed, so much of it that even as the designated driver, she'd inhaled enough to be pretty buzzed.

Still, by the time their little caravan got to the place, Rileigh was the only one among them who wasn't stoned. She'd been so gung-ho back then. She knew that someday she wanted to be a police officer. And she was smart enough to figure out that if she pursued that goal to its logical conclusion, sooner or later — to get into a class, or into the academy or as a screening for a job somewhere someday — she would be asked if she'd ever taken drugs. Likely asked while attached to a lie detector. So she'd made the decision as a teenager not to use anything stronger than an aspirin — which made her enormously popular with the kids who did use, because they could count on her to get them home in one piece.

There'd probably been ten, fifteen kids, standing in the darkness in front of the sagging porch of the old home, all daring each other to go inside. Finally, they agreed they would all go inside together, nobody wandering off like those morons in slasher movies who needed a tissue out of the glove box and wound up with their body parts strewn all over the lawn.

The entry hall was so large, the whole bunch of them could stand in there together, giggling and coughing and farting, making so much noise they'd have scared off every ghost for fifty miles in all directions. And then it had started to storm.

Rainstorms were likely to pop up anytime, anywhere in the mountains. Torrential downpours that lasted a few minutes or all afternoon. This hadn't been that. It'd been a thunderstorm, a bonafide lightning-crashing, thunder-rumbling storm that lashed at the old house, banged the shutters against the outside walls and sent cold drafts down the big hallways and into the entry hall.

She remembered it was Gunther Scroggins who'd bolted first, went running out the front porch in the rain and dived into the front seat of the van with Scroggins Cleaners painted on the outside, closed the doors and locked them. The rest stampeded too, then, and the people riding with Gunny had banged on the windows and the windshield, begging him to let them in out of the rain. Gunny wouldn't budge. The cold shower had sobered all the kids up and everybody was in a foul mood. Rileigh had to jam six extra people into her car so they could get home.

Rileigh watched the car in front of her turn off at an old logging road a couple of hundred yards before the potholed lane leading back to the estate. She slowed, watched the car's lights climb up the side of the mountain. Red brake lights flashed then and the headlights went dark.

What was *that* about?

Chapter Forty-One

LIGHTS SHINING around the next bend showed an approaching car and Rileigh stopped before she turned left and let it pass. She immediately saw the car's brake lights come on, and that car turned up the logging road just like the first one.

Rileigh switched off her headlights. Courtesy of the light-around-corners phenomenon of mountain driving, she'd know when somebody was approaching and she needed to turn them back on. This wasn't a very well-traveled stretch of road. Her car and two others on it at one time was a stretch.

She watched the second car bounce up the logging road until its headlights lit up the first car, which had just stopped about seventy five yards up the road. Then the second car's headlights switched off. She could see a figure briefly as the dome light lit up the interior of the vehicle before that car went dark too. Then she thought she saw little lights, maybe the flashlight app on a cell phone, shining in the trees, but she couldn't be sure.

She spotted lights coming up behind her, so she

switched on her own lights and turned in at the lane leading back to the estate as the car passed by. She didn't continue down the lane to the estate. She was considering the two cars and two drivers who were now in the woods above the property. Doing what?

Rileigh had always had good instincts and she'd learned to trust her gut. And right now, her gut was telling her that something out of the ordinary was happening here. But what could it be?

A thought occurred to her and she very much did not like the implications of what she was thinking. Two people had come out to the hillside above the Wheaton House. They had to have something to do with Ian McGinnis, whom Georgia said had gone there ... secretly. Well, the dudes in the woods appeared to be going somewhere secret, too.

So could it be ... that the men in the woods were associated in some way with what she had come to call the BBDO, Big Bad Drug Organization that the local rumor mill carried messages about and the sheriff knew existed? They had come "secretly" to the Wheaton house to ... what? Meet with Ian, she supposed, since he was there.

She wanted to know who these people were. These people who she had believed ordered the death of Tina Montgomery and ...

Yeah, and tried to kill Rileigh.

She considered the fact that she was packing. Her Glock was snug in the holster at her waist ... like it would do her any good. With her stupid broken finger in a splint, she couldn't even get the gun out of the holster with her right hand. And firing the weapon would be a challenge, since she couldn't bend her index finger around the trigger.

Still, she wasn't defenseless. In a two-hand grip, she'd swap the hand positions, hold the weapon in her left hand,

and wrap her right around it— finger stuck out along the barrel. Her aim would be the same, she'd just be pulling the trigger with her left index finger instead of her right.

Of course even that little change mattered. Everything mattered in the accuracy of a firearm. Using her left finger, her shot would pull to the left, because that finger wasn't as strong as her right and …

She silenced the internal monologue about firearms. She had no intention of getting into a situation where she had to use her weapon. The plan forming in her head was that she'd approach in the dark from the far side, try to get a look at whoever was inside, maybe even identify one or more of the players.

She pulled farther down the lane toward the house, then edged her car off the side of the lane and into the undergrowth. She could hear the limbs of the bushes scratching up the paint on Daisy's car.

When the car was out of sight, deep enough in the undergrowth that it couldn't be seen from the lane, she turned off the dome light before exiting, didn't close the door all the way, then moved to the front of the car … and just stood there. She forced herself to stand a full five minutes, allowing her eyes to adjust to the darkness. And it'd give the men in the woods a chance to get to the house and inside. She didn't want to run into them out in the trees.

The moon was high in the night sky, casting a glow that painted everything with ghostly silver light. Once her eyes had adjusted, it provided enough light to see where she was going as she crossed the lane and headed down the right side of it, keeping to the tree line. The building was dark, appeared as unoccupied and spooky as it had when she was a teenager. Ian and the others must be somewhere in the back of the house and she made her way around it.

But no light shone out any windows on the back side either.

Except. She bent over and ran in a crouch across the weeds that once were a lawn to the overgrown bushes hugging the side of the house. She thought she'd seen a sparkle ...

Moving as far as she could between the house and the bushes, she got to a window that had emitted the glimmer of light. Close enough now, she could see that the window had been fitted with room-darkening shades and drapes, but still a crack of light escaped. There were lights on in that room, and she could hear a low murmur of voices coming from inside.

"You'll want to stay real still right where you are Missy," said a rumbling voice behind her in the darkness, and she heard the distinctive sound of a pistol being cocked.

Under normal circumstances, Rileigh would have instantly leapt into action. Contrary to the narrative of cop shows on television or movies, it is genuinely difficult to hit a moving target. Almost impossible to deliver a lethal shot. And in the dark? She'd have dived to the left, turning toward the voice behind her as she moved, and pulled her weapon.

With her *left* hand? Fire one-handed with her left hand?

"Now turn around, nice and slow. No sudden movements."

She did as instructed.

Suddenly a bright light was shown directly into her eyes, blinding her. The voice who'd spoken to her grunted and she heard muttering. There was more than one person behind that bright light.

"Lift up your shirt and take that Glock out of the holster with your left hand, two fingers."

The man wanted her weapon. The bottom of her stomach fell into a black pit. She'd always ended roll call with some kind of statistic about police work. She made sure to use one in particular at least once a week. "Numbers never lie. If you're forced to give up your weapon, there's a ninety five percent chance that the perp will kill you with it."

"Ain't got all night, Sweetie Pie, let's have it."

"Look, who are you and—"?

"It don't matter who we are. Only thing needs to matter to you right now is handing over that gun — peaceable-like. It won't be peaceful if we have to take it off you."

Rileigh pulled up her shirt, took out the weapon and held it out to him with two fingers, the way you'd hold a dead mouse by the tail.

"Drop it."

She let go and the Glock fell to the ground. Someone picked it up, but it wasn't the man holding the light in her face. They spoke briefly, then a hand emerged from behind the beam of light.

"Put this on" It was a man's stocking cap, a big one, made out of black wool. Why a stocking cap? She fumbled it onto the top of her head with her left hand and finger-sticking-out right hand. It was the kind of cap that rolled up at the bottom.

"Pull it over your face and all the way down to your neck."

"No. I'm not going—"

"You need to understand this real well right now, so we don't have no debate about it. You ain't got no rights. You ain't got no power. You are as close as maybe you've ever been to dying. So shut your mouth and pull the hat down or I will do it for you."

Rileigh did as she was told. It was as effective as putting

a black hood over her head … the kind they used on prisoners about to face a firing squad.

Somebody grabbed her upper arm and pulled her out of the bushes, then dragged and shoved her along with him into the house. She stumbled on the porch steps and would have gone down if the man holding her arm hadn't lifted her up over them in a gliding motion and set her down on the top of the porch. A big man, strong.

Stepping through the doorway into the house, she smelled the aroma native to all old places that have been closed up for a long time, the combination of mold, mildew, rotting fabric, and decaying wallpaper paste.

She could sense people, and could smell them, too. One person was wearing the same kind of aftershave as Patrolman Tyrell Crocker, the Memphis Police Department officer placed on permanent disability after a bullet plowed into his belly. It had torn out a good portion of his colon, and took into the wound with it enough nasty bacteria to give him such a virulent case of sepsis that the undamaged portion of his colon had to be removed as well.

Nobody in the room said anything, not to her and not to each other. She heard some mumbling, some whispering, but nobody other than the big guy with the booming voice spoke aloud.

Then the cell phone in her pocket vibrated. She hoped the movement wasn't noticeable, but the distinctive humming it made was, and on the third ring, somebody took the phone out of her hip pocket.

Somebody looked at the name that came up on the screen and said, "Oh, shit."

Chapter Forty-Two

RILEIGH WAS SWEATING in the wool cap. It itched and smelled like a wet sheep. Somebody had stretched two lengths of duct tape around her wrists and she was sitting on something that might have been an army cot that'd been made into a couch. It had a very thin mat covered in what felt like denim, and the holsters in back were covered in corduroy and didn't appear to be connected to the rest of the couch.

Considering the upholstery. As good a way as any to distract your mind from thinking about all manner of other things that are much more unpleasant.

Was she about to die?

Again, it wouldn't be the first time for that, either. She'd been in a firefight once where she had taken refuge behind a crumbling rock wall, the only soldier left standing, dead and dying all around her and any second her position would be overrun. She'd thought then she only had moments to live.

But a chopper appeared over head as magically as if she'd rubbed a bottle and a genie popped out. Its guns mowed down everything breathing on the other side of that crumbling wall.

Now she was a prisoner of a some kind of drug cartel or distribution system that was piping fentanyl into the region. An organization that had already killed Tina Montgomery and had tried twice to kill Rileigh. In truth, she didn't know why they hadn't already put a bullet in her.

Was she ready to die? Really ready? Was anybody ever really ready to die? She had fought and scratched and clawed her way through life, much of the time just to stay alive. It seemed a shame for it all to be over now, when, for the first time in thirty years, she knew what had happened to her older sister.

There were people in the room with her, but most of them left, then the door opened and closed a final time and she suspected she was alone. This was her chance. She started to reach up with her duct-taped hands and yank the cap off her face when a familiar voice spoke, so close to her she jumped back in surprise.

"This was unnecessary," Ian McGinnis said, as he pulled the stocking cap off her head.

She was sitting beside him on the couch in a large, dim room that had brand new room-darkening shades on the windows.

He picked at the edges of the duct tape to get it loose. "This didn't have to happen. It's not my fault. What are you doing here, sneaking around in the dark?"

Rileigh was so stunned, she couldn't think what to say.

"Look, I'm sorry." He got the tape loose and pulled it off her hands, freeing them. Then he reached behind him on the couch and picked up her gun. Ian didn't like guns, wouldn't go hunting with his brothers.

"Here. I don't think anybody took the bullets out of it

or anything, so it's probably still loaded. So… you know, be careful."

He took a breath.

"Well, say something," he said, and then he really looked at her, and if her life had depended on reading the expression on his face, she'd have died on the spot.

"*Say* something? How about, what the hell's going on here? Who were those men?"

"Just some people I know."

Rileigh was disoriented, trying to put it all together in her head.

"Why did you come here?" Ian asked. "You couldn't have picked a worst time to show up."

"*Some people you know…?*" Rileigh was incredulous. "Maybe some drug dealers you know? Maybe some drug dealers you work for, or with or—"

"Drug dealers?" His surprise seemed genuine. "Why would you think they're drug dealers?"

"Oh, maybe because they sneak around in the night and kidnap people, tie them up—"

"You were the one sneaking around in the night," Ian said. "And the kidnap part … what do you expect? You come skulking around the house, peeking in windows, with a gun—"

"Ian what's going on?"

"I want to know why you're so convinced they're drug dealers."

Well, because I have figured out that you're connected to drug dealers who ordered you to kill Tina Montgomery … and me.

She didn't say that because clearly he had no intention of killing her now, and neither did the others who'd been here. And apparently left, because the house around them was silent.

"Sheriff Webster says there is a drug organization operating here, distributing drugs, especially fentanyl all around the area. He believes Tina Montgomery was a mule for the organization."

"So *that's* who killed her? Some drug cartel? Why?"

This was definitely not the way she expected this conversation to go. None of this made any sense at all.

Rileigh got to her feet. Throwing the used duct tape on the floor, she began to pace, then stopped abruptly and turned to Ian, who was still sitting on the couch made from an army cot. It did have a denim cover.

"Alright, tell me. I want to know who those people were who were here, the ones who kidnapped—"

"They didn't kidnap you. You were the one acting like a criminal."

"Who were they, dammit?" She yelled. "If they weren't drug dealers, who were they and what were they doing here and what do you have to do with them?"

Ian paused and looked at her.

"I don't have to tell you that. I don't owe you an explanation. It is none of your business who those people were and why they were here. I can tell you that they weren't doing anything illegal." He paused, cocked his head to the side, and eyed her. "At least not yet. But I imagine it will come to that. And when it does, I'm not sure what side you'll be on. You know about them now, though, so you'll get dragged into it eventually, and then you'll have to pick a side."

Ian might as well have spouted "four score and seven years ago, our forefathers…"

"What in the hell are you talking about?"

"I'm telling you that I'm not going to tell you what you want to know."

"This ... secret gathering ... in the dead of night —
what is this, a resurrection of the Klan?"

"The two black men here tonight would argue that
point. And the klan was not overly fond of gay people,
either."

"Then what—?"

"It's none of your business!" He drew himself up then.
"But by god, you owe me an explanation for what *you're*
doing here. Why'd you come out here tonight."

"To talk to you."

"How'd you even know I was here?" Before she could
answer, he answered himself. "Georgia."

She didn't nod, but she didn't have to.

"What was so damned important to talk to me about
that you tracked me down here in the middle of the night
and came peeping in windows–"

"I thought you killed Tina Montgomery." She blurted
out the words for shock value, watched his reaction
carefully.

"You *what*—?"

"And I know you killed my sister Jillian thirty years
ago."

Ian just stared at her.

Chapter Forty-Three

RILEIGH DIDN'T THINK Ian was duplicitous enough to fake the level of surprise on his face. His mouth didn't literally drop open, but his jaw had come unhinged and it took an effort of will to keep it shut.

"You think I … seriously? I killed Tina Montgomery? Why on earth would I kill Tina Montgomery? I barely knew her."

"You killed her on orders from the drug organization you both worked for." As Rileigh said the words, she realized she didn't really believe them anymore.

"Right … the gang of cutthroats who were here tonight, the ones who gave you your gun back after they caught you spying on them."

She didn't have a comeback for that.

"How could I have killed Tina Montgomery? I was with your Aunt Daisy."

"Like Crazy Daisy's a credible alibi."

"It doesn't make any sense. I was at the grass hut with your aunt and Tina Montgomery shows up— fighting with somebody else, I might add. I didn't even know who the two people were, just voices. But for some unknown reason, I decided to kill her. And Daisy watched, but I made her pinky swear she wouldn't tell anybody?"

"Aunt Daisy didn't see you. You went into the hut to cut the pie, you could have sneaked away." But Rileigh didn't believe it anymore.

"And used Daisy's butcher knife to do it? Then... what? Wiped the blood off on my pants like a pirate and put the knife back in the picnic basket?" He paused. "And the blood, how did—?"

"You were washing it off in the creek when Aunt Daisy — "

"Daisy was the one in the creek, not me. She said she decided to get a drink of water, but instead of coming inside to get it, she went to the creek, slipped on the wet rocks and fell. She was soaked. I was just wet up to my knees from wading in to help her out. How do you murder somebody with a knife and only get blood on your clothes from the knees down?"

Rileigh gave up. He was right. Unless he was working for the BBDO, he had absolutely no reason to kill Tina. And even if she didn't know what those people were doing here tonight, they certainly didn't behave like members of a drug cartel.

No motive, and the Ian-as-the-killer theory went up in smoke.

At least as the person who'd killed Tina. But he absolutely did have a motive to kill Jillian.

"If you're looking for the person who killed Tina, track down the man she was fighting with in the woods that day. That dude's the killer."

And that dude was Ian's brother-in-law, Chigger Stump. Who had been having an affair with her, got her pregnant, and was desperate to keep her from telling Georgia. Rileigh almost told Ian about Chigger, but didn't. She almost told him that his little sister was about to need all the family support she could get, that her husband was going to be tried for murder, that she was going to have to raise all those children alone.

"What's all this shit about me killing Jillian? Why would I kill Jillian?"

"Because she caught my father molesting Georgia and was threatening to go to the police. You went there that night to talk her out of it."

Ian looked like she'd punched him.

"So Georgia told you. I've been telling her for years she needed to do it, but she just never seemed to find the right time."

"There was no right time to tell me my father had been molesting my best friend. And my sister!"

The words stole Rileigh's breath. It would be a long, long time to feel the full impact of all that Georgia had told her this afternoon. She thought she'd survived the full brunt of the blow and then it would hit her again and knock her flat.

"And you think I went to talk Jillian out of going to the police, and when I couldn't, I *killed* her? You can't really believe that."

No, she couldn't. It had all fit together in her head as abstract concepts, as pieces of a puzzle. She thought she'd put the pieces together to identify Ian as Jillian's killer. Thinking a thing like that was one thing, but now, with Ian sitting there beside her, it seemed unlikely. The Ian who'd fixed the chain on her bike when it broke and took her and Georgia out for ice cream on hot Saturday afternoons. No, the young man she remembered as Georgia's older brother couldn't have killed Jillian.

But if he didn't kill her, how did he know she wasn't going to the police?

"You didn't tell Georgia the next day that you'd talked Jillian out of it, that she'd listened to you and agreed not to report it. Did you talk her out of it?"

"No, there was no reasoning with Jillian that night. I tried, left and then decided to try again. But when I went back, I heard voices. Jillian was telling Daisy the whole story and I knew Daisy would be on her side. I didn't have a chance, so I left again."

Those were the voices Rileigh had heard when she went to put the note in Jillian's suitcase.

"If Jillian said no, why did you tell Georgia that she'd never have to testify? You couldn't have known then that Jillian would … vanish."

Ian let out a big breath, leaned over and put his elbows on his knees, clasping his hands in front of him.

"I knew she'd never have to testify because there'd be nobody to testify against."

He turned away from her then, looked down at his clasped hands and she watched him drag himself back to that time, back to the teenage boy whose little sister had been molested.

"After I left Jillian, I drove around for awhile, trying to figure out what to do. Remember, I was a snot-nosed sixteen-year-old kid at the time, had just got my driver's license, and probably wasn't the sharpest knife in the drawer to begin with. The only thing that mattered to me was protecting Georgia, and I'd tried and failed. I had done everything I could to convince Jillian but she was absolutely not buying what I was selling."

He shook his head. "I was devastated. I would have given my life to shield my baby sister from harm — the button-nosed, gap-toothed little girl who jumped on my chest on Christmas mornings, squealing that the Santa man had "leabed pres-nents."

Tears welled in his eyes but he shook off the emotion, sat back up straight.

"I was in a blind rage at your father, wanted to kill the son of a bitch… and that's when it came to me. The way to keep my little sister safe was to administer justice without a court and lawyers and policemen. It was such a simple solution, I don't know why I didn't think of it first." He took a deep breath, then said:

"I decided to kill your father."

Chapter Forty-Four

IAN MCGINNIS HAD DECIDED to kill Rileigh's father the same night somebody else killed her sister. Rileigh felt like a piñata.

Ian was on a roll now, telling the tale and Rileigh realized that he had probably never told this story to another living soul.

"I had to figure out how to do it and get away with it. Because, as we have already established here, I was a snot-nosed sixteen-year-old kid and I didn't want to die. I had a life out there ahead of me and I wanted to live it. But I was determined that your father wasn't going to live any more of his."

Ian said he came up with and discarded several possible methods of murder.

"But as they say in the movies, it had to look like an accident. I figured I had a week maybe, to get the job done. I mean, Jillian was getting married the next day. She and David would be off on their honeymoon — they were going to the Bahamas, weren't they?"

"Somewhere beachy, but I'm not sure where."

"Well, wherever they were going, Jillian wouldn't be able to go to the police until after they got back, so her father had to be dead by then, clean and neat, she'd be spared all the horror, too."

He paused, turned to Rileigh.

"You know I did think then what a nightmare this had to be for Jillian. She's about to get married, and the day before the ceremony, she catches her own father molesting a six-year-old child. What do you do with a thing like that? All that it must have brought up — how do you go from that to taking the bastard's arm and letting the man walk you down the aisle on your wedding day?"

Rileigh hadn't gotten that far in her own mental reenactment of what'd happened that night and the thought hit her like a wrecking ball.

"How do you go from that to your wedding night? Not to get to specific here, but we all know that childhood sexual abuse is the cause of all kinds of sexual problems for the rest of your life. I don't know if Jillian was a virgin…"

He held up his hands.

"And I didn't want to know. But if she was, how did she go merrily off on her honeymoon to experience sex for the first time the day after she caught her father molesting a child, just like he'd done to her for years?"

It was an unthinkable scenario, but Rileigh was sure she would think about it, would spend hours thinking about it, just like she would think about all the other revelations from today.

"I finally settled on the simplest, cleanest way to kill your father: run him off the road, let the mountains do the dirty work. The perfect place was a spot on Bethel Church Road. It's been fixed for years now, but at that time, water had run down the mountainside and under the asphalt, had eaten away the whole shoulder of the road. I'm amazed that somebody didn't close the road, because if you got too close to the edge of that blacktop, let your tires slip off the edge, you'd go off the road and down into that ravine on the other side of it. You car would be airborne for fifty or sixty feet before it even hit the treetops below."

"Bethel Church Road?"

"Old Bethel Church Road. You can't even see the spot I'm talking about now. The state road department fixed it, then a few years later, built that bypass around it."

"How'd you know when my father would —?"

"No bypass then, remember? It was the shortest way to get from your house to Buddy's Bar."

Buddy's Bar. Rileigh hadn't thought about that place in decades, and the place she was picturing was the new one, the one built after the fire when she was in middle school. Buddy's Bar was the watering hole where all the men in the area spent their free time. Women weren't excluded, but Rileigh doubted there'd been more than half a dozen females in the building since it'd opened. Smoke-filled, loud jukebox, pool tables and beer. Just beer. Buddy Preston didn't serve hard liquor.

"I knew your father was a regular. I just had to follow him some night and set up my trap to get him when he drove home."

"But wouldn't that be dangerous for you? It's not like some movie. In the real world, if you tried to force somebody off the road, there's a good chance you'd join them on the rocks below."

"Oh, I wasn't going to force him off the road with *a car.* I had it all planned out to use only car headlights."

"Headlights?"

"Say you were driving down Tucker Station Road where it hairpins before the bridge, and you came around the bend and saw headlights in your lane, coming right at you. You'd swerve, it'd be knee-jerk, you wouldn't be able to help it. So I planned to get two car headlights, rig them up so I could mount them on the right side guardrail. When your father came around that sharp curve, I'd switch on the lights, high beams, and it would look like he was about to be in a head on with another car."

Rileigh shook her head.

"You figured all that out as you drove around that night, after you talked to Jillian."

"Yup, I planned to start building my imaginary ghost car as soon as we got home from Jillian's wedding the next day."

He looked at her.

"Of course, there was no wedding. And your son of a bitch father saved me the trouble by hanging himself in the garage. I wish he'd told me what he was planning. With his bad shoulder, it was probably hard to get that wire up and over that beam. I'd cheerfully have volunteered to help him do the job."

He stopped then, and spoke more softly.

"When Jillian disappeared, I thought I was the only one who knew why. It was obvious to me— what with all that had happened to her the day before her wedding, she couldn't go through with it. She needed time and space to get over it all, to pull herself together. I thought maybe she even went somewhere, you know, looking for professional help."

Ian reached out to Rileigh and touched her arm.

"Georgia didn't tell me what you saw that night until years later. We were hiking up above the falls on Culver

Creek and your name came up somehow, and the next thing I know she's telling me about you going into Jillian's room that night after I left and finding ... "

"Did you believe it was real. Did you believe I didn't make it up or imagine it or dream it?"

"I *knew* it was real. Georgia said you described Jillian's veil, all torn up, ripped to pieces. She tore it up while I was there. I watched her do it. But the torn-up veil wasn't in her bedroom later. I asked Aunt Daisy about that night once — and by the way, don't ever do that. When you bring it up, she goes postal."

"Half the time now, she thinks I'm Jillian."

"Well, she said the veil was gone, said Jillian took it with her. But why would you take a torn-up wedding veil and nothing else with you when you run away? I figure your father threw the veil away when he cleaned up the crime scene."

"My father?"

"Your father, the murderer. Of course he did it."

Rileigh had long ago tried to make her father the villain in the story, but it didn't fit.

"Obviously your father went to Jillian for the same reason I did. He didn't want her to tell the police. Maybe he was begging her not to tell. Or threatening her. Who knows? It got ugly, and he killed her to keep her silent."

"So what happened to the mess? That's the part that doesn't fit. How would he have cleaned it up?"

Before he could answer, she plunged ahead. "And why bother if he was going to commit suicide?"

"The why bother part, I couldn't tell you. Nobody but your father could tell you that, and the miserable son of a bitch has been rotting in his grave for thirty years."

"But how could he have—? "

"I got one word for you, Rileigh. Desperation. He

managed to hang himself, didn't he? Managed to throw an extension cord over a beam when he couldn't lift his arms above his head. How'd he get that stool under it, get on it, put the noose around his neck? A desperate man can do amazing things. "

Chapter Forty-Five

RILEIGH FELT like she'd blown all her fuses. As she drove the winding mountain roads home, she tried to order her thoughts but it was a useless endeavor. They were moving so fast, she couldn't catch any one of them long enough to think it.

It was too much information to absorb at one time. Her father had molested Jillian. The day she died, she caught him molesting Georgia and he killed her to keep her silent.

What'd he do with her body? Desperation notwithstanding, how did he carry a body out of the house to … where? What'd he do with it? No trace of it had ever been found.

How'd he do that?

Chigger Stump was about to be charged with the murder of Tina Montgomery and Georgia would be devastated, absolutely devastated. Rileigh had to admit in her more charitable moments that Chigger was charming, and handsome in a rangy, disheveled sort of way. She'd never thought he was particularly bright — I mean, how

268

do you deal drugs and stay poor? But the ways of the heart are unknowable. Georgia loved him and now she was about to have to negotiate life without him.

Rileigh would help, of course.

Right, help how?

How do you help somebody raise five children... particularly when your tolerance for being in their presence wears out in about an hour? Realistically, what could she do?

Her cell phone rang in her pocket again and she left it, felt it vibrate with every ring until her voice mail kicked in. She hadn't checked her voicemail, and didn't bother to check the screen to see who the most recent caller was. It was the sheriff, and he was bound to be one pissed off man.

Had every right to be. She'd withheld information from him, went to Chigger with what she knew and she was sure Chigger had bolted. That would be his style, run as far and as fast as he could. And the sheriff could have arrested him on the spot, slapped the cuffs on him and hauled him away without a whole lot of hassle. Now, there was probably a BOLO out on him in Tennessee, Virginia, North Carolina... and beyond that.

Her fault.

He would never trust her again.

And why did she care?

But she did care. She didn't like how it felt in the pit of her stomach to know she had totally torched her relationship with the man.

What did it matter?

She turned to head up her steep driveway toward the house and saw Sid Houlihan cross the side yard and head into the woods. How many times had she warned her mother and aunt about the hooligans? And then for the first time she thought about the scratches on her aunt's car.

Daisy would have a meltdown when she saw them, which wasn't going to make getting her car keys away from her any easier.

Please, just let Daisy be sound asleep—

She bounced over the rocky lump at the top of the driveway and saw her aunt sitting on the porch swing, knitting. Well, something like knitting. She might once have know how to operate the needles so they turned out something usable on the other end, but she didn't know now. She just sat there, happily clacking the needles together and producing a tangled maze of yarn that wasn't usable for anything.

Better than a sweater nobody would wear, she supposed.

She was grateful that the porch light didn't provide enough illumination to see the car very well, parked out beyond the fence as it was. Rileigh did not want to fight the battle of the scratches tonight. She didn't want anything but to take a long, hot bath and go to bed.

Maybe she'd have to talk to the sheriff, though. If he called again, she'd have to take it. No reason not to now. In fact, she ought to call him, stage a preemptive strike, take her tongue lashing, then take a bath and go to bed.

She patted her cell phone in her pocket as she climbed the steps. Her mouth was forming the words "Hi, Aunt Daisy," but they never came out. The instant her aunt got a good look at her, the old woman's face curled up in a rictus of rage.

"What are *you* doing here—*again?*"

No, not tonight. Please.

"I live here, Aunt Daisy, it's my—"

"How can you keep coming back? You're dead, Jillian, but you come walking in here like everybody's gonna be glad to see you."

"I'm not Jillian. It's me, Rileigh.

The look on the woman's face never changed. Whenever she went off on some tangent, about the mystery package the mailman was supposed to have delivered but didn't, or about the tomato plants that weren't growing in the back yard, or about Rileigh being Jillian, it was like she was somebody Rileigh didn't know, some mean, hateful old crone.

"Why, don't you deny—"

"That's enough Daisy," said Rileigh's mother from inside the screen door. Both of them were still awake. Goody. Rileigh had hoped to come home to a dark, quiet house.

"This here's Rileigh, and you got to stop calling her Jillian."

"What was Sid Houlihan doing here?" Rileigh asked.

"Sid?" When Aunt Daisy said his name, recognition showed in her eyes.

"I saw him leave as I drove up. What was—?"

"He done a job for me and I was paying him," Aunt Daisy said. "Done something on my car."

Daisy's car. Rileigh didn't want to go *there*.

She noticed that her mother was leaning against the door frame, and there'd been a pained quality in her voice. Either she had a migraine, or she'd taken the knock-out medicine that would take her to na-na land so she wouldn't get one.

"Mama, you need to get back to bed," Rileigh said, and went to her.

"I'll make some lemonade," said Daisy. "Wouldn't everybody like some lemonade?"

Right, lemonade was the universal panacea that fixed all problems great and small.

Rileigh stepped into the house and took her mother's

arm, guiding her gently down the hallway to her bedroom as Daisy clomped purposefully to the kitchen.

"It ain't started yet, but this is gonna be a bigg'un," her mother said, her words sightly slurred.

"You just lie down here and close your eyes, and when you wake up in the morning you'll feel better."

"If I beat it, I will. If I don't …"

There was some art to timing the taking of migraine medication. If you didn't do it soon enough, you'd get the double whammy of the migraine and feeling falling-down drunk.

"I'm sure you did, Mama," Rileigh said, soothingly. "Did you take out your hearing aids?"

Sometimes her mother forgot to take them out, and if she slept in them, her ears would be sore in the morning.

"I don't…"

Rileigh felt her ears, plucked the hearing aids out of the right and then the left, and put the devices in the charger case on the nightstand. Now, her mother was func-tionally deaf, which was a good thing to be if you were about to have a migraine.

She kissed her mother lightly on the forehead, left the room and closed the door softly behind her.

But when she turned around, she almost collided with Daisy, who stood in the hallway in that droopy dress she wore every day, holding a pitcher of fresh lemonade.

"Made it just for you … dear," she said.

"I don't think I want–"

"Oh, I insist. Come sit with me on the porch and we'll both have a glass."

Aunt Daisy marched out to the porch like Sherman marching through Atlanta and Rileigh followed meekly behind. A single glass of lemonade was a small price to pay for mollifying her aunt so she could take a bath and —

No, call the sheriff, first.

"The sheriff's been looking for you," Daisy told her as she moved past the swing to the rocking chair beyond it. Rileigh sat in her favored place in the silent swing and her aunt shoved a glass of lemonade in her hand.

"Taste it, make sure I didn't put too much sugar in it."

Rileigh downed a big gulp and thought if anything, it needed more sugar, but she didn't say anything to her aunt about it or she'd have to wait until the old woman fixed a replacement pitcher. It was easier just to drink the one she had.

She took another drink out of the glass and set it on the table in front of her.

"Sheriff Webster's been calling, has he?"

"All afternoon long. Most of the time Lily talked to him, but the one time I did, he sounded ... well, he didn't sound happy."

"Oh, I'm sure he isn't happy."

"Why would that be?"

"Let's just say he's piffed at me ... I mean pissed at me."

"What for?"

Rileigh's throat felt dry and she reached for the glass on the coffee table, but almost knocked it sideways. The movement of the swing, had got her off balance.

She took a big drink, but it didn't seem to help the dryness. It was like the dryness was down deep somewhere in her mouth, below her tongue, which was ridiculous.

"I messed something up. It's too complicated to explain."

And she was certain that right now, she wouldn't have been able to explain anything to anybody. Her mind felt jumbled, a disconnected pile of thoughts. She needed to get into that tub now, forget calling the sheriff.

"He will forgive you, I'm sure. A pretty girl like you …
but you're spoken for."

"Huh?"

"You'd have made such a beautiful bride."

Here we go again. Jillian.

"And there will be some people who will be sad when
you don't come home. I won't be one of them, though."

Her face had changed again, the anger back.

"I'm not …" Not what? Rileigh couldn't remember.

"That sweet little sister of yours is going to miss you
terribly, she'll be very upset when you never come to visit
her."

Nothing Daisy said was making any sense. Then she
reached into the pocket of her dress and took something
out of it. She set it down on the coffee table in front of
Rileigh, but the table was moving, swaying back and forth,
and Rileigh had trouble focusing.

"She left these for you."

Rileigh tried again to focus. And when she did, she
couldn't breathe. Lying on the table was the school picture
of a little gap-toothed girl and a piece of lined notebook
paper with words scrawled on it in little-kid writing.

The words blurred, but Rileigh didn't have to be able
to read it to know what it said.

Chapter Forty-Six

MITCH LISTENED to Rileigh's voice advise him that she couldn't take his call right now, but he if would leave his name, number and a brief message, she would return his call as soon as possible.

He'd heard the message at least half a dozen times already.

Where had she gone? She'd vanished as surely as Chigger had, but she was better at covering her trail than he had been.

About fifteen minutes ago, the Kentucky State Police pulled over a car that fit the description of Chigger's, positive ID pending because the car had no license plate. That was smart. If you knew police would be looking for your license plate, just take the thing off. The car was hauling ass up Interstate 65 North near Bowling Green, blowing by a radar check doing ninety-five miles an hours.

Even the stupid criminals on television cop shows had sense enough to drive the speed limit when they were fleeing authorities.

Mitch had gotten word that he'd been apprehended ...

in Kentucky, which was a royal pain in the ass. Now they'd have to go through the whole rigmarole of getting him extradited to Tennessee, and Chigger would be appointed an attorney for that process, who would certainly tell him to "shut your pie hole" and not talk to police.

All because of Rileigh Bishop.

The sheriff put his cell phone away, and pulled his cruiser out of the space where he'd been parked behind the courthouse. Hadn't even gotten out of his vehicle and he was sure his desk was piled high with paperwork he was supposed to be doing right now, but it could wait. He was by god going to find Rileigh Bishop tonight and give her a piece of his mind.

And make sure she was alright.

The sheriff was not looking forward to making his way up her driveway. Just about every driveway in Yarmouth County was approaching vertical, but hers had the added feature of a big rocky bump right at the top that you had to have enough momentum to clear, without blowing through the fence and onto the front porch beyond.

As he pulled into the bottom of the driveway, he could see the porch light blazing. He'd bet Rileigh was sitting on the porch swing right now with her mother and her aunt.

He'd best hold onto his temper, didn't want to explode in front of those two sweet little old ladies.

RILEIGH GAWKED at what lay on the coffee table in front of her, swimming in some kind of mist that made it hard to see.

It was the note she'd dropped on the floor in Jillian's room when she ran away that night, which had vanished as surely as Jillian had. She'd had fantasies about finding

Jillian alive and well, that she'd walk into the house on Christmas morning with her arms full of packages, or she'd be waiting on the porch swing when Rileigh got home from school, or she'd just show up for dinner one night like she'd never been gone anywhere.

Whenever Rileigh entertained those fantasies, which wasn't often because it hurt so damn bad when they evaporated, Jillian would be holding the note and the picture and they'd be kind of scuffed up, and Jillian would say something like, "I take this picture out and kiss it every night before I go to sleep," or "I didn't forget you— that's what the postcards were for, to let you know that I would never forget you, that I would come home eventually."

Now, Rileigh looked from the note to her aunt's face and back to the note.

"How did you ... where?"

"They were lying on the floor in your bedroom, when I was cleaning up the mess you made. I always had to clean up your messes, Jillian!"

Even through the haze, Rileigh's temper flared.

"I'm not Jillian!"

Daisy slapped her in the face. Not a casual slap of mild disapproval. She caught Rileigh in the cheek with the flat of her hand, the blow carrying all the force of her considerable strength. Rileigh flew sideways off the swing and crashed into the coffee table, sending it skidding down the slat porch as it dumped the note and photograph on the floor.

The slap was a wake-up call. Rileigh didn't fully comprehend what was going on until her aunt hit her.

The pain of the slap was off a beat, it didn't register with the blow but a second or two after. Then she fell, almost floating through the air. That was when it finally dawned on Rileigh that she'd been drugged. Daisy had put something in the lemonade. Rileigh couldn't imagine what it was, but her aunt could have mixed up quite a cocktail from all the out of date prescriptions in the medicine cabinet.

"I've been wanting to do that for years!" snarled the old woman, bent over Rileigh as she lay on her side on the porch floor, with one cheek on the slats and the other aflame. "Years! You flitting around the room, such a little flirt. Any man woulda fallen for a routine like that. You little tramp."

Aunt Daisy kicked Rileigh, slammed the toe of her "sensible shoe" into Rileigh's side, sending a bolt of agony through Rileigh's whole body. She couldn't breathe or think, with the pain rolling over her in waves. Her vision blurred with tears, and through her tears she saw head-lights turn off the road in the driveway.

Somebody was coming.

The sheriff. Mitch had come looking for her. Thank god!

Daisy spun around when she saw the lights, spewing a stream of venomous profanity, using words Rileigh never dreamed she even knew. Then she reached down and grabbed a handful of Rileigh's hair, and began dragging her across the porch by it, the way you'd pull a cotton sack between rows of cotton. The pain in her scalp almost eclipsed the pain in her side.

But it would be over in seconds. Her aunt wasn't strong enough to drag Rileigh off the porch before the sheriff got to the top of the driveway. Rileigh was safe.

MITCH'S RADIO crackled to life.

"Unit one, this is dispatch. Be advised that the

Kentucky State Police have confirmed that the subject they have in custody is not, I repeat not, the suspect in the BOLO."

Dammit. Mitch thought they'd had him… and they did, more or less, as he learned when the dispatcher continued.

"And Deputy Hadley just reported he got a private phone call from the subject's neighbor, a man he questioned earlier. The neighbor reported that the subject's pickup is now parked in the driveway in front of his home."

Chigger was at home. The truism of law enforcement — a fugitive always goes home. Mitch used Rileigh's driveway to turn his cruiser around and headed toward Chigger Stump's house. Where the man lived with a wife and five children.

God, Mitch hoped they weren't home.

RILEIGH WATCHED in horrified disbelief as the headlights of the vehicle at the bottom of the driveway flashed on the woods on the right side of the house.

The car was turning around.

Then the lights were gone. Her aunt made some grunting sound of approval and kept dragging Rileigh toward the screen door.

"You ain't gonna get away this time," her aunt said. "I done killed you twice. It's gonna be permanent this time, I'm gonna kill you deader than dead, cut your head off this time 'stead of your tongue. Cut it off with a chain saw so you can't come back."

Chapter Forty-Seven

MITCH DROVE the winding roads from Bent Twig Road on Tucker Mountain, where Rileigh lived, to a doublewide trailer house wedged up against the mountainside into what looked like nothing more than a wide spot on Carter's Mill Road.

He'd been considering as he drove the best way to take Chigger into custody with the least amount of drama. He absolutely did not want to go roaring in there like a tornado and slap the cuffs on a man with his wife and five children watching. But maybe they weren't home.

The options he'd considered were immediately limited when he saw flashing lights ahead, then rounded the final bend in the road and saw both Deputy Beau Mullins and Tony Hadley parked on the road, one on each side of the house. Hadley's cruiser was hanging out into the road, could have been clipped by whoever came around the bend beyond the house too fast, but he had put out flares.

The flashing lights on the light bar atop the two cruisers painted the woods all around in shades of red and blue, and reflected off the white trailer house, like some display for the fourth of July.

Mitchell's plan had been to park in front of the house and walk casually up to the door. No, that wasn't protocol when apprehending a murder suspect, but Mitch didn't believe the man was dangerous, that he would put up any resistance in his own home, with — he hoped they weren't there — his family inside.

He wouldn't have approached with his lights on. Lights were a funny thing, and he wondered why nobody'd done any psychologic studies on the affects they had on people. They were meant to be illuminating, to make your presence known as law enforcement, and to intimidate. They had a way of making whatever you were doing "official".

But some people responded to them irrationally, almost like an epileptic's brain misfires when they look at blinking lights. They could spook the driver of a vehicle you were pulling over for a broken brake light into making run for it. And they seemed to embolden teenagers, some implied I-dare-you. Mitch tried, whenever he could, to pull up behind a car with a little blip of his siren, just to get their attention, and not turn on his lights at all unless they failed to pull over.

Well, the lights and the police presence had already done their damage by the time Mitch arrived. He parked in the road directly behind Chigger's vehicle and got out of the cruiser. Deputy Hadley approached him, and gave him the news he absolutely did not want to here.

"He's in there with his wife and kids. And he won't come out."

Mitch could hear screaming then, a high pitched wail that went on and on.

❧

RILEIGH COULDN'T CATCH her breath from the pain of the broken rib — it had to be broken — and the agony of being dragged across the floor by her hair. The hardwood floors were slick, so she slid easily. In the front door, across the living room, around the area rugs, through the dining room and the kitchen, and out onto the back porch.

Where was—

Then she knew. Daisy was taking her to the garage. There was a chain saw in the garage.

Rileigh struggled to get her wits about her, had to think. But the effects of whatever concoction her aunt had put in the lemonade made her mind so muddy, thoughts dragged through against so much resistance, it took an effort to think at all.

Daisy had found her note in Jillian's room *after* Rileigh left. She'd cleaned up the mess. She'd gotten rid of the bloody sheets and the ... the tongue on the pillowcase and the torn veil.

And Jillian.

Daisy had killed her.

There wasn't anywhere in her mind that could think that thought and make sense of it. Why? What possible reason could she have had?

Well, for starters, she was crazy.

Everybody credited Daisy's irrational behavior to the nervous breakdown she'd suffered after Jillian left and her father killed himself. Nervous breakdown were the words used then. Now, it would likely be "psychotic episode." Or psychotic break. She'd totally lost it. Rileigh had heard her screaming and screaming and screaming. Finding a dead body, hanging from the rafters at the end of extension cords would have rattled anybody's psyche. But Daisy had always been ... different. Fragile. They called it eccentric.

When Daisy returned home after more than two years

in a psych hospital, she wasn't the same person who'd left. Either the treatment had worked, or her worst tendencies were now controlled by medication. Rileigh had never asked her mother any questions about her aunt's condition. She'd been just a little kid, and a diagnosis wouldn't have meant anything to her.

Now she wished she'd asked. It was possible her current break with reality could have been predicted or averted if Rileigh had had any idea that she and her mother were living with a primed land mine.

Daisy opened the back door and the screen, then dragged Rileigh across the threshold and out onto the back porch. She was mumbling, sometimes like she was talking to somebody, sometimes unintelligible words.

"Ain't gonna spoil everything. Not this time. It was all your fault to begin with. How's a man supposed to resist a flirty little girl sitting in his lap, wiggling around on him. Twern't his fault he wasn't strong enough to bear it."

All of that was spouted in disjointed sentences as she pulled Rileigh down the back porch steps and started across the yard to the gate in the fence and the garage. It was harder going in the grass, not so slick, and she paused halfway to get her breath.

Daisy hadn't noticed the gun tucked in Rileigh's waistband. Rileigh had managed to keep her shirt down as her aunt dragged her, so she wouldn't see it. How was Rileigh going to get the gun out of the holster on the right side without her aunt noticing? And how would she fire it?

When she got her breath back, Daisy looked down at Rileigh and shook Rileigh's head, pulling out a huge hunk of hair. Rileigh cried out in pain.

"Hurt, does it? You don't know nothing 'bout pain. The pain in my soul every time I seen you pawing all over him. That's what hurt is. But I saved him and that's what mattered. In the end, it was me kept the world from coming to an end."

Her face changed and she looked confused. "I thought I seen J.R.'s pickup truck lights. I bet he's in the garage. When I tell him what I done, how I saved him, we'll leave right then, not pack nor nothing, just run off to Mexico together."

MITCH WALKED SLOWLY, purposefully across the little yard in front of the trailer, stepping over broken toys, plastic shovels, and buckets. He put his foot on the bottom step of the porch and a voice called out to him from inside.

The screaming from inside never stopped. It was the voice of a small child and it sounded like the kid was either in great pain or madder'n dammit. If Mitch had to pick, he'd go with door number two.

"That's far enough. Don't you get any closer, you hear me?"

Mitch froze. The man who was speaking was at the end of himself. He could hear it in the tone of his voice.

When Mitch was ten years old, he'd climbed up on a chair next to the stand-up piano after the lesson he hated, lifted the lid and looked down inside. He was fascinated by the little hammers that were attached to the keys, so that when you pushed a key down, the hammer hit one of the wires.

The wires weren't all the same size or length. The ones on the far end were thick, about the size of a piece of spaghetti and they were stretched out across the whole width of the piano. The ones on the near end were just wires, thin as a strand of a spider's web and stretched tight, and wound around metal posts. The thin wires were for the high notes, and he never forgot the imagery. You could hear it in people's voices, sometimes, how tight the wires inside them were stretched.

Working for years with criminals, he suspected that some of them lived lives filled with nothing but high notes.

The man who'd called out, "don't get closer?" He was stretched as taut as the highest note.

Mitch needed to back down, literally as well as figuratively. He didn't step up onto the porch. In fact, he backed up three or four steps out into the yard and called out.

"Mr. Stump. Is everything all right in there. Is somebody hurt?"

"That there's just Mayella. She always screams like that." He heard some mumbling, maybe the word 'banana" and suddenly the shrieking stopped.

" I need to talk to you, Mr. Stump. Will you please come out here—"

"I ain't coming out there. I know what you want. And I didn't do nothing wrong, didn't have nothing to do with it."

Closer to the trailer now, Mitch could hear the sound of a woman sobbing inside.

"Mr. Stump, I would rather you come out here than me come inside. And that's what you want, too, so we can talk without the children—"

"You leave my kids out of this."

"I only meant—"

"I know what you meant, but I ain't leaving with you, so you can just back up them police cars and drive out of here. I'm staying right where I am."

"You know I can't let you do that, Mr. Stump. We have to talk."

"I done said everything I had to say on the subject. Go ask Rileigh, she'll tell you what I said."

"I need to talk to you myself."

"I ain't talking to you. I don't trust you. Least I knew Rileigh wasn't lying to me, trying to trick me."

"I won't lie to you or try …"

"You go get Rileigh, bring her here. I'll talk to her, tell her the same thing I said this afternoon, I didn't do nothing."

Mitchell had read the case file they had on Chigger Stump. He was a drug dealer, moving weed and cocaine and crack. Strictly penny ante stuff. A burglary charge, broke into a convenience store, stole a little bit of cash, cigarettes and beer. There was no indication anywhere in his file that he had exhibited violent behavior. There was also no mention of a firearm.

But from where Mitch stood, he could see Chigger's pickup truck and the gun rack in front of the back window. Probably fit a 30.06 deer rifle there.

The space was empty.

Chapter Forty-Eight

EVEN WITH HER mind muddied by drugs and distracted by pain, Rileigh registered what her aunt had said, processed it and understood the implications. She might have been sick to her stomach, might have actually thrown up at the images that raced through her mind, every one of them on a souped-up Harley.

Rileigh's father had been having an affair with his wife's sister.

And molesting his own daughter... and his other daughter's best friend.

And god only knew how many other little girls he'd defiled over the years.

The pure vulgarity of the thought was staggering. Rileigh hadn't loved her father, didn't miss him when he was gone, but he had been her *father*. Who has a father capable of that kind of vile licentiousness? It was absolutely breathtaking.

Her poor mother. Sweet ditsy Lily never suspected a thing, never dreamed she climbed into bed every night and went to sleep next to a monster in a human being suit.

Daisy had dragged Rileigh all the way across the yard and was panting from the effort. Now was the time to act, to jump her, overpower her. Daisy had five inches and a hundred pounds on Rileigh, but size didn't matter in hand to hand combat. If she could just get her bearings, get rid of the dizziness and stand up…

But the world continued to cartwheel around her. The big light on the front of the garage that lit that part of the driveway was swirling around and around in circles, and no matter how hard she concentrated, she couldn't keep it still.

The garage had a front bay door. You had to raise it manually, and it was heavy. Rileigh hadn't seen either her mother or her aunt lift it in years. They couldn't anymore. Rileigh knew that if they were going to use the building for its intended purpose, to house a car this winter, she would have to get an automatic garage door opener installed.

But there was a regular door on the side near the back yard and that's where Daisy was headed, genuinely huffing and puffing now, staggering under Rileigh's weight. Jillian had been big-boned like their aunt, about her height and weight, too as Rileigh recalled. How had Daisy managed to…?

She had been thirty years younger then.

Rileigh looked up into her aunt's face, tried to make the images swirling around college into just one.

"Aunt Daisy, don't do this. Let me go."

"Let you go!" She barked out a bleat of anger. "I done left you laying in the weeds and that was a mistake. Oh, I shut you up, you threatening to tell, stuck my butcher knife all the way up to the handle in your belly, watched your guts gush out. But I shouldn't a' left you there. That's why you come back. Don't do no good to cut out your tongue. I put it in my pocket to keep it safe, thought you couldn't talk without it. But I lost it, washed out in the creek ... and here you are again, come back. "

Washed out in the creek.

Tina! Daisy had killed Tina Montgomery ... because she heard her fighting with Chigger, heard her threaten that she was going to tell. Maybe it was like hearing Jillian threaten to tell. Something must have come unhooked inside Daisy then, and she'd slid off the edge of reality into the dark abyss.

Rileigh tried to wrench free and lost another hunk of hair in the process. But her arms and legs felt weak and heavy. She couldn't get her feet under her.

Daisy opened the side garage door and flipped the light switch, which cast a bilious yellow glow over the dust-covered interior, where all manner of junk had been piled along the walls.

Houses in the mountains didn't tend to have basements — what with sitting on rock mountains and all— but most had attics. What was here in the garage was the flotsam and jetsam of their lives that had overflowed from the attic.

A work bench and tools took up most of the end of the building. A pegboard above the bench bore the Magic Marker outlines of tools — wrenches, saws, a level, and hammers. The outlines were empty, and most of the tools they were meant to contain probably lay in the pile of tools at the far end of the work bench. Two ancient bent wire coat hangers hung from the hook with a hand drill shape above it. The coat hangers were for catching a chicken to fry for supper.

The garage was also where they stowed the lawn equipment. Just a basic gas powered mower, didn't need much for their small lawn. There was also a leaf rake and a hoe to work in the garden. Hanging on the far wall, almost outside the glow of the overhead light was the chainsaw. Couldn't live in the mountains without a chain saw to cut through fallen limbs or make a pile of kindling for the fireplace.

Daisy pulled her across the threshold, gasping for air now. Rileigh managed to grab hold of the door frame with her left hand and held on.

"Let go of that," Daisy said, between gasps. Though the agony on her scalp was almost unbearable, Rileigh curled her body around the door frame, knowing her aunt wasn't strong enough to dislodge her.

"I'm not Jillian! Aunt Daisy, look at me. It's me, Rileigh."

Her aunt let go of her hair and kicked at her in a rage, the blow glancing off her hip. Rilegh reached out her right hand— splint and all— and tried to grab her aunt's foot, grabbed a bit of it, but her aunt yanked it away,

That's when she reached for her gun. She fumbled with her right hand at the gun in the holster, managed to pull it free and grab the barrel with her left hand, tried to turn it over in her hand as the world spun around her.

"Don't you dare pull no gun on me." Daisy kicked Rileigh's arm, but she managed to hold on to the pistol, turning it to fit the grip into her left hand, so she could curl her finger—

Daisy kicked out again and dislodged the pistol. It fell to the floor and skidded a few feet across the concrete. Rileigh lunged for it, reaching out her left hand but missing it, just like she'd missed when she tried to pick up her glass of lemonade.

She tried again, glancing up as she did and caught a glimpse of her aunt, her face a study of maniacal rage, the sledgehammer raised high above her head. Then the old woman slammed the hammer down on Rileigh's hand with all her strength.

Rileigh screamed as the bones snapped.

~

IT WAS a mistake that could get somebody killed to believe Chigger Stump wouldn't put the lives of his wife and children at risk. A man who was stretched as tight as a high note was capable of anything.

Maybe Chigger Stump wasn't a hunter. Just about every other male human being in Yarmouth County was, but perhaps he was an exception. Right. So why'd he have a rifle rack in his truck — an *empty* rifle rack?

If he'd gotten the hunting rifle out of his truck and taken it into the house with him, that made Chigger a murder suspect armed with a deadly weapon. It didn't get much more dangerous than that.

"Back off," Mitch said to the deputies who were standing about fifteen feet behind him. "Easy. Don't spook him."

Mitch backed away across the yard to his cruiser, then stood behind it with the two deputies. If Chigger was armed, this morphed into a whole new level of awful. It was now, officially a hostage situation. Protocol was clear. Mitch needed to call the Tennessee State Police and get them to chopper in their hostage negotiation team. Closest place to land was that meadow on the other side of the road from the overlook, at least five miles away.

Say the whole team is available right now — which it wouldn't be, they'd have to wait for personnel to respond. Say they rounded everybody up and the chopper took off immediately. A helicopter flight from Nashville to the Smoky Mountains — depended on the chopper, but nothing short of a Blackhawk could make the distance in less than an hour. Then another fifteen minutes to get here from the landing site.

Best possible case scenario, they were ninety minutes away from even beginning to resolve this situation. An hour and a half of that man sitting in that trailer, with a crying wife, terrified children, and a deer rifle.

Mitch had a really bad feeling about this. It was going to go south long before help arrived. He and his men were on the hook for this one.

Rileigh lived only a few minutes from here. He could get her and come back before the hostage negotiation team even made it to the chopper. She was his only hope of diffusing the situation, ratcheting the drama and stress down to something manageable.

Mitch didn't take the megaphone out of his cruiser — that and some bright lights was all this powder keg would need to blow.

Instead, he shouted out, "Chigger, I'll make a deal with you. You just sit tight in there, get your wife—"

He looked a question at Deputy Mullians, who whispered, "Georgia."

"—Georgia to make a pitcher of lemonade and chill out while I got get Rileigh. Then we can talk, the three of us— you, me and Rileigh. Deal?"

Hour-long seconds ticked by before Chigger called out, "You bring Rileigh here. I'll talk to her. She don't like me, but she and Georgia are tight. She'll do right by me for Georgia's sake."

The sheriff called dispatch for backup, instructed the two deputies on site to secure the scene for fifty yards both ways. Nobody in, nobody out.

Before he got into his cruiser, he punched Rileigh's number again, let it ring until voicemail picked up. This time he left a message.

"I've been trying to reach you all afternoon, so I'm coming to your house. Chigger Stump is holed up in his trailer with his wife, kids, and probably a deer rifle. He refuses to come out unless you talk to him. I'll be there in about fifteen minutes."

Chapter Forty-Nine

RILEIGH HAD BEEN WOUNDED in combat. She'd taken a round in the thigh on her first tour in Afghanistan, which put her out of commission for six months. Shrapnel wounds all up and down her chest and belly. She had bullet fragments in both arms, and permanent tinnitus from an IED exploding too close. She would never complain about that one, though. That IED had killed two men in the squad.

None of the injuries Rileigh had sustained in battle held a candle to the level of agony she felt when her aunt crushed the bones of her hand with a sledge hammer. She screamed, shrieked so loud and hard that it made her throat raw. Then she blacked out.

She didn't know how long she was unconscious, but it was a sensation that brought her around. Her cell phone was vibrating in her pocket.

When the spinning world stopped spinning and the roaring sound in her ears faded, Rileigh opened her eyes to an impossible sight so she closed them again.

How could she possibly be in the garage? She'd come

home from ... somewhere. She thought maybe she'd talked to Ian, but her memories were too tangled to sort out.

She opened her eyes again, barely, looked out through a forest of eyelashes ... and saw the ceiling of the garage high above. The building was a story and a half, with a loft at one end for storage.

It was from the railing of that loft that her father had tossed the noose end of three tied-together extension cords over a beam in the middle of the building. How many tries did it take him to get the cord over the beam? Then he'd tied the end in his hand to the railing, gone back downstairs, positioned a stool under the end with the noose and the rest, as they say, is history.

Almost unable to breathe because of the pain in her hand and in her side, Rileigh tried desperately to order her thoughts. She was in danger here, she knew that much. But in danger from what? Who was the enemy?

Then she heard a sputtering sound, like a lawn mower starting. No, not a lawn mower, a chain saw.

Forcing herself to roll over onto her side, she spotted her aunt, who had a chainsaw sitting on the workbench and was tinkering with it. Rileigh couldn't see from her position what she was doing exactly, but she knew the intent. Once she managed to start it—

Rileigh looked around desperately for something to use to defend herself, some way to escape. She was lying just inside the back door to the garage. She couldn't stand. If she crawled out the back door, but Daisy would be on her before she got three feet beyond it.

Think!

Daisy muttered to her as she fiddled with the saw.

"Gonna plant you soon's you're dead. Gonna put you in the dirt. That was my mistake the first time, hiding you in the quilt box all the next day. Didn't have time to do nothing else until things settled down, though, and wasn't nobody paying attention."

The hits just kept on coming. Daisy had killed Jillian and then stuffed her body in the quilt box that had been against the wall in her bedroom.

A tiny meteor of memory blazed across the black expanse of her mind. Playing hide and seek. Looking everywhere for Jillian. Then she'd popped up out of the quilt box. She had fit in it just fine.

Then the memory was gone and she watched in fascinated horror as her aunt fiddled with the chainsaw, then cranked it a time or two. On the third pull on the cord, it sprang to life, the distinctive rumbling sound filling the garage, the smell of gasoline and exhaust filling the air.

It sputtered then, and died. It always did that. It usually took three or four tries to get it running, and stay running. In the silence after the engine quit, Rileigh launched out a Hail Mary. Raising her voice to make it squeaky, she cried, "Aunt Daisy, Daddy's looking for you."

Daisy's head snapped up and looked at her.

"He sent me to find you."

"Why'd he send *you*?"

"I don't know … he just said he didn't want me, he wanted you."

A heart-wrenching look of desperate hope bloomed on her aunt's face.

"J. R. wants me?"

"He's waiting on the back porch."

Daisy stood, holding onto the chainsaw, and walked almost dreamlike out the door of the garage.

Rileigh had only seconds. Ignoring the agony, she rolled back onto her belly and got to her hands and knees. She crawled the six or seven feet to the open door of the garage and shoved it shut with her foot. Then she sat back against the leg of the workbench and used both her feet to brace the door to hold it shut.

She had just locked her knees when her aunt wiggled the door knob, shoved on the door. Rileigh held it shut firmly.

"Open this door. You hear me, Jillian? You let me in!"

Her head spinning, her mind burped out, *or I'll huff and I'll puff and I'll blow your house in.*

Her aunt huffed and puffed, shoved with all her weight on the door. But with her back braced, both feet against the door, her aunt would have to break both Rileigh's legs to get the door open. She could cut through the door with the chainsaw maybe, but it was no hollow-core door. It was solid oak. There were no windows in the garage and only the two doors—the one she was holding shut with every speck of strength she possessed, and the big bay door which was too heavy for her mother or her aunt to lift.

Rileigh was safe, for now, cradling her mangled left hand in her lap, she didn't try to examine it as it swelled up huge and purple and the broken bones screamed at her. She would remain here until the effects of whatever drugs her aunt had given her wore off enough for her to function. Her aunt hadn't taken Rileigh's pistol when she left. It still lay where she'd put it on the workbench. Rileigh didn't know how she could use the weapon with mangled hands, but she would figure out a way.

Worst case scenario, she'd stay here until her mother woke up—

Creak! The sound came from the front of the garage. Rileigh tried to focus on that part of the room, but nothing remained still in her vision. Everything twirled and spun and cavorted, moving—

Creeeeak! Louder this time, Rileigh knew what was

making the sound. It was the sound of the big bay garage door creeping slowly upward.

She can't. No way, Aunt Daisy absolutely cannot lift that garage door. Through the spinning blur of her vision, Rileigh saw a light begin to appear under the door, just a sliver of light from the back porch. But the sliver got wider and wider as her aunt lifted the door higher and higher.

It was impossible, but it was happening. She heard her aunt muttering as she grunted with effort. "Got my chainsaw. Gonna cut your head off,"— *grunt!* — "put it down in the hole first."

The door continued to rise into the air, the light no longer a sliver under it but a beam getting wider and wider.

"You fit real snug last time, but you clawed your way out. Wasn't rats I was hearing, it was you, scratching at the bottom of them boards."

The door was up more than half way now. Back when it worked properly, you had to raise it all the way, or it'd drop back in place. Apparently the rollers were gummed up, screeching and protesting. It was stuck in place, would remain wherever she stopped pushing it.

She stopped. The porch light illuminated her from behind, making her a black silhouette in the doorway. The silhouette leaned to the side and picked up a black lump. She pulled on a cord and the chain saw coughed. She pulled again and it coughed again.

But third time's the charm. The engine caught and it roared to life. She pulled the trigger with the blade disengaged and revved the engine.

Varoom.

Varoom. Varoom.

Then she leaned over to pass beneath the half open

door and walked slowly toward Rileigh, revving the engine
of the chain saw Varoom. Varoom.

When she stepped into the puddle of light from the
overhead bulb in the ceiling of the garage, the look of
madness on her face was almost as frightening as the saw
in her hands.

She was smiling.

Chapter Fifty

MITCH PULLED his cruiser into the driveway of Rileigh's house and gave it the little bit of extra acceleration it needed to make it over the hump at the top of the drive.

When his headlights swept the front porch, he saw no one. But the front door was standing open.

He climbed the porch steps and saw that the coffee table had been knocked over and there was something lying on the floor in front of the swing. He bent and picked it up— two things.

One was an old, yellowed school picture. It was a little girl with a familiar face. Vanish the chipmunk cheeks and add in the missing teeth, and the little girl was Rileigh Bishop.

The second was a piece of notebook paper with words printed in little-kid scrawl.

"I WAS GOING to hide something in the bottom of Jillian's suitcase, so she'd see it when she unpacked. I cut out one of my school pictures and wrote a note to go with it."

"What'd the note say?"

"PLEASE DON'T FORGET ME." Mitch read the words out loud.

Was this the note Rileigh had written to her sister three decades ago, the one she dropped on the floor in Jillian's bedroom when she saw the horror of bloody sheets and the human tongue on a white pillowcase?

If it was, how'd it get here, tonight? He thought Rileigh had said that the note was missing the next morning when her family went to examine Jillian's room. It'd been there in the bloody debris, but whatever had happened to the mess had also happened to the note and picture.

And what had happened to them was that *the killer* had taken them away.

So why was the note lying on the porch floor tonight?

There was a coughing sound from the back of the house. Then another. Then a familiar rumble filled the air. Somebody had just cranked a chainsaw in the back yard.

Why would two old ladies decide to cut up kindling in the middle of the night?

The sheriff opened the screen door and went into the house and through it. The hum of the chainsaw grew louder as he neared the back door.

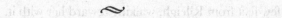

SECONDS TO LIVE. That's all Rileigh had. Fewer than a dozen, she figured. Would it hurt? She didn't think so. She had read somewhere about the death of Anne Boleyn, the first wife of King Henry the VIII. She had been terrified of the guillotine, was horrified by the thought of waiting at the bottom for the blade to fall. Before her execution, she was kneeling in her chambers in prayer, and an executioner sneaked up behind her and slashed off her head with one blow of a sword. They said when her head tumbled to the floor, she was still saying her prayers.

Daisy stalked toward her with the chainsaw in hand, her eyes ablaze with maniacal fury. She was smiling, and a tiny line of drool had escaped through her lips and was sliding down the corner of her mouth.

Rileigh wasn't afraid.

She'd always believed that a person ought to die with as much dignity as the circumstances allowed, so she sat up straight.

THE SOUND of the chainsaw was coming from the garage.

Mitch stepped out onto the back porch and could see that the bay door of the garage had been raised part of the way up. He crossed the yard to the garage, leaned over and peered into the room. What he saw made no sense at all.

Rileigh was sitting flat on the floor at the back of the room, between the workbench and the back door. She was leaned against the bench, and her feet were pressed tight on the door.

That was not, by far, the strangest sight. Daisy had a chainsaw. It was turned on, running, and she was only a few feet from Rileigh, walking toward her with it.

No, not walking toward her.

Advancing on her.

In the next split second, he recognized the look of terror on Rileigh's face and he didn't hesitate. He was speaking before he actually had his weapon drawn, but had it in a firm two-hand grip, pointed at the old lady before he finished.

"Drop the chainsaw! Do it now!"

The old woman turned toward him and he knew in that instant what total madness looked like. Then she ran at him with the saw running, lifted it into the air to swipe down—

He fired, caught her in the upper right shoulder, and the force of the bullet knocked her backward. The sound of the chainsaw's engine instantly silenced when her finger came off the trigger and it clattered to the floor out of Daisy's hand. She kept her balance for a moment, then toppled over backward on the floor and was still.

Mitch ran to Rileigh and knelt beside her. She crumpled against him as though all her bones had turned to sawdust. And then she started crying.

He saw the ruin of her hand. What had hell had happened?

Chapter Fifty-One

RILEIGH SAT in the porch swing, pushing it gently back and forth, silently back and forth, as she listened to the sounds from the back yard. The hammering and sawing was done. Workmen had come first thing this morning and worked until about half an hour ago, ripping the floor out of the storage room that'd been added years ago onto the far side of the garage.

Now they were digging.

She couldn't hear it, but she could picture it and she shuddered.

She'd told Mitchell that she did not want to be there when they dug up Jillian's body from beneath the floor where Daisy had buried it three decades ago.

She said she'd wait at Georgia's and he could come and get her after. The funeral home would take charge of the remains, cremate them, and bring them to the house in an urn. At least that had been the plan.

But Rileigh found she couldn't stay away. She'd tried spending the night before at Georgia's house — not the most relaxing environment under normal circumstances,

and now with Chigger moved out and the kids all traumatized by the split, she'd expected bedlam. But the kids were
mostly calm, probably in shock, but … frightened, maybe?
They were clingy. Georgia had to put them all to bed, one
at a time, all five of them.

This morning, however, Rileigh couldn't do it, couldn't
stay away, so she got Georgia to drive her home. She
couldn't drive yet. The doctors said it would take six
months, at least, for her to regain full use of her left hand.
It had taken surgeons eight hours to repair the damage to
her knuckles and fingers, and she wore a bandage on her
hand the size of a boxing glove. The finger on her right
hand had healed nicely, though. And it was her trigger
finger. There was that.

They'd made a morning of it to keep Rileigh's mind
occupied, went to McDonald's for breakfast, stopped at the
physical therapist's for a session, picked up the dry-clean-
ing, snatched the mail out of the box at the bottom of the
hill, and brought a fresh bouquet of flowers to put in the
vase in the parlor. She'd tossed the junk mail on the coffee
table, arranged the flowers in the vase, and then she'd
made tea — all of those simple tasks unbelievably
awkward and difficult because of the boxing glove on her
left hand.

Mama would be home in a few days. A sanitarium, her
doctor said. She needed rest and a pleasant environment
for awhile. But he made it clear all the rest and relaxation
in the world wouldn't fix what was broke in Lily Bishop.

It wasn't Alzheimer's, they didn't think. But maybe. It
was surprising how far her mother had wandered down the
path to La La Land without anybody noticing. She was
always in the shadow of Daisy's craziness. Mama had
never seemed so bad by comparison.

Rileigh didn't tell her what she'd learned about Jillian,

about J.R. and Aunt Daisy and Georgia. It would be cruel to tell her, and she wouldn't likely remember it if you did.

They were almost certain Daisy had advanced Alzheimer's. It made a vicious cocktail when you mixed it with bi-polar disorder, added water, and stirred.

Rileigh hadn't seen Daisy in awhile. Couldn't really see her anymore without seeing the maniac she had become. Mama had visited and told her that Daisy was as happy as she'd ever seen her. Apparently, she was delusional and thought the other women in the unit were her sisters, the bouquet of flowers — Lily, Iris, Daisy, Rose, Jasmine and Della, for delphinium — gathered together in one vase again.

"Rileigh," the word startled her and she almost knocked over her glass of iced tea. She drank only that now, didn't like lemonade anymore.

The sheriff had spoken, had come around the side of the house from the back yard and up the porch steps while her mind was somewhere else. "They're finished."

That wasn't all of it. Something wasn't right.

"What? Don't make me guess–"

"There's nothing there. They dug out the area under the whole floor. There is no body. Your Aunt Daisy didn't bury your sister under the floor in the storage room."

Rileigh stared up at him, dumbfounded. Of all the possible outcomes, finding nothing had not been one she'd anticipated.

"Sit down," she said, gesturing toward the empty rocker. There was only one now on the porch. Though Mama would be home soon, Daisy would never see the outside of North Tennessee Psychiatric Hospital's criminally insane unit.

He took his hat off and wiped his forehead with his

sleeve. It was hot out there in the sun, though she didn't think he'd done any of the digging.

"Go get yourself a glass of tea first," she said and handed him her glass with her right hand. "Refill mine, too."

She needed something stronger than tea, though. She didn't drink, but if she did, she'd concoct some haymaker strong enough to dissolve the swizzle stick.

The sheriff came back out of the house, let the screen door bang properly shut behind him. He was learning. He handed over her glass and took a big gulp out of his own before he sat down heavily in the chair.

"I'm sorry."

"I thought it was over. That I could lay it all to rest, and now ..."

"There really is no telling where she buried the body. You said she kept her in that chest in her room until she had the time to 'do it right.' That could mean anywhere."

He'd gestured on the "anywhere" and upset his glass of tea, spilling it on the papers on the coffee table — circulars from the local grocery stores, Save-A-Lot and Buy Low, admission tickets to such heart-stopping attractions as Pigeon Forge's Hollywood wax museum where a seventy-five-foot-tall King Kong climbed the outside walls of the building or the upside-down WonderWorks building where you walked on the ceiling with light fixtures between your feet.

There was also a fat envelope full of coupons redeemable at any one of the umpteen dozen tourist crapola stores that lined both sides of the divided highway through Pigeon Forge to Gatlinburg.

Maybe she could use one to get herself a new rubber tomahawk. You couldn't claim citizenship in the Smoky

Mountains if you didn't own a coonskin cap and a rubber tomahawk.

She moved the envelope out of the liquid and that's when she saw it.

Her heart stopped beating. She sat frozen, absolutely motionless. Mitch was still talking. She couldn't hear the words because of the rumble of noise that had suddenly started inside her skull. He stopped when he saw her face, followed her gaze.

A post card lay on the table beneath the junk mail. The picture on the front showed a mountain with a peak that stretched high above the clouds and a beautiful city at its feet. The word "Avila" was printed over the picture.

Rileigh couldn't make herself touch it.

Mitch reached out, picked it up and turned it over.

It was postmarked Caracas, Venezuela. There were no words on the back. But in the blank space where words should have been, someone had drawn a bright yellow smiley face.

THE END

What To Read Next:

Three tourists burned alive. Two disgraced cops. One deranged killer.

Ex-police officer Rileigh Bishop is just trying to be friendly when she gives directions to an impatient tourist. Five hours later, the same tourist is dead. The only evidence? A lit match and the lingering smell of gasoline. It's the first of three murders, all tourists, all burned alive.

It's a race against the clock for Rileigh Bishop and the former sheriff – can they find the killer before more people burn?

Pick up your copy of Fuel To The Flame today.

About The Author

Lauren Street has always loved a mystery. As a kid growing up in bible belt country she devoured every whodunit book she could get her sticky little hands on and secretly investigated all of her (seemingly) normal boring neighbors. Sometimes their pets and farm animals too. All grown up now and living in the UK with her thoroughly unsuspicious (and often unsuspecting) husband, she writes domestic psychological thrillers about families torn apart by secrets and lies. And she sometimes still peers over garden walls to check up on the neighbors.